Breach
of
Immunity

Breach
of
Immunity

Molly Hite

St. Martin's Press   New York

Design by Judy Stagnitto

Library of Congress Cataloging-in-Publication
Data
Hite, Molly
    Breach of immunity / Molly Hite.
        p.   cm.
    ISBN 0-312-06893-X
    I. Title.
    PS3558.I833B74   1992
    813'.54—dc20   91-38162
                                             CIP

First Edition: February 1992
10   9   8   7   6   5   4   3   2   1

For Frank

My thanks to Yaddo, the MacDowell Colony, and the Society for the Humanities at Cornell University for the support they gave to this book. Also to the Ithaca Police Department, Mick Ellis, David Feldshuh, Frank Costigliola, and Margery Hite, who provided advice and expertise.

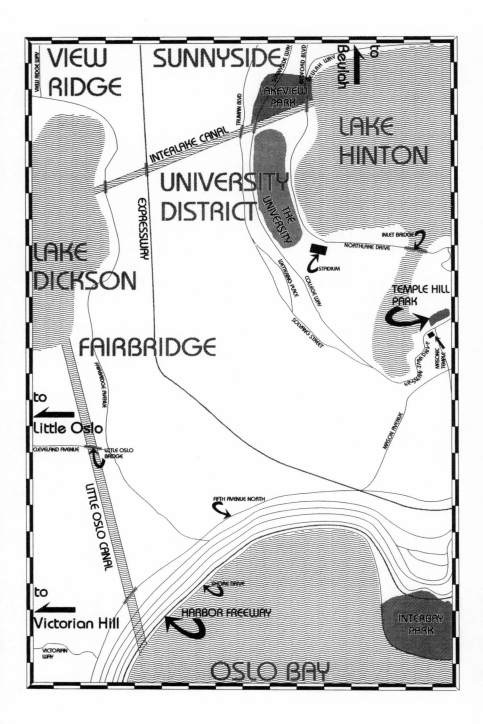

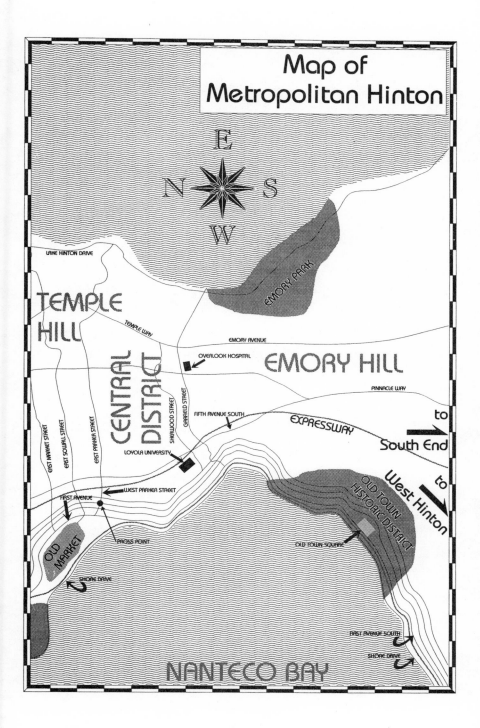

Prologue

As he kept telling them later, he had passed within two feet of the figure without really seeing it. *Really* seeing it, he would repeat, but they asked anyway, then how did you know you passed it; and he would take a deep breath and say he wasn't sure, but there must have been something in the shadows around the dumpster that made him wary. Because he was wary, a little quicker to spin to the left at the sudden scuff of gravel, his elbow lifting to ward off the slash or blow that didn't come because the arm was around his waist instead, and the other arm caught him from the right, where he was unprotected, and clubbed him across his windpipe so that for a moment he didn't know if he was going to go on breathing and could only think: tall.

At that point they invariably asked him how tall, and he invariably said he wasn't really fixated on registering quantitative data like that, valuable as it might be in retrospect, he was primarily concerned with breathing; and his own words seemed to be growing more rhythmic with the repetition until they belonged only to this numbing ritual of telling and not at all to the long moments with the arm across his windpipe, the left hand working now at his belt buckle and then the button of his jeans and then his zipper, and the swaying bulk behind him pressing, rubbing—or slipping, rather, with the odd, cushioned feel of something buffering there, catching at his jeans—

1

and then the arm leaving his throat and the expert tug bringing jeans and Jockey shorts down so that his prickling flesh was suddenly exposed to the slick bulge of fabric over something crumpled and billowing and sibilant.

Holy shit, he told himself, it's wearing a skirt.

It, they confirmed. You actually thought, it. They wrote this down with evident satisfaction, as if he had compromised himself with a pronoun. He knew that they wanted him to compromise himself. That was the way they always went at these cases: Did you say anything, did you put up a fight, what were you thinking? Thinking themselves, did you come? They didn't get to ask that anymore, but you knew that was always the implied question behind all the other questions.

After the first time around this part he tried to address the issue directly. Wasn't the pronoun in fact testimony to his presence of mind in a situation of extreme ambiguity?

But they weren't about to be impressed by his presence of mind. They intimated that he was used to ambiguity. Ambiguity of this sort. Delusions of gender. Anyway, the ambiguity had lasted maybe a second. The skirt and its suddenly scratchy underpart had slid up like a curtain, like the frothy costume of a cancan dancer; in fact, exactly like a cancan costume, engineered to exhibit flashing legs, foaming petticoats. So that he was in the middle of another silent holy shit, another mental gasp of recognition, when he shouted in pain instead, and that shout in turn was cut off by the hand over his mouth.

You did shout, they confirmed. Skeptical, of course. They thought he was used to it. At least used to it. Who can understand the sensations of people who are in no way like us? Wrong category, he wanted to tell them. Nobody is used to this. Very simply, it hurt. Not the hurt of virginity, the hurt of something you did not want, did not request, did not for one moment entertain the need of, jammed right into your body, do you understand that? Although of course they never did, or perhaps had to resist understanding. Maybe in his case it took

2

a special effort. This could never happen to me. I'm not used to it.

Nobody is used to it, he thought, against the current as always. If only you could just relax. Go with it. He was so exhausted. You shouted, they said. I shouted. Shouted or grunted, an involuntary expulsion of breath, voiced, vocative. Then the hand again. Then the pain. It took a long time.

He took a long time, they said. How long? And unvoiced: How long does it usually take?

What do you do while that is going on, the hand over your mouth, the grinding pain of it, the intrusion of it? You try to register impressions, other than the impression you have no choice but to register. Big hand, wide, thick fingers. How big? Knees bent, pinning him. Big man. How big? As if it were a joke. Eight inches, he told them. Eight inches long. You wanted to know, didn't you?

It doesn't get better. You don't get used to it. That thought was censored before they could let it mean anything.

The presumption all around was that he was used to it. All around. Even at the time.

What the rapist had whispered into his ear over and over, more rapidly as the thrusts became more rapid, was "Faggot. Faggot. Faggot."

One

The first call came in while Mary McIvor was sending all the patrols in the North Downtown area to a pileup on First and Rodney. The configurations of the pileup kept changing as Mary tried to deal with it, getting more complicated and idiosyncratic as more squad cars arrived at the scene. Two trucks, two pedestrians was how it first came in: Ten Fifty-Two, ambulance needed. Then it was two trucks, some Japanese businessmen and a taxi: Ten Fifty-One, wrecker needed. Make that two ambulances. Then it was *three* trucks, three Japanese businessmen *in* a taxi, an elementary school teacher, and two winos: Ten Fifty-Three, road blocked. Probably with people waiting their turn to be part of the general carnage. As the dispatch board blinked and buzzed and her earphones squawked, Mary, who had just brewed half an urn of coffee to keep the twelve-to-eight shift minimally alert, started wondering if people dropping by to check out the action found themselves entering into the spirit of the thing by throwing themselves under the wheels of the nearest oncoming vehicle. Come right on in and bleed a little, well don't mind if I do. It seemed hardly possible that so many people could be hanging around the Harbor Freeway on-ramp in the very early hours of a Friday morning. Even less possible that they should be there on foot, with the bars closed and the first pickup trucks and vans from the little farms across the bay not due to pull into the Old Market before 4:30. The digital clock at the top of the board said 1:20.

"I want to report a rape," said the man. He was speaking quietly, but she didn't ask him to repeat it.

"You want to report a rape," she said instead, and typed in SA, the new user-friendly cue for the sexual assault program. When you take incomings you learn to reflect a lot, to repeat exactly what they tell you. Reflecting lets you check the information on the spot and also gives you time to figure out where you are on the new software. "Over eighteen years old?" she said now.

"Of *me*," said the man, and Mary hit A for adult rather than M for minor. The screen went briefly black, then rolled out a new list in glowing green letters. She was relieved to see that her first choice was between M and F. She had begun to notice gaps in the program now she was getting used to it, possibilities that somehow hadn't occurred to the designers. "I'm at Overlook Emergency Room," said the man, who clearly didn't know that his location as caller wasn't part of the Victim menu. "Listen, all hell's breaking loose up here."

"You're telling me," said Mary. Through her headset someone was pleading for a third ambulance. "Have they given you a physical examination yet?" she asked, keying into Medical. Another green list scrolled onto the screen. Overlook was understaffed even on slow nights. Tonight he'd be lucky to get the attention of a social work intern.

"*I* did the examination," the man said.

"You did the examination," reflected Mary, trying to remember which category this information belonged in. That was the problem with retiring the old forms: you weren't always sure where to go with the stuff they volunteered.

"I work here," said the man. "I'm a nurse here. I do rape cases. Swabs, smears, pubic hair combings, blood, saliva, urine, clothing, evidence of trauma. I do everything."

"Oh, right," said Mary, who had found that P on Medical gave her a heading for Attending Personnel. Through her

5

headset she could hear somebody giving directions to two patrols coming in from out-of-area. It sounded like Larsson, which might mean trouble. Larsson gave lousy directions.

"Listen," said the man, "I've got the semen sample all sealed up. All bottled and labeled and in the refrigerator. Nobody was around to help, you know, but I took it. I mean, that counts, doesn't it?"

Mary wasn't sure. It was a good question, given the number of sexual assault cases they'd thrown out lately because of botched evidence. "Any witnesses?" she asked.

There was a little hissing sigh at the other end of the line. "This was *rape*," said the man, sounding impatient for the first time.

"To the semen extraction," said Mary. She wondered fleetingly which orifice it had been extracted from, but that sort of question was detective business, not hers. "We probably should get it on record that you did it properly, preferably signed by a doctor."

"There are whole nights nobody sees a doctor around here," said the man. "I did it properly. I've done it a lot. What I need now is a cop, a cop who can write fast. They're bleeding down the hall, you know."

"I know," said Mary. "There are a lot of cops down there, too. I'll radio somebody to interview you for the initial report, if you've got the medical side under control."

"Nothing is under control," said the man. "We've got two DOAs and a bunch of bleeders and you haven't even asked me for my name."

"Oh, right," said Mary, keying back to the Victim menu. "We'll assign the detectives to your case as soon as the precinct captain has had a chance to review the patrol report," she added, wishing again for the old paper forms where the blanks just sat there and didn't leave you poised like an idiot in front of a screen that said PLEASE WAIT.

"Presuming there is a patrol report," said the man. "I can't see there's any big hurry with the detectives. After all, you probably won't have the lab results for ten days." Mary didn't try to contradict him. "And then you'll have a whole *slew* of information about somebody you haven't caught," the man continued. "It's a nice fresh sample. It could convict the bastard if you had the bastard, which you don't. And since you can't very well stop people on the street and say, pardon me would you mind just jerking off into this *cup*—"

"Look," said Mary, who thought this was getting out of hand, "I'm just the dispatcher here. I just take the information."

"I'm just the nurse here," said the man. "Usually I hold hands. Right now I'm holding my own hands."

"What *is* your name?"

She could hear him drawing a breath. "Bruce Levine," he said. "I'll spell it."

Two

By 8:15 A.M., when Lieutenant Anna Blessing accepted her second cup of coffee from Police Administrative Aide Jane Lowry and set it down on the pile of printouts from the twelve-to-eight shift, the report on the Levine rape included an interview with the victim, recorded in careening longhand at 4:30 A.M. by Patrol Officer Peter Prescott, and a note by Frank Allingham, who was precinct captain for the shift, to the effect that Bruce Levine had been the medical attendant on the Griffin rape case in September. The Griffin case had culminated in a conviction, largely because Levine had succeeded in extracting samples of the blood, skin, and hair of the rapist from Gloria Griffin's teeth.

"He's good, this guy," said Jane, who was leaning over Anna's shoulder, ready to swipe with a paper towel at the coffee ring on the report once Anna had picked up her cup.

Anna shifted her weight, causing the regulation swivel chair to squeal alarmingly. Jane stepped back and took a quick look at the steel pedestal connecting the seat of the chair to the base, which consisted of four utilitarian claws radiating from the bottom of the pedestal and culminating in casters. In Jane's recent experience the pedestal had proved the most vulnerable part of the chair. When it started to bend, you had a tricky situation with balance and those casters could deposit a lieutenant of detectives directly onto the floor of the detective room where she might lie on her back for hours flailing around like a gigantic snapping turtle until someone came along to flip her over. This had never actually happened, largely due to vigilance on the part of Jane Lowry, who had managed to have the last swivel chair replaced when the pedestal started to bow. It was touch and go now, of course, whether Anna would destroy the chair first or whether she would become so massive that she was no longer able to insert herself between the vinyl-padded steel arms. Anna's recent rate of growth was unsettling, especially in view of the fact that she was approaching mandatory retirement age. Jane was not about to apply pop psychology to the problem of Anna's weight gain over the last five years, a period coinciding with Anna's promotion from acting to official lieutenant of detectives, but she did worry that Anna's girth might be perceived as rendering Anna unfit for duty, "unfit" being a judgment with a disconcertingly literal meaning under these circumstances. Moreover, Anna had made a career of fitting, of being the woman who passed. Now she was in charge of detective operations in the most important precinct in the city, and passing was no longer a requirement or even an issue. She made the decisions; everyone else had to fit. Or that was the spirit in which she seemed to be taking her promotion. Jane hoped she wasn't taking it too far.

"He'd better be good," said Anna. "He did the examination on himself. We're going to have to run it past the legal guys." She puffed her cheeks for a moment and then blew out the air slowly, so that the sound was barely discernible, the faint hiss of a rubber toy deflating. Jane sometimes claimed that even blindfolded she could pick her boss out of a lineup, given her eighteen years' exposure to Anna's repertoire of noises. Most of the noises were louder and less polite than this one.

Jane shrugged. "We're lucky anybody did the medical," she said. Five separate patrol reports had been filed on the accident, which had made the front page of the Hinton *Express* after the relevant information had been sorted out in the Overlook emergency room (three trucks, two taxis, four Japanese businessmen, three of them in the taxis, the fourth on foot and in all likelihood accompanying the elementary school teacher, who had turned out to be moonlighting as a call girl). Beyond the pileup and the rape, the stack of printouts on Anna's desk documented two busts for possession (crack and cocaine), the detention of four drunken fraternity brothers in the two cells below the precinct house, a threatened suicide (averted), two home burglaries, one armed robbery of a Mobil station, and a family knife fight. A little more fun than usual for a Friday morning in the greater Hinton metropolitan area, but then spring was in the air.

"Nobody's lucky," observed Anna morosely and picked up her coffee cup. Jane leaned over her shoulder and dabbed at the circle it had left around Levine's home address, 412 Sherwood Avenue. "That's only five, six blocks from the hospital," she observed. "Handy for a nurse." She wadded up the paper towel and pitched it into Anna's wastebasket. "I still have a hard time thinking about guys being nurses. Why would a guy want to do that?"

"Why would anyone want to do that?"

"What?"

"Be a nurse," said Anna.

"I thought you meant be raped," said Jane.

"Why would anyone want to be raped?" asked Anna rhetorically. The chair squealed again. Jane eyed it dubiously.

"What I mean is, why would anyone want to rape a man?" she asked. "I don't think we've ever had a case of rape of an adult male before."

"You'd rather they stuck to adult females? *Child* females? You have a preference?"

Jane ignored this. "It's just that it's all backward. I can't get used to it. I'm getting old."

Anna squinted at her. *"I'm* getting old," she said. "I think it's time for a doughnut. Want a doughnut?"

Jane shook her head. It was a ritual they went through every morning.

"I've got a dozen here," said Anna. She slid open her file drawer, which had a number of things in it, none of them files. "A *baker's* dozen," she said, pulling out a white paper bag. Jane shook her head again. Anna reached into the bag and pulled out a brown doughnut with white frosting and multicolored sprinkles. "Fresh this morning," she said.

"I'll pass," said Jane. "Who do you want to give this Levine thing to?"

Anna took a bite out of the doughnut. "Rape of an adult male," she said thickly. "An adult male *nurse*. What you'd call an example of your changing sex roles." Jane nodded. Anna's little pig eyes disappeared momentarily into the blotchy mounds of her cheeks. "Guess," she said, and the force of the sibilants spattered crumbs and sprinkles over the printout.

Rape, even rape of an adult male, is a high-priority crime. Ordinarily in instances of sexual assault, the detective team assigned to the case moves in to interview the victim as soon as the patrol report has been filed and reviewed by the commanding officer. On this occasion, however, everyone involved in the aftermath of the accident had converged at Overlook, so that an interval of almost four hours elapsed between Bruce Levine's call to the precinct house and Officer Constantine's report. During that interval, Levine himself had not been inclined to make conversation, being busy with the kind of case that cops and emergency room personnel call a bleeder. After he had described the incident and read over Prescott's transcription, he announced that he was going home to bed and that he would be happy to receive a visit from the detectives after noon. In view of the nature of the crime and its implications—and Levine grasped the latter immediately and fully—this restraint seemed remarkable, but Anna Blessing could see no reason to prevent the man from getting some sleep and accordingly sent Detectives Annunzio and Carmody first to the university district, to check out a hairdressing salon that had been burglarized during the night.

The burglars had chiseled one corner of the safe plate from its rivet and then peeled down the plate as if the safe were a can of anchovies. Hardly student work: Annunzio and Carmody suspected that whoever had done the job had gotten more than the day's take, rubber-banded into little packets of fives and tens and twenties and awaiting deposit in the morning. Or more than the day's take from a clientele primarily interested in cuts, perms, and highlights. It was a very chic hairdresser's. "Fast lane," Mike Annunzio murmured as they clattered down the stairs after the interview with the distraught owner, who chain-smoked as they took her statement and kept crossing and recrossing her legs.

"Speedy crowd," Priscilla Carmody murmured back as they reached the bottom of the stairwell and came to a stop in front of an oak door with a frosted glass panel. Cut into the frosted glass were the letters DIAR RIAH.

"Cute," said Mike Annunzio.

"Trendy," said Priscilla Carmody.

Trendy, Mike repeated to himself. More information to file away for future reference. Someday he might begin to assemble the context in which Hair Raid was clearly trendy whereas, say, Michelle's Beauty Spot was just as clearly not. In the meantime, he simply acknowledged his partner to be the authority on trendiness, as on so many other things. He wasn't sure from her tone whether the observation had been offered as a supplement or as a correction.

Now she put both hands to her head and pushed her dark hair behind her ears while he pushed open the door. It wasn't supposed to be a big deal who opened the door. It was supposed to be whoever was first, that was all. They had discussed this early on in their partnership. They had discussed a lot of things. He thought she looked very pretty with her hair behind her ears but he didn't say so. The way she looked was one of the things they never discussed.

"I could use a trim," she said, "but here, I don't know. Flying fingers. You want a coke freak waving scissors around your eyes?" Holly, the dispatcher for the day shift, had beeped them during the interview, and the owner had almost jumped out the window. At that point both of them had made a mental note to check back on the place when they weren't expected. The decision was automatic and understood. A lot of things were understood at this point. They had been working together for over two years now.

When they got to Levine's apartment, Levine greeted them in seersucker pajamas and led them into his kitchen. "It's night for me," he explained, motioning them to sit down at the scrubbed pine table by the window. "Coffee?"

Mike Annunzio laid his notebook and pencil on the table in front of him and accepted with pleasure, observing that Levine's coffee was considerably better than anything he got either in the precinct house or at home. Priscilla Carmody refused, although she did not go on to observe that coffee was certainly addictive and very probably linked to rectal cancer. During the first two months after her abrupt conversion to the principles of *Prevention* magazine, an event that had taken place during spring semester of her senior year at the university and had prompted her to move out of her dormitory and into a short-lived collective called Lifewell, she had learned that such observations constituted surefire conversation stoppers. Now she comforted herself with the thought that if people wanted to put toxic substances into their bodies, that was their business. It was really a question of civil rights, although you did have a certain duty to address ignorance when you encountered it. She had been encountering it in Mike since the beginning of their partnership, and here he was still drinking coffee. But that was his business. Her business at the moment was to ask questions while Mike wrote down the answers.

They took turns doing the questioning and the writing, alternating responsibilities with caution since their initial week as a team, when Mike had proposed that she do all the transcribing because she was better at it. This incident had marked the beginning of Mike's education on the subject of the prevailing sex/gender system, an education that had proceeded with some success during the last two years despite the fact that it tended to expose Mike as culpably naive about the conditions of his own upbringing. She had not been optimistic about the project at the outset. If he wanted to be partners with her, she told him, he was going to have to become conscious of the politics allowing him to be so securely unreflective. Then she wondered whether they would try to find her another partner or send her back to patrol work or even suggest she would discover her true calling over in Clerical. But Mike took the ultimatum seriously. He said he would try to become conscious. He even seemed at times to be working on it, although working on it usually took the form of furrowing his brow until he looked, she thought, like a basset hound. Still, she gave him points for effort. It appeared that he did want to be partners with her.

One upshot of this educational experiment was that half the time he wrote and she asked the questions. The equal division was more momentous than it might have seemed to an observer outside the force because during any interrogation presenting difficulties, detectives routinely fall into the roles of good guy and bad guy. The bad guy is the one asking the questions. He is liable to get pushy or even threatening if the person answering the questions seems to be holding out. The good guy takes the notes and intervenes at intervals to mitigate the bad guy's hostility and threats. At a certain point the bad guy can leave the room and the good guy can pick up the questioning, offering himself as a more credulous and sympathetic listener. This tactic often provokes the speaker into revealing far more than he or she had intended. The bad guy is important because he has to create the situation in which the good guy will be perceived as good. This setup can become confusing, not only to the subjects of an interrogation, who after all are supposed to be confused by it, but also to cops themselves, who habitually live in a whole world made up of good guys and bad guys and who have a hard time thinking of criminals as necessary to the construction of their own ethical identities. Luckily, cops are not inclined to brood about these issues, or at least not during the course of an interrogation. Priscilla Carmody was even less inclined to brood than most, in part because she was still one of the few female detectives in the Hinton Metropolitan Police Department and couldn't afford to have anything so feminine as a scruple, in part because she genuinely enjoyed the role of bad guy.

As a natural soprano who was five feet three, barely the revised minimum height requirement for the force, she had to work to appear ominous, but she did work, and usually she came off as very ominous, unexpectedly fanged and clawed and provocative, like some bright-eyed little forest animal with rabies. She was on her guard now because Levine had delayed the interrogation and had been reported as mildly uncooperative during the patrol questioning. There was no doubt that he had cooperated fully with the medical examiners, but inasmuch as he also *was* the medical examiners, the situation was ticklish enough to make her wary. The good-guy and bad-guy roles weren't often used in rape cases. In fact, during the recent years of Anna's leadership, the victim was usually interrogated by a single officer, a woman if at all possible, working alone. But rape of an adult male had few precedents in the literature and none in Detective Carmody's own professional experience. They were going to play this one by ear, and she was counting on the surprise factor of intimidation originating from such an unlikely source.

"Now Bruce," she began, all charm and chest tones. "We know you gave a statement to the patrol officers, but we'd like to ask you now just to tell us again in your own words what happened."

Levine took a sip of his coffee. "Who else's words would I use?" he inquired.

She raised her eyebrows and looked down the table at Mike. He was writing busily. "In your own words is just a phrase," she said. "Sometimes people worry about verbatim quoting, or they think they have to talk like a court record." Levine only stared at her. She stared back, gauging his hostility. Not a willing witness, although on the face of things he ought to be eager to tell his story. "You don't like cops much, do you, Bruce?" she said.

"I'm a nurse," said Levine. "I work in the emergency room. I see a lot of cops."

"That wasn't what I asked."

He leaned back in his chair, his eyes still holding hers. "No, I don't suppose I do," he said. "In my line of work, I've seen too much of the way cops operate."

"But of course you generally cooperate with them," she said. "You've given evidence in several cases. You do cooperate, by and large, don't you, Bruce?"

Levine only stared at her. She stared back.

"You do cooperate, by and large," she said again. "Look, Bruce, why aren't you cooperating now?"

His mouth twisted. "It doesn't exactly put me at my ease when you introduce yourself as Detective Carmody and then address me as Now Bruce," he remarked.

There was a long silence while she considered. Then she said, "Priscilla Carmody."

"*Priss*-scilla."

"Scilla."

"Oh. Scilla. Very classical."

"If you could just tell us—"

"In my own words, I know. How the brute overpowered me. How I couldn't help myself."

Mike put his pencil down. She narrowed her eyes, feeling for the bad-guy role. "Why are you making this so difficult?"

He was staring at her again. She met his eyes, her own gaze steady and neutral. Power games. Maybe he had played them in school, too. But she had learned how to win; she had learned you didn't have the right to back down.

Finally he said, "Oh shit, Scilla, I do these cases. I have a ringside seat when your boys in blue go at some poor, mauled victim. They like to do it when she's still got her feet in the stirrups, do you know that?"

Her expression didn't change. She had learned to stay impassive while she ran through the possibilities, assessed the comparative weight of her divided loyalties. Friend or foe? As always, those were the options. Good guys. Bad guys. Finally she nodded. She did know, of course.

He acknowledged the nod with a lift of his eyebrows. "So, when that officer finally came in to talk to me, I wasn't too surprised that it was all comic relief. After all, those were bleeding people, dead people he'd been dealing with. Real victims. And then me. What could be better, little balding fairy, big hairy rapist in crinoline and nylons—"

"Crinoline," repeated Mike, looking up from his notebook.

"I'll spell it for you, okay?"

"Just checking," said Mike. "Nylons?"

"It's in the report," said Levine. "Don't you people talk to each other?"

"I meant, stockings or panty hose?"

Levine looked at him with interest. "Very *good*. Your blue boy didn't think of that one. Stockings, definitely, it was well thought out. And a garter belt."

"You saw him," said Scilla.

"I didn't see him. I saw movement. Then he had me."

"But the garter belt—"

"I *felt* it, Scilla." She straightened, surprised for a moment by the hostility in his voice. "You want to ask me if it felt good?"

"What did you do?"

"I shouted. Once. Then I couldn't breathe enough to do anything but stay alive."

"Did you struggle?"

"I tried. Do you know what it's like not being able to breathe, having somebody that big on you? You don't know. I tried. I twisted, tried to get an elbow in. There was nowhere to kick. Pretty passive, right Scilla? Pretty *femme,* don't you think?"

17

She breathed out slowly. It didn't matter whether she was in or out of the role; he saw her as the bad guy. "Just what do you have against me, Bruce?"

He smiled tightly. "Me? What could I have against you, Scilla? You're a lady pig, just as good as a man pig any day. Just as macho, just as bigoted. And I'm between Scylla and Charybdis on this one, you get the allusion, Scilla? I mean, I watch your pig brothers talking to women so beat up they don't know where they are, and the pigs say, 'You sure you don't know the guy?' 'You sure you didn't *enjoy* it a little?' I've watched them get hard-ons, Scilla."

"I don't get hard-ons."

"No, you get dis*gus*ted, Scilla, that's all the difference between you. Like I said, I'm between Scylla and Charybdis here, because if I don't tell you the whole dis*gus*ting story, my alternative is to shut up and worry. I'm talking to you because I want this on record, not because I think you're going to do diddly squat about it."

She took a slow breath and concentrated on letting it out completely: *o*-kay. They had taught her that at the beginning of the first karate class she had ever taken. Get in touch with your own ability to control the situation. Wonder how you got out of control of the situation. Try to figure out what's just part of the bad-guy role here and what's something that's personal, you, something you can't take off. Keeping her voice conversational, she said, "You're between Scilla and Mike on this one, actually. I'm beginning to think you have something against sucking vortexes, Levine."

She could see it register. Blink. Not stupid. There's bigotry and bigotry, she thought. You could be gay. You could be a woman. They had those things they could hold against each other. If they held those things against each other, they could be pigs, too.

His shoulders sagged and he was suddenly smaller and older, a lean, olive-skinned man with a fringe of dark hair and a neat mustache. He peered across the table and she had the feeling that he was seeing her for the first time. Maybe because she was finally here, just Scilla, for first time.

"Vortices," he said gently.

"What?"

"The plural of *vortex* is *vortices.*"

"Spell it," said Mike.

"Only one vortex here," she said.

He nodded. "I'm sorry."

"It's okay."

"It's not okay. There are enough victims as it is."

She nodded. "Tell me what you're worried about, Bruce."

Mike looked up from his notebook. "Victims. Vortices. Could you kind of give me the gist of what's going on here?"

"You don't have to take down this part," Scilla said.

Levine was still looking at her. "What I'm worried about," he said, "You know what I'm worried about. I used to joke about the new celibacy," he said. "You know?" She nodded. "I mean, I'm a medical professional and I'm an activist. So about three years ago I stopped. It wasn't a conscious decision. I just knew too much. Too many victims already."

"Three years?"

"Three years of *nothing*, Scilla, if you can imagine. Not for lack of opportunities, either. I used to try not to think about how long it might last, my new celibacy. I used to try not to think it might last a lifetime."

"And now."

He shrugged. "Now I'm thinking about how long a lifetime might last. About how it might not be very long. Six months, more if I'm lucky. Luck being relative to the situation, which hasn't been all that positive."

"You don't know this," she said.

"I don't know *anything*. That's the point. The whole problem is just that, not knowing. What I do know about is the test. and I know enough about the test to know I'm going to be doing a lot of testing."

"I'm sorry," she said at last.

19

"You know about the antibodies, how they don't show up at first, how they sometimes don't show up for years, and how even if they do show up you don't know for sure, maybe not for eight, nine years, maybe more, whether that's going to mean the other."

"Oh hey," said Mike. "I should be getting this part, shouldn't I?"

"Probably," said Scilla. "Jesus. Probably."

"You're saying the guy might——"

"First you catch him," said Levine. "You catch him, maybe we can test him. Presuming we don't need his *consent*. For the record, he didn't ask for mine. But first you have to catch him. That's where we start."

Three

Levine had been attacked in the parking lot behind the pharmacy that adjoined the main tower of Overlook. The pharmacy closed at 5:30 P.M., and at that point the parking lot became a pay-by-number operation, where people parked their cars in the numbered spaces and jammed folded dollar bills into the correspondingly numbered slots of a green metal box located by the only entry and exit, off Garfield Street. The box was frequently jimmied, despite the fact that someone from the company that operated these lots all over the city was supposed to come by regularly and empty it out. Parking was scarce for the inhabitants of the high-rise apartment buildings that over the last ten years had sprung up all over the neighborhood surrounding the hospital, so the lot was usually full by six or six-thirty.

"Very little action after six or thereabouts on your weekday night," explained the man who had been introduced to Annunzio as Mr. Wasson. He was sitting in a swivel chair in front of a computer screen that displayed in four throbbing colors a schematic rendering of the Hinton North Downtown and Central areas. Because the background of the map was black, the configuration of streets and freeways showed up as a gorgeous nighttime neon. The areas identified as Sullivan lots were acid green. As Annunzio watched, a red arrow moved up from the black emptiness that was the only indication of Nanteco Bay, through the galaxy of white and yellow lines and green squares where Sullivan had clearly struck it rich with the crowds patronizing the Old Market, across the red slash where the new expressway severed the downtown from Temple Hill, and up the hill to the thick streak of white that was Mason Avenue.

"You with me so far?" Wasson was clearly enjoying his role of helping the police with their inquiries. Mike sometimes wondered if your average television viewer had the tone of an investigation down much better than real detectives, who were hampered in their pursuit of crisp, professional brevity by the fact that they had to find real things out. Wasson hit a key with the panache of a concert pianist. "Okay, then let's zero in on the Central–Temple Hill area." The screen went black for a second and then sprang into more subdued life. The expressway had vanished, so that the only red now was the arrow, pointed at a thicker Mason Avenue, which dominated an enlarged grid of regular white and yellow lines. Green Sullivan lots were spotted decorously along its route. "Here you've got your movie theaters, your restaurants, your boutiques," Wasson said. "Down the avenue, however, as you move south, you get into the Central area. What you call your residential, your mixed. Weekends, people park down here, walk north on Mason, go to a movie or something. Weekends they get all the way down to the Overlook area, that's your area of concern." Mike nodded. "Regulars go in and out, too, sometimes after midnight," said Wasson. "But that's weekends."

"What about Overlook?"

Wasson shrugged. "They have their own lots. Also, they tow." He shrugged again. "This area, this kind of heavy transient stuff, on weekends, you understand, you have to tow. Hey, we tow."

"I know," said Mike. The precinct got a lot of the calls, missing vehicle, officer I just put it there while I ran in. Sullivan Parking was ruthless. "But you don't expect much action on a weeknight around Overlook, is that what you're saying?"

"Naw," said Wasson. Maybe we have a man swing by there about seven, then again about eight, then maybe once more the entire night."

"When would that be?"

Wasson shrugged expansively, swiveling around in his chair. "Ask him."

Richie Borkman lived in one of the bungalows off Cleveland Avenue in the Little Oslo district. His mother answered the doorbell and seemed worried at being confronted with a working detective. Richie, however, was delighted.

"What *kind* of assault?" he demanded through a mouthful of mashed potatoes. Richie's mother had explained that Richie ate dinner early in order to begin work at six in the evening. Richie was eating two TV dinners in front of the TV when Annunzio walked into the Borkman living room.

"Just an assault," said Mike.

"Come on. I mean, gun, knife, razor? What?"

"Have you seen people with those kinds of weapons in the course of your job?"

"It's a jungle out there," observed Richie with satisfaction.

Despite his acquaintance with the life of the streets, Richie had missed being present at the scene of the crime by a good hour and a half. After some prodding from Annunzio, he was persuaded to consult the logbook required by Sullivan as documentation of his visits to the lots on his beat. "Last I swung by last night is maybe eleven-thirty," he reported hopefully. "Just two new cars in, all-nighters. Four bucks apiece. That's eight bucks."

"Out of how many?"

Richie consulted his logbook. "In the Overlook drugstore lot we got thirty-two spaces."

"And the lot was full?"

Richie looked superior. "All our lots in that hospital area are generally full-up by the time I swing by second time round.

23

Seven-thirty to eight-thirty, maybe nine. After that I just cruise them a little. Look for illegal parkers, violators, like that."

"And there was nothing going on in the pharmacy lot when you went by?"

"That's a quiet lot weeknights," said Richie. "Quiet neighborhood. Lots of old people. Anyway, everybody knows we tow."

Detective Carmody was verifying these observations as she checked out the pink concrete high-rise alongside the parking lot. Quiet neighborhood. Lots of old people. Not many of them in the high-rise, but those inhabitants of the high-rise that she found at home were unanimous in their assessment of the locality. "Old ladyville," according to Sasha Friedman, mother of two preschoolers and soon to be owner, with her husband Jeffrey, of a cedar-shingled four-bedroom contemporary rising from an erstwhile cow pasture east of Lake Hinton. Sasha had architect's drawings of the contemporary, which was one of a dozen in the process of being built. "It's not really a development," she explained. "Each house is unique to their owners. We're just here till Jeff finishes his internship." Scilla admired the drawings and asked about the parking lot. "It's criminal," said Sasha. "You just pull *in* there, they show up with a tow truck." She had heard nothing unusual, but then she was dead on her feet by the time the kids were asleep. Ditto Elizabeth Forrester two floors down, wife of Jonathan, mother of Ashleigh. Ditto Barbara Dieter, ground floor, wife of Christopher, mother of Jonah and Jennifer. Young mothers make indifferent witnesses. Seth Miller on the seventh floor worked nights at Domino's, the dance club. Roger Liebowitz and Jill Doty, eighth floor, were manager and bartender, respectively, at the Chapel, a Lutheran church that had metamorphosed into a fashionable restaurant specializing in microwaved frozen seafood. Expensive building, part of an upgrade that ought to be countering the impression of old ladyville. But the impression was still there. Scilla resolved to come back after dinner, but she wasn't optimistic about what any of these tenants were likely to have seen or heard.

Across the street, in an ancient three-story house with MARI-DON stenciled across the top of its front door to commemorate the owners who had renovated it with glitter stucco during some enchanted moment of fifties history, she found what she was looking for. In apartment 2B, front south, directly across Seventh from the entrance to the pharmacy parking lot, she was greeted by Mrs. Lily Johannsen, who seated her in a second wicker armchair by the front window, offered her tea (which Scilla refused: caffeine is caffeine), and related breathlessly her newest evidence that the neighborhood was in decline once again.

"You can always tell," said Mrs. Johannsen, fixing Scilla with a bright blue gaze. "They carry these big purses. That's for the wigs. And those high heels is a giveaway. You can't walk too good. Not that you need to walk when mostly you got your legs in the air. And that's just some of what I could mention. I know what they do. Nasty."

"This person had a big purse," Scilla repeated, noting the fact on her pad.

"Person is right," said Mrs. Johannsen. "I don't dignify them with the title of nothing else. Big square purse like they have. And blond hair that wasn't hers I'm telling you. Sometimes you see niggers with that blond hair, like it was fooling somebody. Me, I had blond hair till I was fifty, never had any gray in it, not that you could see, and then suddenly it was all this white. You believe me?"

"I believe you," said Scilla. "You think it was a black person, then?"

"I think it was a *person,*" said Mrs. Johannsen. "That's what I think. I wouldn't stoop to the other word."

"You think it was a Negro," said Scilla, pronouncing very carefully.

Mrs. Johannsen shook her head, a little regretfully. "Not this person," she said. "This person wasn't blond but I wouldn't go so far as that. I saw her, you see. With her wig off."

Scilla leaned forward. "When was that?"

"When she came *out*," said Mrs. Johannsen. "You know, I wouldn't put it past her to be doing it right there, in a car maybe. You gotta be careful locking your car. Or on the car, even, right on top, they got no shame these persons. Right by the hospital where people are dying."

"Do you have any idea what time this was? Was there maybe a television program you were watching, or did you have the radio on—"

"I don't do any of that trash," said Mrs. Johannsen with heavy finality. "What they got on now, that's just filth. When I was younger, now, they had your comedy, they had your dramas, they had your game shows, they had your pet shows, they had your kid performers, like those acrobatic dancers you don't see no more, they had your Lawrence Welk—"

"If you have some idea, even, what time she came out—"

"Oh, sure," said Mrs. Johannsen. "That was about two minutes before one. I hear the chimes from Saint Dominick way down here even. You keep your television off, your radio off, you hear *everything*."

"Right," said Scilla, making another note. "What did she look like?"

Mrs. Johannsen closed her eyes as if summoning up an image. "Big girl, especially in those heels, which she didn't handle so good. Tall but thick, especially in the legs. No beauty, I can tell you. Straight hair, dark, with bangs, down to her collar. Like those Chinese girls have, except that big she was no Chinese. And no blond either, I can tell you."

"What was she wearing?"

"Same thing as when she went in. Big skirt, real full. Down to the middle of her calf. It stuck out, too, like she was wearing one of those petticoats. Then she had a jacket on that was dark, too, sort of square. And that purse that had her big blond wig in it."

"But you didn't see the wig," said Scilla.

"I don't have to see to know," observed Mrs. Johannsen enigmatically. "You know why they have those wigs, it's for the excitement." She leaned across the table toward Scilla. "You have to use your imagination, dear, I can't tell you too much. But I happen to know they use their mouths."

"Really!" said Scilla.

"I can't say no more," said Mrs. Johannsen. "You have to use your imagination."

Scilla made another note. "I don't know quite how to broach this," she said, "but I need to ask you. Is there anything about this person that might lead you to believe that it wasn't a woman? I mean, that it was a man?"

Mrs. Johannsen looked shocked. "Oh, no, dear," she said. "She was wearing a big full skirt and high heels and a wig. Why would a man want to wear any of those things?"

Scilla, who had never been certain why a woman would want to wear any of these things, told Mrs. Johannsen that she had been very helpful.

Four

"Circle skirts, mostly," said Lieutenant Blessing through a mouthful of doughnut. She leaned back until her chair squeaked ominously. "Taffeta was very popular for evening," she continued. "For school it was felt, with appliqués. My oldest girl had one of those, with a poodle on it."

"No poodle," said Scilla, looking down at her own gray gabardine knees. "Taffeta sounds more like it. He said it rustled." Rustled and bunched around the crinoline, Levine had told them. There had been a bulge of shifting, muttering fabric against his back, with the arm above, across his windpipe, and the hand below, squeezing and then prodding his legs apart.

"The poodle had a rhinestone collar and a rhinestone leash that spiraled around the skirt and up to the waist. The rhinestones fell out one by one." Anna Blessing took another bite out of her doughnut. It was the second doughnut she had eaten since Scilla had come in with her report on the Bruce Levine case.

"Crinolines are back," said Scilla. "I stopped in at Joan Etten on College Way." She had been heading for the fast hairdresser's to get a look at their late afternoon clientele when it occurred to her to check on the availability of transvestite rapist gear. According to the manager of Joan Etten, all the gear was readily available. "They've got garter belts and stockings, too. Stockings with seams."

"The more things change," Anna observed cryptically. "Once upon a time, they all had seams. Everything was stockings, too, held up by garters attached to something else, belts or girdles. Mostly girdles. And we all wore stockings, always. That was part of my uniform for twenty years, appropriate legwear. Appropriate with the skirt, that meant."

Scilla didn't want to think about Anna Blessing in a skirt with appropriate legwear. It was bad enough dealing with the question of where she got her uniform trousers. Most of the precinct agreed that she had to have a tailor somewhere, some visaless immigrant hoarding bolts of blue serge against the reappearance of the monolith in a still more massive incarnation. Almost six feet tall, Anna had been gaining weight steadily during the four years Scilla had been working under her supervision. The Hinton Metropolitan Police Department required a yearly physical examination, but nobody had yet suggested to Lieutenant Blessing that obesity might be grounds for early retirement. Given the tendency of upper-echelon officers to spread into their desk jobs and the recent success of affirmative action suits involving public servants, it wasn't likely that Anna would be the test case for a fat purge, but in the precinct there were periodic attempts to guess her weight, with the median guess well above 300 pounds.

"Appropriate legwear," Scilla said. "I suppose his will turn out to be appropriate if we can figure out what he has in mind." Granting that rape was on his mind, she could see that stockings had the advantage over panty hose, but that didn't answer the question of why he chose in the first place to rape in prom-queen drag. She could tell it was going to be a tough one to figure. "He seems to have been pretty big, even for a man," she continued. "At least six four in heels. But evidently, it's no problem getting stockings that long." It occurred to her belatedly that this would not be news to Anna, given Anna's history in regulation skirts. "We don't even know how he figured Levine was gay," Scilla went on. "There's nothing obvious about Levine, he's just a man. And we have what he was wearing—sport shirt, khaki pants, bush jacket, running shoes. They don't take their scrubs and lab coats out of the building. We're wondering if the guy was following him for a while, maybe picked up his pattern over a period of several days. Evidently, Levine usually took the same route to the hospital. Mike and I walked it after we talked to him." Levine claimed to do it in four minutes. Up the hill for two steep blocks on Sherwood, then cutting over on Monroe to the alley between the big pink high-rise and the pharmacy, then down the alley and diagonally across the parking lot. He'd come out on Garfield, kitty-corner from the street entrance to the emergency room. They had done it in four minutes forty seconds and had emerged from the parking lot breathing hard. Levine was in good shape.

Anna looked hopefully into the doughnut bag before wadding it up and dropping it into her wastebasket. "He could have been followed. On the other hand, it could have been a lucky guess. Or the rapist could just have been *saying* faggot, not realizing he'd actually got it right."

"Levine isn't feeling very lucky," said Scilla. "Levine's got a hypothesis."

"A hypothesis!" Anna looked enchanted. "Scientific type, isn't he? Little brain just chugging away. Helping the police with their inquiries."

"I think we should take it into consideration," Scilla insisted.

"Let's see if I can figure it out. Okay, it's going to be a con*spir*acy."

Scilla withheld comment.

"A conspiracy against *queers,* am I close?"

Put that way, it sounded ridiculous.

"And let's see, the whole point is to give them, what's that disease?"

"AIDS," said Scilla.

"Yeah, give them AIDS, get rid of them all, except the

problem is the rapist has to have AIDS first and if he hates queers how did he get it?"

"He's raping them," said Scilla. "Gays," she amended. "I mean, he's got to be sexually aroused by them or he couldn't do it. But that's beside the point because you don't have to be gay to have AIDS."

"Sure, it's a free country," Anna agreed. "But listen, your guy have any hard evidence for any of this? Like, has he *got* this disease?"

Scilla cleared her throat. "They're estimating now that the HIV antibody takes anywhere from two to twelve weeks to show up after infection, but it could be longer. In fact, it could be a lot longer. They just don't have enough data to say with any certainty that somebody *hasn't* been infected."

"HIV?"

"Human immunodeficiency virus. It can lead to a whole range of symptoms, which is to say that with your immune system under attack, you might get all sorts of diseases. But here's the next hitch, it might not lead to anything. Not necessarily to AIDS, in other words, although it's always present when AIDS is present. We don't know yet whether HIV infection necessarily means AIDS one hundred percent of the time, and it may be a long time before we do know. The studies just haven't gone on for that long. Two to five years is what they're calling the average incubation period right now, but there's no saying that you're ever *not* at risk, once you've been exposed."

Lieutenant Blessing whistled. "You've been reading that Harvard Medical School newsletter again," she said. Scilla had once made the mistake of leaving a copy of this publication on Anna's desk, opened to the results of the newest study on cholesterol and heart disease.

"I've been reading the *Hinton Gay and Lesbian Advocate*," said Scilla stiffly. Bruce Levine had presented her with a selection of back issues as she was leaving his apartment. She had pored over them that evening and emerged impressed with the volume and quality of medical reporting they contained.

Anna's little pig eyes lit up. "Swinging that way, are we?" Scilla concentrated on not changing anything in her expression. Anna nudged her with a large elbow. "What's *Mike* going to say?" Scilla shrugged. It didn't help that she could predict this response. Some time ago she had worked out that these gross joshings had to be a legacy of Anna's early days on the force, when everybody put up with a sole big girl among the uniformed patrols because she was the captain's daughter and in effect one of the boys. Anna had been good at acting the part, too, and you could only guess at the work she must have put into making the transition from cop's widow and mother of two girls to just plain cop. That was the fifties, after all, when uniformed police were presumed not only to be men but to be unreflective parodies of Hollywood masculinity. In the middle of all that bluff and testosterone, Anna had maneuvered from her clerical position as precinct manager into the traffic division, and from there into patrol training school, where she had established a marksmanship record that stood unbroken for six years. Four years on the beat and she took the detective exam, establishing another record. And nobody complained, or at least not loudly enough to make a difference. She'd had pull, of course, coming from a family of cops with Daddy on his way to the top, but pull alone wouldn't have done it. You still have to have pull, even now; they always wondered why a nice girl like you wanted to do this dirty thing, and almost the only answer that would get you through was the answer that Anna had given, that Scilla had given twenty-eight years later with rehearsed demureness while the recruiter looked for outward and visible signs of perversity. My father. In Anna's case, also My husband. Two blood connections. My late husband: play it for maximum sympathy. Cop families. They wanted that assurance that you'd understand, or maybe it was their only assurance that they'd be able to understand you. Art's widow but more than that, Daddy's girl. Anna Blessing was her father's daughter. But she'd also paid her dues. She'd passed. In 1963, ten years after she had joined the force, she was a real detective, an honorary man. And a precedent.

My role model, thought Scilla. Dear God.

"Mike's going to be sor-ry you're going lezzie," crooned Anna in playground singsong.

"Don't say lezzie," said Scilla tonelessly. The woman had the emotional responses of a ten-year-old. Not to mention the eating habits.

"He's gonna lose *all* hope."

Scilla wished she could tell Anna to lay off. She liked Mike and had a good working relationship with him. This infantile teasing should have been beside the point. The fact that it wasn't quite beside the point tended to make her wonder if some of what Anna was saying about him might be true.

"Well, okay," Anna conceded. "That's your private life. That's your own business. That's the right line, isn't it?" She squinted malevolently at Scilla. "I'm being politically *correct*, aren't I? You can answer that."

"It is my own business," said Scilla, feeling somehow that she'd been outdone.

"You get some pertinent information from that gay and lezzie newsletter, you let me know. Don't bother to bring it in, just let me know. Okay?"

"Okay," said Scilla. It didn't feel like a victory.

"Otherwise, you don't presume there's something being transmitted by this here act of aggression," Anna continued, suddenly very serious. "Humiliation, sperm, that's gotten passed on. That we know about. The other stuff, we got no evidence. None. Anybody that says so is spreading irresponsible rumors. You got that?"

Scilla nodded.

"Including this guy Levine. He leaks that kind of thing to that gay and lezzie paper, he could be obstructing. You let him know."

"I will," said Scilla, although she didn't think it would stop Bruce.

"Now getting back to the business at hand," continued Anna, waving her own pudgy hand airily, "which is the homosexual rape of a homosexual man, if that clarifies the crime. Which it doesn't, necessarily."

Scilla eyed her warily. "Now you're saying it could be more."

"Not out loud I'm not. Pay attention. But if it is more, we have to ask what kind of crime we have here. And the minute I ask that question I find I gotta call up all the legal guys. You see what I'm getting at?"

"Oh," said Scilla. "Yeah. Right." It always unnerved her that someone so insensitive could get at the implications so fast.

Anna beamed at her. Perhaps because of her general build, perhaps too because of an unkind tendency to delight in embarrassing the officers under her command, Anna often looked inappropriately jolly. Mike sometimes referred to her as Mrs. Claus. "You realize what this faggot might be doing?"

Scilla closed her eyes.

Anna's smile got broader. "No good? We can't call them faggots even when they're the bad guys? Okay, this pervert then. You don't have trouble with pervert, do you?"

Scilla had a lot of trouble with pervert, but she knew Anna. "Okay," she said wearily. "And yeah, I can see we might want to put the legal guys into it."

"You suppose some asshole has figured out a swell new way to murder people?"

"Some asshole," said Scilla, "is how he does it."

Five

The lab report on the semen sample came back to the precinct house in a record eight days. "Rush job," observed Bruce Levine when Scilla called him. "I'm touched that you gave me such a high priority."

"It's type O positive," said Scilla. She wished Levine wouldn't put her on the defensive. They were on the same side, after all.

"Progress!" cried Levine from his end of the connection. He seemed to be in a good mood, or perhaps this was despair. Scilla had learned in patrol school that despair took different people different ways. Same thing with panic, anger, fear. Psychology, they'd called it. None of it had proved very helpful.

"I don't suppose they did any other tests while they were getting this important information about blood type," Levine continued with something like exuberance.

"We don't have the equipment here," she told him. "Also, the sample wasn't fresh enough."

"Of course it wasn't fresh enough!" he caroled. "Nobody even showed up to talk to me for almost two hours." Scilla thought about reminding him that there had been a major accident, but she decided against it. *Major* seemed like a fairly arbitrary designation: was his own rape minor compared to a lot of cars and trucks slamming into each other? She wished he wouldn't make her feel she had to explain these things. A lot of times when she had to explain something about procedure to a member of the general public, she ended up feeling like a fool.

"Well, maybe next time," said Levine. She had the uneasy feeling he was reassuring her.

"We're still working on your case," she said. "What do you mean next time?"

"I mean next time this guy *rapes* somebody," he explained with exasperated patience. "He's taking his own sweet time about it, but then he can afford to."

Probably, she thought. Oh yeah, probably. They don't just stop. "You think it's going to be another guy?" she asked.

"Another gay guy. He's got us figured now. Easy marks. You wait."

"I don't see you as easy marks," she objected. "You're men. You're still conditioned to resist, most of you."

"Most of us," he echoed. "Hey, so is it better if we resist? More *manly*, Scilla?"

She winced at the receiver. Inept, Scilla, she told herself. You try and try, but sometimes you're just a pig. "Not necessarily," she said. "It depends on the circumstances. It's better if you survive, that's the bottom line." And found herself wincing again.

But he let that one pass. All he said was, "Well, let's hope the next one is butch. Then we can test your hypothesis." She didn't think she had a hypothesis, but she wasn't about to continue the conversation.

As it turned out, the second man punched and kicked and was generally very butch, all as Levine had suggested. With a fine sense of restraint, Levine, who was on duty at Overlook emergency room the Tuesday night eleven days and twenty-two hours after his own rape, did the examination and forbore mentioning that the punching and kicking had produced no consequences beyond a nasty bruise on the throat of the victim.

"It'll be the same guy," he predicted, elevating the sealed

and labeled vial in front of Patrol Officers Larsson and Day, who had driven the victim to the hospital. "We won't know who he *is*, of course, but we'll know he's done it twice." Larsson and Day knew this was probably true, but they would have preferred a little more faith in the mysterious ways of the HMPD.

Because the man had made such a commotion, several of the inhabitants of the looming turn-of-the-century houses around the Masonic Temple that capped Temple Hill had been moved to dial 911, and the wailing squad cars had brought in their wake a number of representatives of the media. These men and women, at loose ends during the wee hours of an otherwise dull morning, had hung around the waiting room fiddling with their cassette recorders and directional microphones and cameras and portable lighting equipment until the victim joined them, attractively framed by the blue serge bodies of Officers Larsson and Day, who blinked at the unexpected explosions of light and tried to keep their latest casualty from talking to the press. But Alan Lindgren wanted to talk to the press, whom he claimed as his brothers and sisters. In a fine display of family feeling, the press took him to its collective bosom in a great whirring of electronic equipment.

Lindgren had the kind of rangy blond good looks that prompted men in the gay bars of San Francisco and Los Angeles and New York to speak longingly of Hinton as a homoerotic Valhalla. He could have been displayed in the posters for the *Hinton Gay and Lesbian Advocate* that had gone up last month for the first time ever in selected city buses, so perfectly did he embody the *Advocate*'s updated position on sexual preference as a manifestation of something called Lifestyle. Indeed, his presence on the editorial board of the *Advocate* may have stimulated the other members to spring for the transit advertising campaign, which represented readers of that journal (one male and one female, although not in the same picture) as exceptionally fit and well-dressed individuals who were occupied, respectively, in placing a cut-crystal bowl of roses at the center of a long dinner table set for twelve and in adjusting the already taut spinnaker of a racing yacht. The campaign had been aimed at generating subscribers for a new home-delivery service, which would allow readers to discover the *Advocate* already on their doorsteps, perhaps snuggling with the *Hinton Herald*, when they came home on Thursday afternoons, and thus would spare them the potential embarrassment of asking for it at newsstands. Initially, several of the members of the editorial board had seen the home-delivery service as a move toward greater openness among members of the gay community and had proposed a poster that invited "Come Out, Come Out, Wherever You Are." This slogan was squashed by more temperate elements, and the pictures in the buses carried the caption "The Advocate Goes Where You Do," with the full name, *Hinton Gay and Lesbian Advocate,* at the bottom in small but readable type along with the home-delivery telephone number. A not altogether unanticipated bonus of the campaign was that it brought in a great deal of new advertising, not only from the usual clothing stores (Uomo, Don We Now) but also from shops selling high-tech kitchenware, crystal and silver, sterophonic components, coffee-table books, and sporting equipment. The man in the photograph was not Alan Lindgren, although he looked something like Alan Lindgren. Alan Lindgren had taken the photograph.

Lindgren's first act upon entering the waiting room was to hold up his smashed Nikon, a gesture that elicited murmurs of pain and outrage from the press and surges of light from their arrayed photographic equipment. When the disturbance had died down and the television cameras had dollied into position around him, he indicated the gauze bandage that Bruce Levine had applied over the purpling finger marks of the rapist and announced hoarsely, "This is an act of calculated homophobia." There was a little murmur from the back of the room, where the *Advocate* staff had assembled on short notice. The stringer for the *Herald* raised his hand. "H-O-M-O—" said Lindgren.

Larsson elbowed Day. "We're never going to get him out

of here," he muttered. "Better tell Mike to come over and join the party." Day stepped back out of the warm aura of the lights and faded from the room. Annunzio had been located at home, where he was having a fight with his wife, Sally, and had been persuaded to come interview Lindgren at the precinct house. Scilla Carmody was not home, and the recorded message on her answering machine had stated only that she would return calls when she got back.

"This is the second sexual attack on a gay man in a space of twelve days," announced Lindgren, who had grasped immediately the connections that Larsson and Day were still groping for and was now tracing the outlines of a page-one story. "In both cases, the men were assaulted in public parking lots. I was at the edge of the lot in back of the Masonic Temple, shooting the view of Hinton Harbor that you get from the lip of the hill up there. It's a beautiful night, perfectly clear. The Perth Island Ferry had just moved into my viewfinder."

"Were you on assignment?" called a woman's voice from behind the lights. Like all spontaneous questions during press conferences, this one came from a representative of the print media. The TV people would film this part, but the bulk of their coverage would come later, when their own attractive interviewers shared the space of a close-up with attractive Lindgren, and one by one these interviewers would ask Lindgren the same questions and be given the same answers. Trust a newspaper reporter to horn in on a natural process.

"I was shooting the harbor," said Lindgren. "There's not much of a story there. I mean—" and here he gave an ineffably poignant wave of his hand, "spring. Little buds just coming out on the Madrona trees." He smiled wanly into the bank of cameras. "Well, actually I was thinking of a front cover on the *Weekly Reader* or maybe even the Sunday magazine of the *Herald*. Providing they turned out as well as they looked like they were going to." Little moans of sympathy went ululating through the press corps. He'd created a hook to three of the papers present, noted Rita Freeling, who had asked the question on behalf of the *Weekly Reader*. She didn't hold it against him. She admired professionalism in whatever circumstances she found it.

At this point, Alexander Radley of the *Express* began the relentless questioning that had won him the state Best Journalist, Print Media, award last year and that would be necessary if the *Express* was going to have the story all over its front page in the morning. Mindful of deadlines, Lindgren hunkered down and began matching terse answer to terse question. Had he seen his assailant? No, he was setting up a spectacular shot when the assailant was moving in. The man had made some noise approaching, but he hadn't sounded dangerous enough to warrant turning around. What did that mean, he hadn't sounded dangerous? He hadn't sounded like a man. You see, he had been wearing high heels. Pop, whirr, scribble. One of the two AP reporters scooted out of the room to make a telephone call.

What were the police doing? Officer Day, returned from the emergency-room telephone, moved into the range of the cameras. Large, black, and amiable, he had been earmarked by his superiors early on as a soothing presence in potentially unruly crowd situations. Neither he nor Officer Larsson had consciously decided that the journalists massed in the Overlook emergency waiting room constituted a potentially unruly crowd situation, but both policemen were instinctively responding just as they had one evening last fall, when thousands of otherwise sober citizens took to the streets to celebrate the unprecedented occasion of the Hinton Hornets taking the NBA championship title. Well, now, Officer Day said, the police were currently awaiting the arrival of one of the detectives assigned to the case. What detective? Officer Day believed it would be Detective Michael Annunzio.

Was there a reason for assigning this particular case to Detective Annunzio? The question came from the very back of the room this time, where most of the editorial board of the *Advocate* seemed to be holding an informal meeting.

"Well, now," said Officer Day, but at that moment Mike walked in the street door to the waiting room. Cameras swung around to greet him; lights beamed crazily over the walls before settling down to glare in his eyes. And Lindgren, who had been containing his shock and humiliation for over two hours, finally cracked, crying out in a voice that trembled with passion, "Are you one of us?"

Mike blinked. "One of us what?" he asked. On balance, it was probably the right response. Even dazzled by the lights, he could see that Lindgren didn't look Italian.

It became clear shortly thereafter that Lindgren was in no shape to continue fielding questions from his professional family. Larsson and Annunzio led him back into the emergency room in a final tumultuous popping of flashbulbs while Officer Day stayed behind to handle residual questions. The police would have a statement tomorrow morning. It was possible that there would be a press conference, he couldn't say. Yes, they were pursuing with all deliberate speed a number of leads as to the identity of the rapist. Yes, the bizarre details of the rapist's costume had also been a feature of the previous assault. No, the police were not willing to advance any theories about the motive just yet. Yes, this case also fell under the jurisdiction of Lieutenant Anna Blessing, who had headed the investigation of the Hinton Hooker Hacker two years ago. No, there were no similarities between the two cases, aside from Lieutenant Blessing's involvement. Yes, the crime was rape. No, the police were not anticipating the possibility that a more serious crime had been perpetrated.

"What we got here is a felony all by itself," Officer Day said. "Now don't you people go jumping to any farfetched conclusions."

In the banging and snapping of equipment cases that followed this peroration, Rita Freeling thought she could detect the muffled thud of a whole band of journalists coming down hard on the same farfetched conclusion.

41

Six

The conclusion was there, for anyone who cared to jump to it, on the front page of the *Express* three hours later. Normally allergic to neologisms, the staid night editor had seized on HOMOPHOBIC RAPIST STRIKES AGAIN for the headline. As he explained to the *Express*'s publisher, who called him at home after the paper had been delivered to readers all over the greater Hinton metropolitan area, there really was no simple and familiar language for the unfamiliar phenomenon of a man who sexually assaulted homosexual men. Anyway, Alexander Radley had begun his byline article, top center on the front page, by defining the term, quoting Alan Lindgren to the effect that homophobia was fear and hatred of homosexual persons. The publisher was not mollified. His concern was not with the word, open to attack by the university's Department of Classical Philology as it would doubtless prove to be, but with the smaller headline above Alexander Radley's byline, which read AIDS DANGER CANNOT BE RULED OUT. Was there really evidence for this assertion? If so, what sort of evidence could it be? Wouldn't they be liable for a lawsuit if the headline turned out to be a manifestation of what the *Express* most ardently despised and opposed, Irresponsible Journalism?

And who was going to bring this lawsuit? demanded Alexander Radley, who by this time had also been reached at home. Was the publisher perhaps persuaded that there was a group called Fans of AIDS who would worry that the name of their disease was being taken in vain? Perhaps the rapist himself would emerge to charge defamation of character, alleging violation of the confidentiality statutes applying to medical information? But in either contingency they really had an excellent case, as he, Radley, had never maintained that the rapist had AIDS, only that the possibility could not be ruled out. Did Responsible Journalism really entail hiding a source of danger from members of the Hinton community? Was the publisher perhaps willing to see his prizewinning reporter depart for the more popular, if commensurately less Responsible, *Hinton Herald?* For his part, Radley was more concerned to scoop the evening *Herald,* which would certainly play up the AIDS angle if it got there first but at this point was left only with remnants of the story like FATAL PHOTO WAS FOR HERALD SUNDAY MAG SAYS HOMO RAPE VICTIM. The publisher withdrew to consult his legal staff, and the night editor and Radley both went to bed.

Scilla Carmody arrived at the precinct house at 8:00 A.M. to find Anna Blessing already at her desk, which was covered with a collection of discrete pages from section 1 of the *Express.* Sitting open on top of the front page, with its headline, was a large book that Scilla, reading upside down, identified as the *Random House Dictionary of the English Language.* On the right-hand page of the dictionary was half of a chocolate doughnut. Crumbs from the doughnut had slid into the crack between the pages of the dictionary.

"Sit down," said Anna, abstractedly pulling a second doughnut out of the bag at her feet.

Scilla sat. The new doughnut was covered with white powdered sugar, which settled like snow on the blue serge of Anna's shelflike bosom. She wondered whether it had some sort of effluent jelly or custard center, and what would happen when Anna reached that center. "How many of those have you got?" she asked suddenly, feeling as if the question had been dragged out of her.

"Dozen," said Anna. "You want one?"

"No. No, thank you."

"Some of them are whole wheat."

"No, thank you."

"Whole wheat is *good* for you."

Scilla stared straight ahead. "Not in doughnuts it isn't."

"Oh yeah?" Anna looked only benignly interested. "How come?" She had acquired a clot of red jelly on her chin, but Scilla resisted mentioning it.

"Doughnuts are cooked in hot fat," she said reluctantly.

"Yum," said Anna and pulled out yet another doughnut, this one covered in dandrufflike flakes of coconut. Scilla stared resolutely over Anna's shoulder at the framed photograph of Captain Donald G. "Bud" Dorf, commanding officer of the precinct, which occupied a position of prominence on the far wall. A universally observed custom among the brass in the HMPD was to display a large and intrusive portrait of the officer who was immediately superior. Captain Dorf had on his wall a picture of Chief Henry Considine, who had succeeded Anna's father, Robert Swenson, as commissioner. In turn, Henry Considine had a picture of the mayor, Walter "Skuggy" Norman. Skuggy Norman had a picture of the President of the United States, but most people thought this was because he had managed to get the picture autographed. The people who worked with Skuggy didn't take him very seriously. A trained observer, Scilla had noted immediately that by placing Dorf's picture directly behind her, Anna had managed to force it on the attention of anyone talking to her without having to look at it herself.

"You're not telling me about hot fat," Anna pointed out. Scilla wished she would swallow before she spoke. "Oh hey," said Anna. "Looky here. I forgot this one when I was only halfway finished with it and it's my favorite, chocolate." Scilla smiled distantly. "Okay, so don't tell me about hot fat," said Anna. "Tell me about this homophobia."

Scilla cleared her throat. "Homophobia is fear or hatred of homosexuals."

"Actually it isn't," said Anna promptly. "Phobia does mean abnormal fear or dread with the attendant implication of hatred or aversion." She tapped the open dictionary, sending little crumbs of chocolate doughnut skittering across the page. "But homo could either be from the Latin, in which case it means man, or from the Greek, in which case it means the same. So homophobia means either fear and loathing of man or fear and loathing of the same."

"In *usage*—" said Scilla.

"What you want," concluded Anna, "is homosexualphobia. That's what you want."

"What you want," said Scilla, "is a newer dictionary."

"But that's not what I meant," Anna insisted, having registered her small triumph. "I meant all of a sudden there's discussions of this homophobia everywhere, even in the *Express*. All of a sudden everybody's an expert on the motive. You get what I mean?"

Scilla looked at her with new interest. "Yeah," she said.

"I mean, supposing this was murder." Anna stopped and shook her head. *"Attempted* murder, you can't get a murder conviction."

"You mean because death occurs so far down the line."

"Yeah. You catch the guy, you gotta prosecute him. You can't hold him until you see if it's fatal or not, that could be seven years."

"You've been talking to the legal guys."

"I've been talking to Sandra." They both nodded. Sandra Rubin, one of the deputy prosecutors on the sexual assault unit, was the lawyer both of them preferred to consult because she tended to produce comprehensible explanations the first time around. "You can't prosecute later, after the victim dies, because of course that's double jeopardy. A real pain in this particular situation." One of the things Scilla hadn't anticipated when she joined the force was that the Bill of Rights of the

United States Constitution would present so many headaches. Double jeopardy protected citizens from being tried twice for the same misconduct. A prudent safeguard, you'd think: imagine going back to trial again and again if the prosecutor didn't like the verdict last time. But then you got something cute, like long-term homicide. Like assault with a *potentially* deadly weapon. Those were the times when just the words *civil liberties* made you feel like turning in your shield and taking up something with tangible results, like geriatric nursing. Some days she felt just like the other guys, that it wasn't even worth discussing with people who weren't police, that nobody else would understand. It was all very disorienting to a person who had majored in political science with a concentration in women's studies.

"And you can't charge murder unless you've got a victim who actually *has* AIDS and you can show the rapist has AIDS, too," continued Anna. "And then I suppose you have to prove the rapist's AIDS caused the victim's AIDS, however you do that. But that's pie in the sky, because AIDS takes so long to show up. I mean, you can't hold a suspect for a few years while you wait for the symptoms, there you've got habeas corpus." Scilla nodded glumly. Anna was looking jolly again, now that she was warming up to her subject. "On the other hand, the legislature just passed a law so you can charge *attempted* murder, provided—well, provided a lot of things. That's no picnic either. But getting back to my point, if this is a homicide, we're sure all of us acting like we have the motive even if we don't have anything else. And I want to know why we're so sure. I mean, so the same guy went after Levine and Lindgren. Are we saying these guys don't have anything in common beyond the fact that they're queer?"

"They have the letter *L* in common," said Scilla. "Please don't say queer."

Anna waved her hand. "I keep forgetting. No queer either, huh? No faggot, no queer."

"No lezzie either," said Scilla, feeling unaccountably prim.

Anna extracted another doughnut from her bag. "What I just love about working with you is how all of a sudden I've got to watch my language and it isn't even the same language I've normally got to watch."

Scilla chose not to respond.

"Not that I'm not all for affirmative action," allowed Anna. "Getting back to the two guys, though, the two victims, you get my point, don't you?"

Scilla thought about it. "Lindgren says the guy called him a faggot, too, but I suppose that doesn't really prove much. The rapist might have had some other reason for wanting to rape them both. They were handy. Or pretty. Or they'd both done something to him. Or he thought they had. Or there was something to do with money, although that seems pretty far-fetched here."

"Nothing to do with money is farfetched," said Anna sententiously. It was an article of faith among detectives. "So we check out connections between them, okay? But we also have to do whatever else we can to get our hands on this guy, and that won't be easy."

"No," Scilla agreed. They had gotten a description from Lindgren that checked almost perfectly with the things Levine had told them, but precisely for that reason it didn't give them much more to work with. How do you go about looking for a guy whose distinguishing characteristic is that he dresses like Loretta Young?

"If you were going to buy those things for yourself, where would you go?" Scilla asked Mike when they were clattering down the stairs from the detective room, and Mike knew he was going to have another one of those days he couldn't tell Sally about.

Unlike Loretta Young, the man they were after was memorably blond, at least during the active part of his assault. In this respect, Mrs. Lily Johannsen corroborated Alan Lindgren, who at one point in his struggles had pulled two longish hairs out of the wig. These had been sent on to the forensics lab downtown. A call at 10:30 that morning established them as human hairs, both from the same Oriental source, subsequently bleached and permed into pale yellow crinkles. Crinkles conducive to an Afro or maybe a curly bouffant in the opinion of Jane Lowry, who had surprising pockets of expertise. Mike began with Lovely Lady Hair Specialties on West Parker Street directly across from the main downtown bus transfer point, a concrete island in the traffic. Patrol cops called the island Pross Point.

At 11:30 in the morning, the island contained only the usual weekday assortment of shopping mothers, teenagers who for reasons of their own were not in school, and street people, plus the occasional pimp checking out the teenage action. Inside Lovely Lady, however, the day was well under way. When Mike walked in, there were six customers in the place, two of them women who looked as though they would shortly be strolling back and forth on the traffic island and four of them men. One of the men was trying on a wig, auburn with ringlets. He was wearing a three-piece gray suit with a subtle blue stripe. As Mike stopped to get his bearings, a very small Indian man glided toward him, crooning, "Something for a lady friend, sir? Or perhaps for yourself?"

An hour and a half later, Mike had visited four wig stores in the downtown area and the wig departments of all three major department stores. He had come to the conclusion that not only did men buy wigs, with a preference for blond, curly wigs made out of Oriental hair (cheaper than European hair, he had discovered), but that he was probably the only man in the greater Hinton metropolitan area who had not yet done so. He had learned that men bought wigs for the girls in their offices, for the girls they were dating, for the girls they were trying to get into bed, for the girls they were trying to recruit to the life. They bought wigs as a gag to surprise their friends, their wives, their coworkers, their mothers, to wear to costume parties, to wear in transvestite clubs, to wear in productions of *Charlie's*

Aunt, to wear in bed with whomever they went to bed, and the choice of partner was by no means consistent or obvious. If Mike could describe the man he was looking for, then perhaps the staff of these varied boutiques and departments could be of service. But Mike had only the vaguest description of the man. He knew more about the wig, and after an hour and a half downtown he also knew the wig was ubiquitous.

The high-heeled shoes seemed a more promising line of inquiry, in that they required trying on, but here, too, Mike ran into trouble. From a chinless young man in one of the downtown chains, he learned that men around six feet tall generally took a ladies' ten or above and that such sizes were hard to get, especially in the wide widths, men's feet being commensurately wider than women's. Moving two blocks west to Harriet's Tall Shoppe, he discovered that men indeed bought high-heeled shoes there occasionally, and that Harriet herself could remember and describe the three men who had done so in the last two months, inasmuch as she disapproved heartily of such behavior even though her disapproval did not go so far as to jeopardize a sale. None of the three resembled Mrs. Johannsen's description, however, whereupon Harriet gave him the clue that established his whole morning as a waste of time. "If current fashion isn't a big deal," she told him, "you might check the racks down at Salvation Army."

Filled with foreboding, Mike got into the dented Plymouth that he and Scilla had drawn from the motor pool for the week. As he joined the sedate mid-morning traffic moving south on the interstate, he tried to remember when it had first dawned on him that there were men who enjoyed wearing high-heeled shoes. Probably not in college. In college he had thought all men wore wing tips, even the ones in soutanes. He had believed without question that was what you did when you grew up and turned in your Nikes. Something had happened, though, and he had never turned in his Nikes—he was wearing them now, in fact—and chasing around after men who wore high-heeled shoes, very large ones. He certainly hadn't anticipated this turn of events when he got the scholarship. All he had wanted was to play baseball. In the Salvation Army shoe department there were two double aisles marked SIZE 10 AND UP, and on the floor in the middle of one of them were two young men with their shoes and socks off who didn't even look up when he was standing over them.

In the meantime, Scilla was going house to house in the vicinity of the Masonic Temple and confirming that here was another neighborhood to have upgraded recently. Even ten years ago, the decaying remnants of the lumber and shipping aristocracy that had built these Gothic castles were still in residence, and renting out rooms to students, drug dealers, and old-age pensioners in covert defiance of the zoning regulations. These days, however, the turreted and crenellated fortresses had reverted to single-family status, and no Mrs. Lily Johannsens peered from tower windows like hoary Rapunzels keeping watch on the street and environs. Instead, the area had been reclaimed by families who derived their hefty mortgage payments from aerospace or microchips or some other of the trisyllabic industries that had been vigorously recruited to Hinton by a new wave of elected officials after the depression of the early 1970s. In a way, Scilla felt nostalgic about the passing of the old order, although her own mother had habitually crossed herself when anyone mentioned Masons. These new executives went to bed early so as to get up early and nose their Mercedes diesels and Acura Legends and Saab Turbos and perennial Volvo station wagons onto the Harbor Freeway toward the old city, site of the financial district and the vast renovated brick and ironwork towers housing the trendiest of the new industries, while the night shift was still coming back from the packing plants in the South End. They weren't porch-sitters, even on unseasonably balmy spring evenings. And they weren't window-watchers, now that even the most congenitally snoopy of them could get a nightly dose of prurience from prime-time network television.

What was interesting, she told herself as she walked down

the worn, immaculate sidewalk between a vaguely ecclesiastical house with lurid crimson and amethyst stained-glass windows and a stucco neo-Tudor twinkling with leaded glass, was that the regular patrol had not spotted a gargantuan hooker stalking on unsteady high heels along the thoroughfares of this sedate and moneyed community. The area had been well patrolled, as it was every night, and the first 911 had brought two more squad cars, disgorging pairs of cops who combed the area for an hour after the incident and stopped anyone unlucky enough to be out. The net had yielded one male dog walker, five feet six and terrified, and one male teenager, who had been apprehended in the act of climbing a tree that abutted on his own second-floor bedroom window. Lieutenant Blessing had called the two men patrolling the neighborhood on the twelve-to-eight shift, Mehlman and Parrish, first thing that morning. No blond hooker, nope. No six-foot, brown-haired hooker either: listen, you want me to list all the hookers that *weren't* there? Because they *all* weren't there, if you get me. That was Parrish; Mehlman just grunted. Which information might point several ways. For instance, the rapist might have driven up fairly close to the parking lot, pulled over, waited. Not into the parking lot; Lindgren swore the space was clear, and he would have heard a car coming. But pretty close, seeing as Lindgren was right at the lip of the hill and down there under the drop-off, albeit muted by distance to an oceanic murmur, was the Harbor Freeway. Or the rapist might have walked in wearing civvies—clothes that went with the neighborhood, male executive clothes. In which case he would have had to change somewhere, and the question was where. And then walk out, with all those swiveling blue lights and sirens. She couldn't see it. So was someone hiding him? More disturbing, did he live in the neighborhood?

Right now the big houses hummed with the concerted energy of all the vacuum cleaners and dishwashers and food processors and VCRs and other electronic appliances running in anticipation of the moment, well after six o'clock, when the

Saabs and Acuras and Mercedes and Volvos would start pulling into the carriage-houses-turned-garages, and the new executive-class men would begin easing into their weekends. She wouldn't be able to talk to them until evening. That left her with the wives again, young mothers of the still more affluent, partisans of this new movement where you *chose* to remain in the home with your children and your appliances and your cleaning woman and your Valium and your deep suspicions about what was going on in those trendily refurbished office buildings downtown, just off notorious First Avenue. Scilla sighed. She didn't expect much from the wives, and the cleaning women wouldn't have been around at night. She thought about bearding the executive men in their executive lairs, but it made more sense to talk with them tonight and in the company of Mike, who would impress them as serious. It occurred to her that she wasn't looking forward to visiting these homes of the art nouveau riche, and that on her own she preferred more color and less class. After she had finished with the wives, she decided, she would go have a chat with Missy.

Seven

Ogden's Tasti-Bake had for thirty-two years occupied the northwest corner of Mason Avenue and Sowall Street in the heart of the upwardly mobile Temple Hill business district. Next door was a boutique called Swash, which specialized in leather goods. Across the street was a restaurant called O.K. McFarland's, where on weekends patrons lined up on the sidewalk for the privilege of sitting at a counter and watching young men in chefs' caps fry things over an open flame. Both of these establishments had opened twelve years ago, when rents on lower Temple Hill had suddenly doubled, driving out the mom-and-pop grocery stores and the dingy, furtive Smoke Shops that had characterized the area in its less fashionable days. Ogden's had stayed, benefiting from the upgrade without being of it, so to speak. Young urban professionals need their sugar fixes just like anyone else, even young urban professionals who have special shoes for speed walking and would die rather than serve store-bought pasta. The original clientele saw no reason to take its business elsewhere and remained loyal to the chipping beige formica counter with its twelve revolving stools and the four formica-and-chrome tables bolted to the floor at the rear of the premises.

Ogden's had, in fact, entered local legend as a gathering place. OPEN 24 HOURS, as its neon window sign proclaimed, it had a reputation among the trendy and the sleazy alike as a night spot, a haven when the bars had closed, a temporary shelter where for thirty cents you could warm your hands over a paper cup of watery coffee (refills, fifteen cents), and for another thirty cents you could raise your spirits and your blood sugar level with a plain or glazed cruller (specials and fills, fifty cents). Musicians, waiters, hookers and their patrons, dealers, the homeless, and the elderly indigent who had homes but very little else in the crumbling apartment buildings that had so far escaped renovation, along with assorted couples in various gender combinations who were nodding or tripping or speeding or coming down or cooling out or drying out or waking up, all congregated at Ogden's in the mournful hours between two and six in the morning. For all these reasons the place was, as the saying goes, known to the police. It was known to Anna Blessing for these reasons, plus some others.

At one-thirty in the afternoon, while Scilla Carmody was finishing her rounds of the houses at the top of the hill, and Mike Annunzio was adhering to the letter if not the spirit of his wife Sally's admonitions about red meat by consuming an order of deep-fried chicken nuggets in the driver's seat of the dented Plymouth, Anna Blessing was seated at the rearmost table at Ogden's in front of a paper cup of coffee—heavy milk, heavy sugar—and a paper plate on which were two each of the glazed crullers, the double-chocolate iced specials, and the raspberry fills.

Inasmuch as the surge of business between quarter of twelve and quarter after one could be called lunch, the lunch crowd had come and gone. Ogden's did not serve anything so identifiable as a meal, or rather it served meals that were the same no matter what time of the day or night you partook of them. If you were a fat-and-carbohydrate junkie, you got your buzz when you could, which meant that during the hour and a half when the posher eateries of the avenue were turning up their tapes of Vivaldi fast movements the better to turn over their tables, Ogden's was full of architects, interior decorators, realtors, the secretaries and receptionists for all these glossy professionals, retail sales personnel from the surrounding boutiques, and a number of staffers from the *Weekly Reader,* which was housed on the second and third floors of the Aird Building two doors down. A little later and everybody went back to work, leaving Ogden's to its drowsing regulars until the after-school crowd hit. Anna qualified as a regular. She neither lived in the neighborhood nor worked in it, except in a technical sense, by virtue of the fact that Temple Hill in its entirety was part of the Third Precinct, but she graced one of the back tables at Ogden's at least three times a week, in the course of a round that took her from Dunkin' Donuts downtown to its chain sibling in the university district to the funkier bakery storefront called Sticky Fingers overlooking the Little Oslo bridge to Reinert's Home Bake Shop in Little Oslo proper to two branches of an eastern franchise called Bess Eaton that was invading Hinton by way of Victorian Hill, out of her precinct but closer to home.

Rita Freeling was also a regular, at least in part because she did in fact work in the neighborhood. She was, moreover, free to enter and leave the *Weekly Reader* city room as she pleased, one of the perquisites of a role she habitually described to herself as Girl Reporter for a Great Metropolitan Newspaper. As a consequence she too could avoid the lunch rush and, not incidentally, fraternize with Anna. Anna was one reason that Rita was walking into Ogden's Tasti-Bake now, but only one. As she liked to tell her chicly anorexic city editor, she wouldn't have got that prizewinning angle on the Hacker story if she hadn't liked bear claws.

The bear claws at Ogden's were large, deep brown, shiny with sweet glaze, crisp at the edges and ridges. Rita bought two, along with a large cup of coffee, black, no sugar—the way Hinton natives and obsessive Scandinavians everywhere were reputed to drink it. She was not a native, having grown up on a farm on the other side of the state, and not even a Scandinavian, but she made a certain number of concessions to the locals out of a chameleon capacity to adapt that over the years had persuaded some of the most antisocial, if most newsworthy, people in the city to confide in her as a kindred spirit. Her secret was that she was genuinely flexible, genuinely willing to consider the merits of someone else's tics and quirks, never motivated strictly by reportorial guile. For example, she had found that coffee black and unsweetened, even watery Ogden's coffee, balanced the sugary crispness of a bear claw: set it off, was how she put it to the svelte city editor, who was half Danish and half Swedish, never under any circumstances drank coffee of any sort, and regarded such accounts of what other people put into their mouths with inadequately veiled incredulity. Rita had shrugged and gone out to interview a prostitute who had successfully evaded the Hacker and who eventually digressed into a clinically detailed description of the difference between a twenty-dollar and a forty-dollar blow job. Rita had listened with the intensity of a neophyte. She wasn't at all sure how, or even if, she would ever be able to use this information, but it was information and of a privileged sort, so she accorded it the respectful attention she always paid to knowledge, however unlikely, however esoteric.

Crack newspeople sometimes claim their particular brand of gnosis has its own identifying smell. Rita asserted, rather, that she was simply ready, largely because she possessed a curiosity bordering on the pathological. She maintained that this attitude only seemed to engender different, or at least preternaturally acute, sense capacities, and that she used her eyes and ears like everybody else. Despite these stolid assertions, however, there was something a little unnerving, if not uncanny, in her facility for getting wind of a story. Certainly she had not been observed to glance down the row of tables to where her source crouched spiderlike in the back, but after she gathered up and paid for her coffee and pastry with placid insouciance, she looked up and gave Anna an unsurprised nod. Hunkered down before her plate of assorted pastries, Anna nodded back. Her expression was ferocious, but then, as Rita knew, it was often ferocious. That was the effect of the squinnied eyes, the mouth rendered tiny and malign by an untoward expanse of cheek and dewlap. You couldn't read Anna the way you could read thin people or even pleasingly plump people, the latter designation one that Rita sometimes applied to herself. If you were wise you kept yourself unreceptive to Anna's facial movements, which invariably contradicted what was coming out of Anna's mouth. Rita sometimes wondered if the lieutenant of detectives had anticipated this consequence of her momentous weight gain. Certainly the effect produced by her inveterate expression of malevolence made her a daunting interrogator, most horrible when enacting overlarge sympathy.

"Okay if I join you?"

Anna bared her teeth briefly, displaying evidence of the chocolate glaze. Rita set down her plate and her cup of coffee and eased into the molded plastic chair that Ogden's provided for its sit-down patrons. She had always felt the chairs demonstrated inadequate recognition of the kind of patron Ogden's was by nature liable to attract. She herself was wary about settling too abruptly into their slick concavities, which after all were supported by nothing more than four slender and usually splayed chrome legs. How safe could Anna feel entrusting her entire bulk to such frail supports?

They sat for a while without speaking, the only sound the glottal clunk of contented swallowing. Neither seemed concerned to make small talk. The fact was especially remarkable because Anna was known among the press as the Big Lady or sometimes the Pig Lady—often it was unclear which—and despite a certain degree of disparagement in the label—whichever label you had, in fact, intended to apply—it also indicated that she was not to be messed with. Rita's casual self-invitation and Anna's apparently benign nonanswer were testimony to the strength of their prior relationship; also, of course, to Rita's ability to insinuate herself into the most resistant, not to say repellent, company when on the track of a story.

"You think this is a story, huh?" said Anna suddenly. She hadn't bothered to clear her mouth of raspberry filling.

Rita considered while she tucked the last bit of bear claw between her lips. "What do you think?"

Anna snorted, causing the elderly couple at the next table to jump. "You can *make* a story if that's what you want. You can make connections. You can make this be a series. Series of two. That's a story, right? Connections. Series."

"Like the Hacker," Rita replied promptly.

"Oh I grant you, sometimes there are connections," allowed Anna without animosity. "But connections are what we look for at my end, they're not given, they're not something you can *assume* just because you want some nice, oh, plot development." She bit down on a plump, powdery doughnut with such vehemence that raspberry squirted onto the table top. Rita ignored it.

"Serial killings, you mean?" she asked, as blandly as if she were asking what time it was.

Anna leaned back so suddenly that for a moment it was unclear whether she was going to stay upright. "There's no *killings* here," she thundered. Several patrons sitting on stools at the counter swiveled around to look at her. Rita remained impassive. "You guys go jumping to conclusions, you're gonna create like a hysteria situation, which is not what we need to solve crimes, as you very well know. So you just stop that kind of talk."

"It's in the air," said Rita. "Stop it till when?"

Anna eased her enormous forearms onto the table and then glared across them. "Till I tell you you can," she said. "You want your story you just listen, okay? You don't go pushing me."

Rita nodded amiably. It was the same deal they had made early in the career of the Hooker Hacker. "Serial rape, then?" she asked. There was pushing and pushing.

"Maybe. Same setup, same drag queen props." Rita nodded. That much had come out during Lindgren's impromptu press conference. "On the other hand," Anna continued without enthusiasm, "great minds think alike."

"Or monkey see, monkey do," Rita contributed. Anna accepted this maxim without asking for elucidation. Their relationship was predicated not only on a shared respect for fried pastry but also on a mutual appreciation of the shorthand value of clichés. Even one transvestite same-sex rape had been novel enough to be covered prominently by both the *Express* and the *Herald,* albeit on the inside front page of the first and on the Local News, Central Area, page of the second. An aspiring molester with a yen for the theatrical might well take the assault on Bruce Levine as a precedent. Monkey see, in other words.

"Monkey do," said Anna. "Hell, what if this turns into a trend? What if faggot rape is gonna be the new nighttime *sport,* what if that's the connection?"

"You don't call them faggots anymore," said Rita.

Anna finished off her coffee noisily. "You're as bad as Scilla."

"That's the policewoman you've got on the case. I mean the detective. Scilla."

"Scilla Carmody," said Anna. "Detective Carmody. Detective Third Grade."

Rita nodded without apparent interest. "That's Pat Carmody's girl."

"That's right."

"What's he doing these days?"

Anna shrugged. "I don't see him. Coaching the Little League over in View Ridge is what I hear. That and the O'Dea football team. Meaning he's helping Whitey Hunter out there. Pat was always a jock."

"Whitey could use some help," said Rita. "O'Dea's having another doghouse season."

Anna shrugged again. "So Pat's helping. So he's keeping busy. That's what I hear."

"How's he moving around these days?"

"He moves," said Anna.

"With a cane, right? I mean, the knee isn't coming back."

Anna looked at her with disdain. "They don't," she said.

"They don't," echoed Rita. "You think he should have done that? Gone in there by himself, I mean?"

"He could have got somebody else shot up with him," Anna said. "Would that have been better? More correct?" Almost ten years ago, Detective Second Grade Patrick Carmody of the First Precinct, West Hinton and selected districts in the South End, had kicked down the door to an apartment located in the university district, only about four blocks from Third Precinct headquarters. Inside the apartment three middle-level heroin distributors had been having a business meeting. The middle-level heroin distributors had shot Carmody in the thigh and in the knee before fleeing. Carmody had subsequently described them, but there were no arrests. HMPD higher-ups surmised that his attackers had left the area. To be replaced by other hoods, of course. Middle-level heroin distributors are infinitely replaceable.

"You had an investigation going," said Rita. "I hear you even had that place bugged. So what was he doing there?"

"Following a lead," said Anna tonelessly. "He said he'd traced stolen goods to that address."

"That address was in the Third Precinct," said Rita. "He should have been working with you guys."

Anna's pig eyes grew smaller and colder. "You got another story here? Is that what you think?"

"Well, do I?"

"Not from me, you don't."

"Come on. You got some of the ring, but not till almost two years later. That heroism of Carmody's really screwed you up."

Anna shrugged.

"I'm not saying there was anything criminal in what he did. But it was stupid, you know that. Dirty Harry stuff. Going in on his lonesome to show the wimps how it's done. But you didn't even investigate him. He was wounded in action. So you gave him a citation and sent him home."

"You forget it wasn't me," said Anna with heavy forbearance. "I was only a detective myself then. Anyway, he wasn't in my precinct."

Rita leaned forward, her elbows propped on the sticky formica. "What would you have done if you'd been in charge?" she asked.

Anna looked at her for a while and then began to smile. The smile grew wider and more sinister as Rita watched, finally taking over Anna's face to the point where most of her other features were eclipsed. Strong men had been known to burst into tears in the presence of that smile. Rita waited.

"I'd do exactly the same thing," said Anna. "You know that."

Rita sat back, admitting defeat. "Sure."

"Sure," said Anna. She pointed a thick forefinger at Rita. The smile had not abated. "You got your ideas about what stories are, about how you've got to get underneath stuff to get at other stuff, which other stuff is, by virtue of being underneath, the *real* stuff. Like there's always something hidden with you, and what's hidden is what you mean by the truth. You peel back enough facts, you get other facts. But those facts are the right facts, the real facts. They've got to be. They're the ones you peeled back the other facts to get."

It was Rita's turn to shrug.

"I can understand how you'd get to thinking that way. That's your job. Investigative reporting. Getting the in-depth story, you call it. Get underneath, that's where you find things. So you think."

"Sometimes it is," said Rita.

"Sometimes it is," admitted Anna. "But you can't always assume that connections are going to take you deeper. To that underneath stuff. To the real story."

"How will I know till I follow them?"

"Sometimes following them makes you think you already know," said Anna. "At least you figure that if you follow them, you must be on to something. But sometimes you're not. You're just following a connection that shreds into a dozen, two dozen little leads, each one a slightly different story depending on who's telling it. None of them's the real story, they're just versions. That's all there is, is versions. So you figure you might as well give the guy a medal and send him off with a lot of flashbulbs and the mayor shaking his hand. Why not? It's not all that different from the other versions you're getting, and if you look at it close, it's still pretty sad, not a very good story at all. I think you got a lot more future sticking to this here story, the faggot raper. That one's got possibilities."

"The two stories are related," insisted Rita.

"Only because he's her father. That's like a minimal connection. It's like circumstantial, you know what I mean? Like any judge would throw it out of court. Like your editor would see a little flashing sign that said *Libel*. So you back off."

"It's a sidelight," said Rita.

"Don't put it in the middle then."

"I won't," said Rita. "I like her. She's good, isn't she?"

"She's good," said Anna.

"What does she think about her father?"

"She thinks he's God's gift to Hinton," said Anna. "And he's a big asset these days. Little League, O'Dea football. Who are you to say she's wrong? You've got your own story but there's nothing saying it's any better than the official version. Plus, it comes with that little light says *Libel*."

"I see the little light," said Rita.

"You keep your eye on her," said Anna. "She's the one to watch. I'm going now."

"You have any comment on these crimes? For your friends in the press?"

"Your paper doesn't go to bed till tomorrow night," said Anna. "Lucky you, you get to cover the chief this afternoon, get some nice photos of those flip charts of his." Rita made an offensive noise into her coffee. "Hey, that's the chief himself."

"Big duty," said Rita. "Bobby Evans covers this one. Chiefs on chiefs." Robert Wilbur Evans was the founder and managing editor of the *Weekly Reader*.

"Not enough Indians," Anna murmured.

"Tell me," said Rita. "Okay, so you don't have any comment at this time, is that right?"

"You're going to go quoting me as No Comment, aren't you?"

"That's the dailies. We don't use No Comments unless we're doing an exposé."

"Absence of Comment in the Hinton Metropolitan Police Department," said Anna.

"A Local Scandal," said Rita. "Speaking of which, how are they going to prosecute an AIDS rape as attempted murder? I mean, just starting with the confidentiality statutes—"

Anna rose majestically from her plastic chair, scattering crumbs over the tiled floor. "Not my department," she said. "We bring 'em in, they prosecute. We're in enough trouble trying to *arrest* the bastard legally."

"What kind of trouble?" Rita asked, but Anna was already heading toward the door.

Eight

Like most of its neighbors on First Avenue, Chez Plush opened around noon, but Scilla knew better than to look for Missy there before five o'clock. Just to be sure, she peered through the display window (where one or more of Missy's employees had stood waving and beckoning to passersby until the city had passed an ordinance declaring this sort of display a traffic hazard) into the dimly lit pink reception room, but once she had ascertained that the front desk was being handled by the stocky Chinese woman who acted as Missy's lieutenant and whose name, King-Kok, had been shortened predictably to Kinky, she moved on down the street. It was another clear, breezy afternoon and there were a lot of people around. Not so many patrons this time of day, or not the kind you could immediately spot as patrons; more of the young lawyer crowd, mixed in with local sightseers taking advantage of the weather to check out the progress of the First Avenue renovation. Scilla noted the evidence of sandblasting and decided rents were still going up. The days were numbered for places like Chez Plush. Although maybe not for Chez Plush itself: Missy had a way of adapting to changes in her environment. It wouldn't take much, after all, maybe just a little Victorian wallpaper and a discreet overlay of golden oak, to turn the place into some version of a yuppie spa. Guaranteed relaxation for legal professionals of all sexes. Put the staff in designer sweats and you're in business all over again. She was pleased with the idea and resolved to run it by Missy when she got the chance.

Drifting with the sightseers down the sidewalk in the direction of the Old Town Square, she began checking out the other windows. No time like the present to update your knowledge of trends in the booming sexual accessories business. There was leather underwear, for instance, a longtime favorite given a brand-new look with an industrial zipper that went all the way around. Interesting pain possibilities there, once you really thought about the zipper snagging in your pubic hair, but then S and M had proved the hardiest perennial of them all, blossoming periodically into new materials (polyvinyl chloride, silk, human hair) that could lead you to rethink completely the significance of the old forms (mauve suede leg shackles). Scilla did not find any of this surprising. If you were going to sell sexual aids, you'd lean toward the things that were essential, as opposed to the scents or flavors or textures that were intended only to enhance activities that could be carried on perfectly well without them. In dominance games, the whips and ropes and goads and shackles *were* the sex; different fetishes changed the nature of the act completely. If bondage and flogging were on the rise since the entrepreneurial eighties, this tendency was at least consonant with the fact that sex relying on specialized equipment was better for business. She suddenly remembered the boyfriend of most of her junior year at the university, a skinny, intense econ major who used to harangue her about class struggle. What was that phrase he had used? Commodity fetishism. She gazed at the male and female dummies crowding the window and at the crotchless, cupless garments that exposed not genitals or nipples but only chaste expanses of beige plaster, and suddenly hugged herself. That was the thing about an education, you went along for years with words like *commodity fetishism* in your vocabulary that corresponded to nothing at all in your experience, and then all of a sudden something clicked.

She moved down the sidewalk to a flyspecked window

where variously shaped and colored jars were arranged on a ground of dusty black velvet. At the front of the window were three pump containers, the kind used for hand lotion or liquid soap. Lubricants were going upscale, which made sense given the condom revival. More rubber means more need for things to make the rubber slippery. More slipperiness, and maybe you started looking for other rubber to grease, she thought, transferring her attention to a dildo that seemed to be shaped like a streamlined bear. Maybe you could derive another economic principle, more commodities, more fetishes. She squinted at the bear. There seemed to be something or someone riding it. Of course that made sense too, something sticking out to provide additional stimulation, an improvement on the original model. Safe sex as impetus to innovation. A little man was what it looked like, and he seemed to be holding something. Another dildo? Infinite regress? She had her forehead against the glass before she realized that someone was standing next to her, watching.

She straightened up, squared her shoulders, turned away. Mouth tight, prepare to repel boarders. Those were the responses, learned before she could remember where or how. Don't get caught looking. Looking meant you were sexual. Sexuality meant you were vulnerable. It sometimes astounded her how little it mattered who she was, what she was wearing, what she was thinking. What mattered was whether she was wary enough, and after that the state of her karate and the fact of what she carried in her shoulder holster. She was no better equipped than any other woman to stop them from trying. Her edge was that she could probably stop them from succeeding. Like other women, she would prefer they didn't try.

She could sense the man behind her as she strode down the sidewalk, eyes front, but when she stopped at the corner with the little knot of people waiting for the walk light he seemed to have vanished. She crossed First and went back up the entire block, watching for him through gaps in the traffic, before deciding that he had given up. Her maneuvers had served to establish her as something, probably as not worth the trouble.

When she pushed open the front door of Chez Plush, activating the wind chimes that were part of Missy's early warning system, Missy was behind the desk taking money from a balding man with a briefcase. She raised her eyebrows to acknowledge Scilla's presence but went on talking to the man, who had turned to look at Scilla and seemed to be trying to place a poplin raincoat, pleated pants, and Reebocks in the overall scheme of massage-parlor attire. "Yolanda is the one you like," Missy was saying. "Paula is the other one you like, but Paula's on vacation." Scilla gazed steadily back until the man turned away. One of these days she was going to run into a senior detective here. Or one of her old professors. Or her father. On the other hand, her presence had none of the potential for disruption that, say, Mike's would have. The man had been confused by her appearance but he hadn't jumped automatically to the conclusion *cop* any more than the man on the street had. And wasn't likely to, she decided, watching him lean confidentially toward Missy's cleavage, spectacularly exhibited in a U-necked cerise T-shirt. "Yolanda's the one with the ponytail?" he asked.

"Today I think she has a braid. One braid. It's very *nice,*" said Missy firmly, and Scilla wondered how this information keyed into the desires of the man with the briefcase, how his excitement waxed and waned with ponytails and braids, nice girls and nasty ones; what it was, finally, that he was paying for. But at that moment Yolanda appeared, white-smocked and round-cheeked with a thick caramel-colored braid that hung to the middle of her back, and led him through the bead curtains that separated the reception area from the corridor connecting with the four private studios.

Both of them waited for the sound of a door opening and closing. Then Missy said, "Hey."

"Hey," said Scilla, sitting down in one of the director's chairs flanking the front desk and shrugging out of her raincoat. "You're looking good," she observed.

Missy looked down into her neckline with satisfaction. "I've been keeping well. It isn't easy this time of year. God knows what's floating around, pollen, dust. But I've got this new balsam tea. It smells like compost and sometimes the clients complain, but I'm up to four, five cups an evening." She patted her stomach. "It really flushes you out. Want to try some?"

"No thanks," said Scilla, who did not share Missy's enthusiasm for purges. "Business is okay?"

"Business is booming. Business has never been so good. I've taken on two more girls." Missy grinned at Scilla's reflexive wince. "*Girls* is a technical term, you know. It's not a diminutive, it's a name for what they do. If I called them women, the johns wouldn't know what I was talking about."

"*Girls* and *johns*?"

"*Clients* to their faces. *Girls* to their faces, too, the johns' faces. Hey, but really, we're all women around here. Nobody here but us women." Missy stretched expansively. "*You're looking good.*"

"Thanks." Scilla supplied the qualifier: considering. Considering the way she dressed, did her hair, didn't do her makeup. Missy, despite her passion for branches of knowledge that might not have seemed obviously aligned with her kind of massage therapy—disciplines like acupuncture, biofeedback, and herbal medicine—could never understand why other women chose to look any way other than flamboyantly sexual. On the occasion of their first conversation, over chamomile tea after the Natural Healing class they were both attending at the Alternative University (the Alternative University was physically the same university as the degree-granting institution from which Scilla had graduated four years earlier, but at night and, as it were, on the side), Scilla had tactfully tried to put the issue in terms of personal style. "I look good in dark colors," she had objected in response to Missy's abrupt offer of a make-over. "I'm not the type to stand out, that's all. *You* look—"

"I look like a hooker," Missy had said, pouring more tea for both of them from the dented brass teapot provided by the restaurant they were in, which was called Sprouts. "I *am* a hooker, more or less. Except now I'm on the administrative end."

"I'm a cop," Scilla had confessed. Missy hadn't batted an eye.

"You look like a cop."

"You're kidding," said Scilla, who had shed her patrol uniform after she came off her shift at four and was wearing one of the monochromatic pants-and-shirt outfits that she thought of privately as her civvies.

"No, I don't mean that. I mean you look like . . . plain clothes. You're wearing *very* plain clothes."

"I always have," said Scilla humbly.

"If you'd let me fix you up," Missy had insisted, "you'd be a knockout."

But Scilla had not felt that anything Missy could do would improve her situation in the HMPD and had declined. She continued to decline every time Missy renewed the offer during the subsequent five years of their acquaintance. The exchange of confidences was important, however, in that it had made them friends. They had remained friends, as well as cop and informant, the latter perhaps the more intimate relationship.

The informing began because of their shared concern with preserving the human body in a state that both of them were inclined to call natural, although as Scilla generously pointed out, there was a sense in which activities as disparately therapeutic as standing upright and not dying of the Black Death might be called artificial. Partly out of the same nexus of convictions that included the Natural Healing class and the balsam tea, partly out of some commitment far more personal and passionate, about which Scilla was careful not to inquire, Missy hated drugs. During Scilla's first visit (off duty, very strained) to Chez Plush, Missy had shrieked "Recreational substances my ass!" at a startled insurance executive who had been reported to her as wanting to do a line during his twenty-dollar special. She had gone on at the top of her voice to inform him, along with Scilla, all the masseuses on the premises, and a good half-block of First Avenue in either direction, that she ran a clean shop. "Clean" was of course in the eye of the purveyor, since Missy's shop regularly purveyed hand jobs, blow jobs, and the occasional vaginal penetration for the truly conservative and persistent. But those activities were themselves clean in the sense that Missy meant the word, which had nothing to do with the law and little to do with the notion of prurient activities as good, clean fun that the First Avenue Association was currently trying to sell the city council. "Clean fun is when you don't get anything from doing it," she had told Scilla on a later occasion, when they had learned to relax with each other's professional identities. "Crabs, pregnant, the dry heaves—"

"Busted?" Scilla had inquired.

"You can always get busted. By the way, I never said any of this."

"I'm not even having this conversation," Scilla had affirmed. But she had understood the principle. Sex at Chez Plush meant that people didn't go out with anything they hadn't come in with. John people. Massage-therapist people. Microorganisms didn't circulate at Chez Plush; they remained at their point of origin.

The principle had become increasingly popular as the AIDS epidemic gained momentum and attention. Last year, over another battered brass teapot at Sprouts, Missy had announced that she was raising the price of hand jobs another ten dollars. "It's like I just invented this new way to get off," she crowed. "Guys who've always figured that was one thing they could do just as well themselves are coming in now talking about technique. I ask you, technique!" She had waved the waitress over and in an uncharacteristically expansive gesture demanded carrot cake for both of them. "Complex carbs, sweetie," she had explained. "It's cold out on those streets." But Scilla had still been surprised. Missy's attitude toward the gooey end of the health food spectrum was usually more suspicious, Adelle Davis rather than Jane Brody.

"I'll tell you about technique," Missy had continued after they had put down their smeared forks and allowed the waitress to add more hot water to the soggy chamomile flowers. "They can talk about it like it was expertise, developed finger muscles, *timing*. But what they really come for is information." Scilla shook her head in disbelief. "I'm *telling* you. And they're shy about it, that's the other thing. They edge in on the subject. Like, the other day this guy was lying there and Petra was sort of moving in on his dick, you know how we start out like it's just this massage and then gradually we sort of center on this protruding *thing* here, like hey, here's something else I can rub?" Scilla, who didn't know, stored this piece of information away for consideration at leisure. "And this guy sort of cleared his throat and then he said, I notice you're not wearing *rubber gloves.*" She whooped, and Scilla began to laugh with her. They hunched over the table snorting and muttering "Rubber gloves!" until Missy finally combed the auburn hair back from her forehead with the fingers of both hands and resettled herself in her squeaky cane chair. "So of course Petra goes into a kind of holding pattern around the dick and says, why no, you see the issue is *exchange* of fluids, and off they go, twenty minutes of question and answer, like Petra was the AIDS hotline. Which in a sense she is. We charge for the extra time, of course, but I keep thinking we should charge for the learning experience. Like here *I'm* the Alternative University."

"You're rendering a great service," Scilla had assured her. "Speaking of which, does this mean there's less demand for the other stuff? Other than hand jobs?"

Missy had grinned. "That's the beauty of it, it's *all* booming. They know I'm clean and suddenly that's all that matters. Like, I'm buying dental dams by the *gross!*"

Looking around the reception room now, Scilla was inclined to believe that business had gone on booming since that last conversation. The walls were newly painted, in a calmer and somehow more suggestive pink than the mottled salmon of her previous visits. The red chenille draperies around the display window were clean, if balding in spots, and Missy's desk was a fairly elaborate three-sided white unit that might have been intended to house a computer terminal. Maybe the computer was next, Scilla thought, but then dismissed the idea. Missy would never display anything to suggest that she kept records. Although of course she did keep records, meticulous records; that was part of her value as an informant. Not just in her head, either: there was a safe-deposit box to which Scilla would be directed if anything happened, as Missy ominously put it. So no computer, but distinctly upscale, like so much of First Avenue these days. It was a short step to golden oak and designer sweats, and Scilla wondered if she should introduce her idea. But at that moment Missy got to the point.

"Hear you got yourself a rapist," she said.

Scilla shifted uncomfortably in her director's chair. Missy was due to replace these, she reflected; they were a short-term solution. Something cushioned that swiveled. Puffy and pink wouldn't be bad, in keeping with the implicit motif of vaginal walls. Not golden oak. "Me and Mike," she agreed. "Mike was all over the TV news this morning." She had been eating cereal when his face filled the screen, blinking and mint-colored. He wasn't the best choice for a nighttime close-up, had been her first thought; too pale, pasty under flourescent lights, worse here, with the quartz lights bouncing off the institutional green Overlook walls. Off camera, Lindgren had cried, "Are you one of us?" and Mike had furrowed his brow as if he had been asked to name the twelfth president. Not calculated to reassure, but that couldn't be helped now. She herself had been determinedly out of reach; out of her apartment and her plain clothes, too: off duty. The guy had been a carpenter who restored old wooden boats. A winning combination. She preferred men who were good with their hands. There was more to be said for technique than Missy was allowing.

"I saw him," said Missy. "I can't get over that he's your

partner. Your work partner, I mean. You should send him down here sometime, I'd do him special." Scilla shrugged. "Not your type," said Missy. "My type. I like dark and sensitive. He's got a great mouth."

"He's got a wife," said Scilla. Missy mimed horror. "Oh come on, he's not the issue. The issue is, you're right, we've got this rapist. Or really, we haven't got him, haven't got anything more than the stuff that was all over the *Express* this morning."

They sat in speculative silence for a moment. Then Missy asked, "So what do you want from me?"

"I'm not really sure." Scilla reflected that she had gone to Missy in the same way that she might have consulted one of the professors in the psychology department, except of course that she granted Missy more authority. "I don't know why. I thought you might know about rapists. Rapists in general: that's the level I'm on right now."

"I know about rapists," said Missy grimly. "You think because guys come here they don't go out and knock women over the head? They get rid of it *peacefully* or something?"

"No," said Scilla. "I don't think that. You know I don't. But you'd be surprised at the people who do." Missy's formulation in fact summed up prevailing popular wisdom on the subject of rape. Never mind that the theory making rapists thwarted hedonists, virile types prevented from expressing their sexuality by a repressive society, had gone the way of orgone boxes once the first studies of convicted rapists began coming out in the mid-seventies. Old lore dies hard. Even in patrol school she had learned that rapists were just men pining to get laid. At the same time, she had been instructed that they were an entirely different species from the heavy breathers and flashers and Peeping Toms and First Avenue porn shop and massage-parlor aficionados, that there was a category of harmless sexual exploitation rigidly demarcated from the physical violence of rape. If you carried that logic to its conclusion, you'd come up with the idea that it was impossible to rape prostitutes—thus the attitude of the HMPD to the first depredations of the Hooker Hacker. Presumably that embarrassment had led to changes in the patrol training course; presumably new recruits to the force weren't being led to regard voyeurs and exhibitionists and johns as harmless and rather sweet. Presumably, although Scilla wasn't going to put money on it.

Furthermore, popular wisdom maintained that there was no crossover: heavy breathers didn't evolve into flashers; flashers didn't escalate exposure into attack. The studies of the last decade and a half, the only studies to have been done of actual rapes, actual rapists, blew these theories out of the water. But Scilla had already known better from her experiences on foot patrol in the North Downtown area, and before that from her experiences in the bars of the Old Town Square area, and before that from her experiences on the campus of the university. It was all a matter of degree. The jokes about the guys standing unzipped in the bushes around the sorority houses during finals week weren't jokes anymore when one of the guys jumped a woman going to her 8:30 exam, kicked her in the head until she was unconscious, and dragged her into those same bushes for a leisurely fuck. Or maybe it was a matter of audience. There were jokes about that guy being told in the fraternity houses, that funny guy with his direct approach. Scilla tried not to think too much about the popular wisdom.

"The problem is that the kind of rapist I get here probably isn't the kind you've got." Missy rubbed the spot between her eyebrows where mystics and certain partisans of holistic healing locate the Third Eye. "Yeah, we get them here. A lot of them are proud of not paying for it. Not *having* to pay for it, is how they talk. As if forcing somebody was the same as having her offer it to you. And they really believe those two things are the same. I'll tell you what I think about those guys, the kind of rapist I get here. I think they believe the girl automatically wants what *they* want. He wants to be whacked off, she must want to whack him off—as if it makes her *hand* feel great, you know what I mean?" Scilla nodded. "So, he wants to fuck her,

74

she must want to be fucked. By him. Like she's advertising her desire just by being."

"I know what you mean," said Scilla. "We had a guy who broke into a woman's apartment when she was sleeping, raped her, and then wrote down his telephone number in case she wanted to get together again."

Missy looked dubious. "You sure it was the right number?"

"You think we didn't follow it up? Sure, it was the right number. We traced it and there he was, getting ready to go up another fire escape. That's an extreme case, of course. I wish more of them would write down their phone numbers."

"Well, I don't think you have one of those right now," said Missy. "I think you've got a murdering bastard, like that guy your boss finally got a couple of years ago. The guy that killed prosses and buried them in the state parks. That kind of psycho. That kind can pass, too." Scilla had still been a patrol officer when Anna directed the decoy operation that netted the Hacker. The decoy had been a patrol academy classmate of hers, Laurie Brangwen. Laurie had left the force on a disability discharge after the grab. The disability discharge was also Anna's doing and technically didn't apply because the cuts had healed into scars and there was no permanent nerve or muscle damage. But a psychological discharge on your record could jeopardize your professional standing for your entire life, even when you went into something that had nothing to do with police work. Eventually, Laurie would go into something that had nothing to do with police work. Right now she was still at home with her mother.

"A lot of people think he's a murdering bastard," said Scilla. "But at the moment we have no evidence that it's murder."

"It's murder on his mind, anyway," said Missy. "Look at the way he goes after gay guys. Look at what he says to them."

Scilla looked startled. "How do you know what he says to them?" That information was one of the few things that Anna Blessing had insisted on withholding from the press.

Missy combed back her hair with her fingers again. "I have

my sources," she said. "You're not the only person with good contacts." Scilla knew she couldn't push this one any further.

"So far it's gay men," she said. "On the basis of two incidents, we can say we've got a murdering bastard who's possibly targeted gay men. Or possibly he's targeted people alone in parking lots after midnight. Or people whose names begin with the letter L. Two incidents don't let us define a pattern all that well."

"He calls them faggots," Missy pointed out. "But I get your point. We can't assume anyone's safe."

"There's no reason to assume it's restricted to gay men," said Scilla.

"Sounds familiar," said Missy.

Nine

"Listen, you really don't have to do this," said Mike. He was acutely aware of smells in the diner, of cigarette smoke drifting in from the next booth, of grease hanging in the steamy air. Across from him, Scilla was hunched over the plastic-coated menu as though she were in physical pain. Her knuckles were white. He knew better than to suggest a salad, a tuna fish sandwich. She had told him about those.

"Eggs," she said. "Over easy."

She had committed again: in for a nickel, in for a dime. Cops eat in diners. Her father had eaten in diners. Cops die of heart attacks in their fifties unless they get shot first, like her father, who however had not died and who continued to eat in diners although not, as it were, professionally. There was ideology and there was tradition, and right now Scilla was giving tradition its due, Mike could tell. Grin and bear it. Which is not at all the same thing as liking it. It was only in moments like this that she reminded him of his wife, Sally.

"Me too," he said. "And coffee."

"Water," said Scilla faintly.

The waitress with the skinny arms collected the menus and ambled across the linoleum to the order window at the left of the counter. There were four people at the counter, spotted at intervals along the row of stools. They all looked sleepy.

Scilla looked sleepy, Mike decided. He wasn't about to

wonder what had kept her up and unreachable last night, while he was blinking into the cameras in the Overlook emergency room. That was part of their partnership, that he didn't ask and she didn't tell. Anyway, she wouldn't be unreachable again until they had their rapist. With the advent of a second victim, Anna had put them both on 24-hour call so that although they were technically on the eight-to-four shift until the end of the week, they could be summoned by beeper and sent anywhere in the city at any point in the day or night. Just their luck to be on the eight-to-four, too, Mike reflected. No odds on the rapist haunting parking lots in the early afternoon. But he didn't really mind. He wasn't very comfortable in his own house these days. Presumably Scilla minded, but Scilla had her eye on a promotion and had to be willing to put up with a certain amount of deflected desire.

"Coffee," said the waitress. She didn't say anything as she put down the water. "You want cream?" Mike nodded. She pulled a handful of little plastic containers out of her apron pocket and deposited them next to his saucer. Scilla shrank back at the sight of them.

"That's not cream," she muttered. "That's nondairy whitener."

"Some people make a fuss about what you call things," observed the waitress. Mike decided she had enormous presence.

He pulled back the foil lid from one of the containers of nondairy whitener and poured it carefully into his coffee. Were things supposed to be dairy or not? He had a hard time keeping track of Scilla's prohibitions, but he usually could tell what he was doing wrong from the way she wasn't commenting. She was very obviously refraining from comment now, looking at him sneakily over her water glass. Something he was putting in his body, maybe just the coffee. She wasn't about to say anything. He knew that look. He took a guarded sip. She lowered her eyes. It had been a long day for both of them, he decided charitably, but then he remembered that he had been the one taking Lindgren over and over the same ground until four-thirty in the morning. Over and over, backward and forward, pawing through Lindgren's recollected sensations for some undiscerned lump of hard matter, data, evidence. Could Lindgren get a sense of how tall the man really was, of how much of that height came from the shoes? Did Lindgren feel that the shoes hindered the man in any way, made him un-steady as he moved, grabbed, clubbed, pushed? Yes, yes, Lindgren had murmured, monotone after hours of this, going backward and forward over that ten minutes of his life; maybe six-one, six-two at the most if you weren't counting the heels; yes, he handled the heels all right but you kept thinking, the right move and he'd be thrown off balance. Lindgren hadn't found the right move, ergo the bruise on his throat.

Martial arts, Mike had thought. Karate, kung fu, and akido had spread through the feminist community; there were classes offered through the Women's Center on campus, the Athena Gym downtown. Women had always known they were vul-nerable. Did the gay male community have its own athletic facilities? It perturbed him that he didn't know and in fact had rarely considered the phenomenon of a gay community here, weaving its own strands into the webs of family, religious, ethnic, generational, gang, and professional partisanship that interconnected the denizens of metropolitan Hinton. They hadn't talked about it where he came from, hadn't covered it in any of his classes at Kennedy or Loyola Downtown except in terms of sin: against nature, aganst the Holy Ghost, he wasn't sure now which. There had been other kinds of indications of course, meaningful gestures whose meaning he hadn't ever quite decoded. Father Leo liked to throw his arm across your shoulder. Jimmy Caughie was one. That was the way they'd represented it: one, the singular, the unfathomable sport. What did it mean, then, a gay community? Community had always meant priests, or Irish or Poles or Italians. Or the Church, a community of believers. In patrol school you learned more about them, how sometimes they were prostitutes servicing others like them, how they could be law-abiding citizens despite the inescapable criminality of their private lives, how it didn't make sense to try to enforce the sodomy laws except, of course, in certain cases. A new atmosphere of tolerance. The privacy of their own homes. Alone. In private. You assumed they were in hiding. You assumed you'd know them if you saw them. You assumed you didn't know them.

Scilla was chewing her ice, surreptitiously, as if someone had warned her all through her childhood that if she kept it up, her teeth would crack and fall out. Mike found it heartening that she did things that weren't good for her. At such moments, feeling both conspiratorial and protective, he tried hard not to look as though he'd noticed. He liked the way her eyebrows twisted as she gazed into her water glass, as if there were a message at the bottom she couldn't quite read. She was very pretty when she was doing something that qualified by her own lights as bad.

Staring into her water glass, Scilla was ruminating about the living rooms in the Temple Hill houses. They were cavernous, shadowy, enormous, some of them with fireplaces you could roast an ox in. She and Mike had been told repeatedly how wonderful these living rooms were for parties. In every house they visited, they had been seated ceremoniously at the end of one of these living rooms, in one of the little huddles of furniture that she was given to understand were called conversation groups. Nobody kept televisions in these living rooms; they kept them in television rooms. Sitting in the conversation groups, hearing sometimes the muffled sound of recorded laughter from the television room, they had asked their questions, taken their notes. Sometimes Mike asked, sometimes she did. It didn't matter. There were no bad guys. The men didn't know anything. Their wives didn't know anything. Summoned from the television room, the children reported having been in bed. Some of them had heard the sirens. She had wondered if these families would notice the bomb dropping, swathed as they were in their period houses. The ice cubes creaked between her teeth as she bore down on them.

Mike rubbed his eyes, partly to disguise his wince at the sound of ice splitting catastrophically and partly because he was tired. It was already late, so late that Sally would be asleep or pretending to be asleep when he got back. He didn't call her about being late anymore. She knew he was somewhere with Scilla, and Scilla was one of the big reasons they fought, so it was useless to say he was working or had just finished working and was grabbing a bite. None of that was innocent or an excuse.

He frowned. Scilla, who was eyeing him furtively, wished he wouldn't bring his eyebrows together like that. It made him look anxious and ineffectual, prematurely old, *Catholic*. She hadn't noticed until she saw him on television this morning that his hairline was receding. It was all coming together in his face now, that twist of the eyebrows, that mannered agony, those scruples. Sooner or later, everything those priests put in was going to show. Probably his father looked just like that, all those tormented little furrows in for the long haul now. She knew the look. Her mother could spot them in any crowd, there's a nice boy, wonder whose boy that is. One of ten, one of the Kelly boys, the Kaufman boys, the Kolodny boys. There were four Annunzio boys, Mike had told her. Three Annunzio girls. He was second from the top, top boy; sister in a convent, sister a Sister. She had run screaming from the whole thing, no nice Catholic girl here, no thank you. Mom scuttling around with plates while they sat and argued and ate, demanded seconds, demanded milk and dessert and clean plates. Dad burping and picking his teeth and smiling down on all of them. Mom somewhere in the kitchen, scuttling. Daddy's girl here, thank you, burps and all. Gun and all, that hard bulge of power and professionalism. Daddy's girl, sharpshooter, high school state champion marksman. Markswoman? Oh yes, isn't it symbolic, I think so too.

She took another swallow of water. If Mike would only stop

looking so sensitive. That look they got, preoccupied with ultimate things, and here the plates are all clean again and we don't ever wonder how they got that way. Maybe she could offer to coach him on facial expressions. Maybe not, he'd probably be grateful. The best thing would be to keep him off television altogether, not that he was the worst thing the HMPD had sent over the public airwaves in the last twelve hours, not after the six o'clock news when Chief Considine went on with his flip chart and his best Copspeak to reassure the world that everything was proceeding forthwith and post-haste in pursuance of the perpetrator on whom it was hoped deadly force would not be necessary. Considine was an okay cop if you kept him with the cops, but give him a civilian audience and he was your man for artists' renderings and Victorian turns of phrase. Mike might have looked inept, but Considine looked like a gold-plated fool. Terrifically reassuring when you had deadly force embodied in that thing your gun was supposed to be a Victorian euphemism for. Armed and dangerous, this rapist, a weapon unto himself without any help from technology. Considine had kept trying to evade the issue. Of course, he hadn't put Anna in his show either, and probably not just because Anna filled everybody's viewfinder. Anna was a favorite of the press, who knew her well enough to squat there like baby birds waiting for anything that might drop out of her mouth, usually something long and pink and wiggly. Considine wouldn't risk that. Scilla bit down on another piece of ice and wondered for a moment if that was her molar.

Mike looked away, wondering what she was thinking to make her look so vicious. When she was looking vicious, her nose wrinkled and he could see the tops of her front teeth. She looked like a mean little animal, a ferret or a weasel. He wasn't clear why he liked her so much when she looked that way. Some things you just don't wonder about. He had been brought up to believe there were practical limits to wonder, what with so many things being divine mysteries. On the other hand, he reminded himself, there were things he hadn't wondered about enough, like the gay community. He felt some-how relieved to be turning his attention back to the problem of the gay community. It was one of those things he'd have to find out about, he could tell. Scilla's sort of thing, the sort of thing she had found out about when she was a teenager, an adolescent, he was amazed at how much she had bothered to look into. That she thought to *ask:* it filled him with awe and humility.

By definition, police forces are conservative institutions, dedicated to the preservation of the status quo, the rule of law. Because of this conservatism, even detectives, whose job it is to find things out and who consequently like to describe them-selves in terms of biting or being bitten, hard, can be curiously naive about the lives of ordinary human beings. Mike was familiar with male homosexuality as a street phenomenon. He had dealt with teenage hustlers, pedophiles, lavender movie theaters, and steam baths that generally didn't get busted for the same snarl of practical and furtive reasons that the massage parlors didn't get busted. All these things belonged to a large category of operations that didn't surprise him. What did sur-prise him was that he liked Bruce Levine.

He was so surprised at liking Levine that at first he hadn't been able to identify the emotion as liking. He just found himself wondering whether Levine was really gay. After he thought about it, he decided it was an odd thing to wonder: surely Levine would know. When he was sitting in Levine's kitchen drinking Levine's coffee, he began imagining how it might feel to be raped. It hadn't occurred to him before to imagine anything of the kind. It hadn't occurred to him that he could be raped. Sitting there while Levine and Scilla engaged in incomprehensible hostilities, he thought about how it might feel to have an arm across your windpipe, to have somebody you couldn't see yanking down your pants. Not good. It was odd discovering you were granting a point of view to a kind of person you hadn't thought of before as having one. Of course, that was where he'd had it wrong, he decided. This wasn't a kind of person; this was Bruce Levine, nice guy. Somebody he might have gone to school with, you did get a few of them at Loyola Downtown, "them" meaning Jews as well as that other thing. He wondered if Levine played baseball. That was when he knew he liked the guy. He could imagine playing on the same team with Levine; he'd most likely be a shortstop. Mike was a catcher. At that point he realized that he and Levine had something in common, even if he'd just made it all up. That was why he could even imagine being Levine, a little bit, for a short period of time. Nothing in this process of reasoning made a lot of sense, he knew, but there was something there anyway. The point to hold on to was that you could imagine being somebody else if you took it very slow.

He wasn't sure he had ever tried before imagining being someone else. Or rather, he had been brought up required to imagine being his father, a priest, a businessman, a policeman. Sequentially. Period. Maybe he hadn't known that anyone else actually existed? He'd have to think about it; that was the sort of thing Scilla was inclined to accuse him of, eyes narrowed so the lashes stood up in little spikes, words coming out clipped and pointy. He shivered. God, she was pretty when she lectured him like that. Her immediate response to him, almost the first thing after they were introduced and shook hands, was rage that he wasn't making an effort to see her side of things. Her attacks had been a revelation to him. He was dumbfounded by her capacity to anticipate his defenses before he had the wit to articulate them. He had never met anyone like her before. He felt immediately that she understood him, and then he felt guilty that he didn't understand her. She seemed to expect understanding, as a sort of ground condition. But he was equally struck by the way she would get so lost in an argument that she could have no idea what she looked like. She would lean over the table at him, both hands spread out and trembling a little, and begin enunciating very clearly, as if the thing he weren't getting were so simple, so self-evident, so glaringly obvious that there was something criminal in the fact that he'd never thought about it before. Worst of all, he wouldn't get it then, either. He'd find himself instead marveling that she could look so intensely lovely without even knowing it. He had never known a woman who wasn't aware when she was being pretty. He had never known a woman who wanted first and foremost to get something across to him. Except maybe Sally, and that had come afterward, too late.

Scilla swallowed the remnants of the last ice cube and looked around for the waitress with the skinny arms. It was already past midnight, and first thing in the morning Anna would probably put them on a house-to-house in the areas adjoining Temple Hill proper, looking for dog walkers, drug dealers, people like that, out at night and maybe in possession of some fragmentary clue. That was what you did when your leads went dead; you moved out, snuffled around for new leads. You did that unless you got lucky and there was another crime. Then you were bound to get something more in the way of evidence, although of course you lost something, too. Certainly that was the case here, with Lindgren hustling the media and the *Advocate* staff already rumbling about a Gay Pride march on something, please God on the mayor's office or Considine's office and not their precinct house. Three strikes and somebody might be out. Mike was dead on his feet, she decided. He had that mopey look. She wrinkled her nose again and he looked away, feeling confusedly that she had just done something he shouldn't witness, like taking off her blouse.

Ten

It had been an unexpectedly good night, so good that after the last customer had been nudged out and the doors were locked, she sat down at one of the tables and sorted the grubby singles and fives into piles with all the Washingtons and Lincolns face-up and gazing stoically over her right shoulder. She decided to leave the two twenties in the little velcro pockets she had sewn into the underside of each bra cup. Nothing like a crisp new bill for uplift. And it was wise not to let management know about everything you made. Let them handle the ones and fives while you complain about how hard you had to hustle. Tell them weeknights are full of deadbeats and stiffs and you're sick of swinging your ass in the face of guys who push dollies around warehouses. Act as though you're fed up. What they don't know won't hurt you.

She was humming "Proud Mary" as she brought her money up to the bar. Great dance song. About half the speed of that disco crap they want you to jiggle to, aerobic Muzak, workout tapes. You sweat like a pig and where's the glamour? If a table was willing to pay for the song—an extra five dollars that might go into your tip, but what the hell—she always asked for "Proud Mary." Good beat but nice and smooth, gives you space to play around, develop a little drama in the routine. With a song like that what you were doing was art, or at least craft. Otherwise, it was just jiggle jiggle, look at me. I have tits.

That was when it was demeaning, if you wanted to get into what was demeaning. Not the job itself, not the poses and moves, not the hands, not even the dirty mixing at the back tables where you made your real living wage. You called all those things. That was why she liked this job so much better than waitressing, even apart from the money. It was that sense of control over sexual exchanges. When you were waitressing and got groped, that was just part of what you'd signed on for. Here a grope had immediate cash value and you could demand cash. You want to feel them a little, that's maybe five bucks with possibilities for the future: you called those, too. She didn't mind. It's not sex, she had to keep explaining to Nancy; it's not sex for me, from my side; it's business. But I like the way they feel about my body, sure. I like making them excited. Nancy leaning on the doorframe, drying while she washed. Dubious. Maybe hurt. But not condescending anymore: that part they'd worked through.

The control, the power even, that she felt when things were going well was what made the disco stuff so demeaning. Then it was just jiggle jiggle, come on, baby, shake it faster, as if they were trying to get her body away from her, trying to turn it into a mass of inadvertent heaves and bulges, jellied meat. Sometimes she was sure those guys hated her body, wanted it flaccid and vulnerable, pure prey to the laws of motion and gravity. Which was certainly overstated, extreme. But sometimes she felt that way. And she normally didn't mix with that type. You developed a sixth sense about these things. On the other hand, you could be wrong sometimes; events could prove you wrong. A pushy, insistent bastard could get off in five, ten seconds, practically from the moment you touched him, all that strenuous self-assertion doing the work of arousal for you. And he had been amazingly generous. She had learned something new tonight; there's always something new you can learn. "Rolling," she sang under her breath, "Rolling on the river."

Curt gave her a twenty for the small bills and another sixteen dollars for her percentage off the bottles. The percentage, along with the four dollars an hour that was figured down to the quarter hour on the paycheck allocated to her every two weeks, with deductions for taxes and Social Security, was supposed to be her real income, what she reported on her tax form. Sometimes she thought it was remarkable that the IRS didn't write to congratulate her on supporting herself and Benjy on that amount. Nancy didn't count, of course, and all the side money from her job stayed on the side, so she was Unmarried, Head of Household with a reported income so far below the poverty level that anyone who could do math would have concluded that she and Benjy had already starved to death. She was grateful for the inefficiency of the system. It wasn't that they didn't care; never make the mistake of believing they didn't care. They resent every nickel and dime you get away without reporting: she had learned that when she was working at the coffee shop and suddenly the owner was making them turn out their pockets before they could punch out and go to the dressing room. Waitresses were a known quantity. Everybody knew waitresses got tips. Nothing like what waiters got, but that wasn't an issue. Table dancers were still an ambiguous category. Tips for what? Well you might ask, and so the management of Pete's Good Time was less eager to collaborate with the Feds than the management of the Copper Kettle had been. Not because they were on her side, understand. Nobody was on the side of the table dancers except the other table dancers. She had thought at one point of bringing in a union. Which was a laugh, of course, as several of the veteran dancers had pointed out. First of all, which union?

The dressing room was empty when she finally wandered down the long hall past the rest rooms, past the door that said DO NOT ENTER, through the door that said EMPLOYEES ONLY, not to be confused with DO NOT ENTER, total privacy being reserved for Mr. Downing, Curt, and Buddy. Employees got relative privacy: at least this door didn't say MEN. Smoke hung in the damp air. She sat down in the middle chair of five metal folding chairs lined up to face the long formica-topped counter and the long speckled mirror running above it. There were dark smudges under her eyes again. So much for the claims of her new waterproof mascara. She reached for the communal jar of Noxema, gouged by other fingers, and began spreading the cream over her face. "Rolling," she sang softly, watching her lips move, purple-red against white. They were getting low on Kleenex again. It wasn't her turn to buy, but maybe she'd bring a box anyway. Better to put out than run out. She smeared Noxema over her mouth and wiped. Lipstick never came entirely off unless you stopped putting it on for about a week; it just wore in and changed color. Nancy said she looked like she was hemorrhaging. Nancy said it tasted, too, especially this kind, the theatrical kind. Although who knows, she may have been tasting the Noxema. The T-shirt was still damp under her arms. She pulled it over her head, felt briefly for the slight stiffness under the cups of her bra, and pulled on another T-shirt, oversized, black. Above her left breast was a small black pin with a glowing pink triangle. Last night Lillian had asked, "That some sort of dyke eye-*dee,* honey?" and she had laughed and explained and offered to bring one for each of them, but there were no takers. Nobody wanted to be reminded, although most of them were pretty careful. "I got it from Nancy," she had said, wondering if she sounded apologetic. Down here you were what you were. People accepted you, but by the same token you weren't supposed to go around making converts to anything.

Even though she was sticky with sweat, she didn't bother to change her underwear. No point until she had taken a shower, and there was no shower here, Downing being such a mingy bastard that he'd rather have the girls smell. She pulled her jeans over the yellow bikini underpants she had been wearing all evening and stepped back into her sandals. If you left your shoes overnight they were as good as gone, and anyway these were good shoes, metallic gold but with only one-inch heels so she could still move, didn't feel like some toppling edifice up there on spikes. You could break your neck with the wrong shoes, especially if you had some assholes who thought it would be a great idea to tip the table. Some assholes couldn't stand to think you were in control.

She threw her denim jacket over her shoulders before she moved to the outside door. The dressing room opened onto an alley, but it was only a matter of feet to First Avenue, still lit up and winking at the through traffic from the Harbor Island Bridge. Once on First Avenue she walked quickly, swinging her arms. Nobody looked at her. She loved this moment, when she metamorphosed from Exotic Dancer into no one in particular, short young woman, short-haired, a little stocky, a little abrupt, a little butch. Only the gold sandals complicated the image, clacking smartly on the gritty pavement.

Two blocks up from Pete's she turned onto a narrow side street that led down to the waterfront. Here too there were plenty of lights, these determinedly old-fashioned, gas lamps rewired to burn yellow-white in the new Chamber of Commerce spirit of Olde Hinton. The bars were closed now, and under the frosted windows with their period gold lettering, an assortment of Hinton's homeless were taking their places for the night. She clacked by, her pace picking up just slightly with the grade of the hill. The sidewalk sloped more sharply as the bars thinned out, to be replaced by plain brick facades, loft buildings, some of them now housing lawyers and galleries, some still dark with soot, their inconspicuous entrances locked to the public, loading dock in back, unrenovated. At the bottom of the hill were the lights from cars moving up and down the Shore Drive. Across the drive, the clusters of upscale restaurants and gift shops on the Old Downtown piers glittered in duplicate, their neon signs and white pier lights reflected wetly and upside down on the quivering surface of Nanteco Bay. After the bars and warehouses ended but before the little street crossed the drive to peter out in a pedestrian walkway down one of the piers, it ran for two blocks under the overpass that carried the Harbor Freeway along the waterfront. In this strip of prime downtown real estate, which stretched north another fifteen blocks and south another four, Sullivan Lots had established dominion. The entire area under the overpass was a parking lot, segmented into block-square areas, each with its metal box, each box with its twenty-four numbered slots.

At 6:30 this evening when she pulled in, all the lots were virtually full, but there was a lot of action because the late drinkers from the surrounding offices were vacating places that immediately filled with diners heading for the Old Downtown restaurants and clubs. She had cruised for only three or four minutes before she got lucky and found herself nearly on top of an El Dorado backing majestically into the traffic lane, white-haired lord of creation with no eye for his rearview mirror. She had braked hard and heard brakes slamming in sequence down the street behind her, domino effect. Driving in this town you developed lightning reflexes. Although she didn't really give a damn if someone rear-ended her little Toyota, especially someone with insurance to burn. It was a good car considering its age, but she would rather have money than a trunk any day. There it was now, edged up alongside one of the massive concrete pillars that kept the freeway from falling into the water or the Old Town Square, clearly visible now that the lot had cleared. The only cars around this late belonged to other club workers or to the few loft tenants who had not rented permanent garage space. Or to whores, she supposed. She was eyeing a shiny little Renault Encore parked in the far corner of the lot as she stepped off the curb into Grover, the last cross street. Call girls arrived in taxis when they came to this part of town; streetwalker were sometimes dropped off by their pimps, in those ubiquitous El Dorados. But a lot of the working girls in Hinton worked solo and provided their own transportation, more power to them, she thought. Not everyone succumbed to the lure of protection. Satisfied that no one was in the Encore, she crossed Grover and stepped under the looming bulk of the overpass.

The traffic above was loud but not overpowering. You

could hear individual engines of individual cars, the muted rumble as a badly loaded truck hit one of the potholes. It was almost soothing, like being near a river or the ocean. She had learned to listen under the noise for footsteps, to scan the whole space of the lot as she walked for any unaccountable shapes, any movement. Tonight there was nothing. No late scuffling footfall when she stopped suddenly, breaking the rhythm of her one-inch heels on asphalt. No edges of a figure dissolving into the shadows. Just her little car sitting alone there by the pillar. Nobody behind her, nobody ducking between the shadowy masses to meet her. She was carrying her keys, the one she needed at the ready. She had gone through the drill so many times it was automatic: key into driver's door, open door, in and close door, lock door, key in ignition. A couple of seconds' vulnerability and she was out of there. A couple of seconds where she had to be damned sure nobody was within jumping distance. Then slam, click, engine on, out of there. She had been doing it for almost a year.

On the home stretch now she picked up the pace, letting her heels strike the pavement like hammers, clack clack, here she comes, ready or not. The noise felt authoritative, made her feel stronger. No movement anywhere as she rounded the back of the car, extended her arm. And then the figure came out from behind the pillar, gigantic, huge-headed, and before she considered and dismissed the possibility of flight, regretted the shoes, remembered knees and especially elbows, she thought you don't fool me, you're no woman. Then she bit down hard on the heel of the hand sliding over her mouth and felt the first blow on the side of her head knocking her into the driver's door. She took most of the impact in her shoulder and bounced off, letting the impetus turn and roll her toward the back of the car while she concentrated on keeping on her feet, getting clear. She damned the shoes, thinking about the second or two it would take to kick them off so she could run, never mind gravel or broken glass. Then he had her by the wrist and she was snapped out of her spin and almost off her feet again, the other shoulder hurting this time, possible dislocation, possible concussion, possible death by resistance, but no, she knew about this bastard, she wasn't going to let him. When he reeled her in, she would be able to kick. Possible broken toe. Never mind pain, she told herself, pain is God's way of telling you you're alive. His breathing was heavy. "No!" she screamed, and kicked, but he caught her foot and now she was off balance, squirming on one leg, pivoting to use his weight, to make him hold her while she swung the other leg up. Then he had dropped her foot and was whirling her by the wrist so that suddenly her arm was behind her own back. Good move, she thought, nothing like brute force; he could break my arm. And then, here's where we kick. But his breath was in her ear now and there was something in his other hand. The whisper was so physically intrusive, warming and then tickling her ear, that she couldn't understand the words. "What?" she gasped.

"Don't make me cut you," he whispered.

Anna Blessing lived in a one-bedroom condominium near the top of Victorian Hill. Her building was not Victorian, any more than most of the hill other than a patch of the desirable North Slope was Victorian. Her building was angular, squat, and constructed of aggressively orange bricks, one of the many apartment complexes thrown up in the mid-1960s, when a profusion of defense contracts turned Hinton into a boom town, and transformed into condos in the mid-1970s, when Hinton began to pull out of the economic slump occasioned by the end of the Vietnam War. At that point in the mid-1970s, Anna Blessing was a Detective First Grade in the Third Precinct, her youngest daughter, Marilyn, had just accepted a job teaching junior high school social studies in San Diego, and coffee at Ogden's Tasti-Bake, which was all Anna usually ordered, was ten cents. The condominium had cost 30 thousand dollars, 10 thousand down, hoarded from the pension of the late Arthur Blessing, twenty thousand financed at 6 percent. Right now the condominium was worth something in the neighborhood of 150 thousand dollars and Anna owned it outright. Lying under an electric blanket on a queen-size mattress, which rested on a queen-size box spring, which rested, prudently, on the floor, she could take satisfaction in having gotten a deal. If this knowledge proved an inadequate source of satisfaction, there was also a box of chocolate chip cookies on the floor by her left elbow.

Widows of cops are not richly remunerated for their loss, not even when the lost one was a Detective First Grade on his way into the administrative ranks, not even when the widow is also the daughter of the commissioner. Not even when the defunct cop lost it in the line of duty, which was not the case with Arthur Blessing unless medical science reveals some un-guessed-at link between the stresses of detective work and cancer of the colon. Or perhaps between a domestic history of indifference bordering on what the state divorce courts now call Mental Cruelty and cancer of the colon: in the annals of medicine there are occasional instances of poetic justice. At any rate, Anna was left with two little girls and very little income. Precincts traditionally take care of their own, which means that widows traditionally receive a lot of casseroles during the first few months of their bereavement and then are encouraged to do housewifely tasks around the station house: making up the beds in which harried cops take catnaps when they are putting in long hours on tough cases, for example. Anna chose to go the less traveled but no less traditional route of becoming a part-time police administrative aide in her husband's home precinct, the First. This meant that she spent mornings in the relatively serene wasteland of West Hinton typing and filing patrol reports, and afternoons making after-school snacks for the girls and cleaning the two-story frame house purchased by her taciturn and now dead husband. It seemed inevitable, if slightly less traditional, when she moved into a full-time clerical position after Marilyn went into first grade, and plausible, if not quite inevitable, when three years later she approached her precinct captain, a genial career administrator a year from retirement, about going to patrol school.

At that time uniformed patrol officers still directed a lot of traffic as well as riding around in squad cars peering out at the dubious life of the streets, and it seemed reasonable to assume that someone like Anna would find her vocation in a role no more disruptive of the HMPD's rigid sense of gender arrangements than, say, school crossing guard. In addition, there was a new theory that police officers should function as somewhat more frightening social workers, especially in areas involving juvenile offenders, and once you thought social worker and not cop—especially if you had juvenile jammed somewhere into the same thought—you were probably going to think woman. Sort of a soft cop, you might say. Anyway, Anna had waltzed on two-inch heels into the patrol school and had come clumping out twenty pounds heavier but still discernibly feminine—as her commanding officers were quick to assure each other—in the new regulation black oxfords over nylons with seams but under a very no-nonsense blue serge skirt. After that she never looked back. It had taken her six years in the HMPD before she even got to become a cop. After that she just became more of a cop. If there were remarks about her loss of femininity, nobody made them to her face. After a while it was a little hard remembering if there had been any femininity to get lost, and after more of a while the conjunction of Anna Blessing and femininity became unthinkable. Whatever femininity was. Eating a chocolate chip cookie out of a box labeled FAMILY SIZE in her queen-size bed at two-thirty in the morning, Anna Blessing considered briefly the possibility that it was aligned with Arthur Blessing's capacity to spend a whole weekend in her presence without uttering a word that wasn't a command. She had acknowledged this connection soon after her husband's death, after the visitors with covered casseroles stopped arriving with any regularity but before she had discovered the heady pleasures of typing and filing and making coffee in a twenty-cup urn and bringing home her own paycheck. She had been in advance of her time, she sometimes thought. The other version was that she had always been too smart for her own good; too smart to pass for long as a policeman's wife, for instance. That was why Art stopped talking to her maybe two years into the marriage. It was eight years before the cancer got him, right in the asshole. She didn't have theories about the propriety of this development—about poetic justice or about justice of any sort. She was a career cop, not the sort of uniformed philosopher you ran into in novels if you weren't careful about what you took home from the library. But while she had welcomed the visitors and eaten gratefully out of the covered casseroles, she had never kidded herself. She was glad he was dead. And she was perfectly willing to get rid of whatever it was that had made her look good to him, young and big and blonde and healthy and welcoming and farm-girl Swedish. Good wife material. Never again, she had decided, eating out of other people's serving dishes, contemplating the prospect of an income that wasn't anyone else's.

Now she was eating cookies out of a foil-lined bag and thinking about femininity in the abstract. About what it meant to wear nylons with a garter belt, taffeta circle skirts with a crinoline, shoes with high, precarious heels, all of that when you had rape and maybe murder on your mind. Times had changed, but nylons and crinolines and spike heels were close enough to the regrettable era of her own salad days that she recognized an inversion when she saw one. The guy hated a lot of things, she thought. Not only faggots. Maybe not faggots at all, if you looked at it a certain squinty way. Something here being said about femininity, although it all smelled fishy and probably psychological when you took it that far. Anna Blessing had the veteran cop's deep suspicion of psychology, in all its equivocal forms.

Now she crumpled the foil bag and threw it at her wastebasket before rolling onto her side and reaching for the lamp. A lot of things smelled fishy at this point. A lot of things weren't making a lot of sense. They needed a break, was how they all put it. They needed another assault, if you wanted to be blunt about it. A break usually meant another crime, the perpetrator breaking the surface again, giving them something to look at. Another assault and you'd have a series. Rita Freeling would have a story. The gay community would have a cause. Presuming, of course, that the next victim was also gay.

Or had a name beginning with the letter *L,* Anna Blessing reminded herself as she slid into her habitual rumbling sleep. They needed that continuity. They needed an identifiable link between victims. Otherwise they had the cop's worst nightmare, violence without a system, chaos and old night. Detective work is grounded on the premise of meaningful patterns. If police investigators don't live in a world radiant with intelligible purpose, they do assume the existence of local networks of explanation, chains of events that carry their own internal justification even if in a larger context these justifications are palpably insane. It would make things considerably easier if the police had overwhelming reason to believe the two rapes were the work of a single rapist. If there were only one rapist, the various aspects of his behavior would constitute clues as to what he had on his mind. If there were only one rapist, they could think about his motives, weird and implausible as these motives might be. They could begin to make predictions about what he would do next.

But even to establish that there was only one rapist, they needed more information. That was the irony of the criminal justice system: to get your perpetrator you needed evidence, and you got more evidence when you got more crimes. So they were looking for another rape now. Not hoping, exactly, but there was definitely this sense of anticipation. With luck, just one more rape.

Or attempted rape, Anna Blessing reminded herself as she was jolted back to consciousness by the sound of her telephone ringing. The jolt was familiar. She was not startled by the noise, any more than she was disoriented by the intrusion of theories about rape into the intimacy of her dreams. Even sound asleep she held on to her train of thought, which was one of the reasons she was Lieutenant of Detectives, or one of the ways she was too smart for her own good, depending on which observer you were and which Anna Blessing you were thinking about. You didn't need the crime to get your evidence; all you needed was the attempt. Of course, Anna thought as she picked up the receiver in the middle of the second ring, the problem was that serial crimes tended to be committed very efficiently. The attempt generally succeeded: that's how they got to be serial crimes. And this bastard, if he was one bastard, was having some flaming successes despite the risks he was running with that costume, those adult and athletic victims. A lot of risks, in fact. Why was he running them?

"Yes?" she rasped into the receiver. "Oh shit."

Eleven

At two fifty-five in the morning the beeper might have been a gentler way to wake up, but at that particular moment gentle wasn't on anyone's mind. Scilla was wrenched out of sleep by the shrill ringing of her bedside telephone. The voice on the other end was Anna Blessing's.

"Did I wake you," it said.

Scilla noted that Anna herself was evidently alert and functioning although technically off duty. "Um," she said, unwilling to commit herself. "What happened?"

"Number three happened," said Anna. "Two-thirty, two-forty, something like that. Passing motorist called it in."

"Oh," said Scilla.

"Victim's in intensive care at Overlook."

"Oh shit," said Scilla in her turn. "Are you there? At Overlook?"

"I'm here. Mike's on his way. How soon can you be here?"

"Ten minutes." She was already standing at the foot of her bed rummaging through her top dresser drawer for underpants, with the receiver squeezed between her cheek and her shoulder. "What's the name?"

"Alvarez. Christopher Alvarez."

She paused in the act of stepping into a black cotton bikini with a monarch butterfly embroidered on the crotch. "No L," she said.

"No L," said Anna.

"Is he gay?"

There was a pause, in which Scilla could hear the wheezing exhalation that Jane Lowry claimed as one of Anna's distinguishing noises. She felt around the back of the drawer for a bra.

"*She* is," said Anna.

"Oh shit," said Scilla again.

Two of the networks were already in evidence on the sidewalk outside the main entrance of Overlook when Scilla walked through the double doors. All heads swung her way but only Rita Freeling recognized her. Scilla waved, hoping the signal would defer questions, and looked around. Nobody here but us press. The real action was going on upstairs. Two uniformed patrol officers stood by the bank of elevators. She had to show one of them her shield before she was allowed to go up.

The intensive care unit was on the ninth floor. When the elevator door opened, she was greeted by another uniformed patrolman who again checked her shield. Heavy-duty protection. This one must have seen something. Amazing the woman was alive. But then maybe she wouldn't be alive much longer. "Hey," she said to Mike, who had come around the corner to the elevator foyer and was waiting patiently behind the uniformed patrolman.

"Hey," said Mike. "Long time no see."

"I have to do this for everyone," said the uniformed patrolman, who looked very young.

"That's okay," said Scilla. She looked up over his shoulder where Mike's head was bobbing. Mike was looking a little green again, she noticed. Maybe it wasn't just the quartz lights and the paint on the walls of the emergency waiting room. Maybe he was just naturally green at this hour of the morning.

"How come she's named Christopher?" she asked.

"Named for her father," said Mike. The uniformed patrolman handed back her shield. "Good work," she told him, sliding it into her wallet and slipping her wallet back into the inside pocket of her raincoat. The uniformed patrolman looked embarrassed. "So her father is a nice guy or what?" she asked Mike.

"Her father is a dead guy," said Mike. "Died before she was born. Knifed. She was named in his memory."

"How is she?"

Mike shrugged. "She's in surgery now. One finger probably goes. Nobody's clear how many more."

Scilla whistled softly. "He had a knife."

"He had a knife. She grabbed it. By the blade."

Scilla shook her head in admiration. "She really didn't want to get raped."

Mike looked at her in surprise. "Who does?" he asked. She reached up and squeezed his shoulder before moving ahead of him into the waiting room.

Two more uniformed patrolmen, conspicuously large ones, were standing just inside the entrance. In the far corner Anna Blessing oozed like a blue serge swamp over the edges of a chrome and plastic armchair. On the chrome and plastic couch beside her sat an obviously exhausted woman in jeans and a faded blue sweater, her graying brown hair pulled back into a hasty ponytail. On the woman's lap was a little boy wearing shorts and a sweatshirt, profoundly asleep. His bare legs dangled down from the woman's knees. On his feet were fuzzy Garfield slippers.

"This here is Nancy Werner," said Anna, motioning them to pull up more chrome and plastic chairs so that the corner was transformed into a little huddle. Scilla wondered if anyone else was going to be allowed into the intensive care waiting room. Probably there were visiting hours. "This is my detective team on the case," Anna continued, waving her hand over them magisterially. "Priscilla Carmody. Mike Annunzio." They all shook hands over the head of the little boy, whose eyelashes fluttered briefly. A beautiful boy, Scilla thought. Clearly Asian of some sort, or part Asian. Four, maybe five years old.

"Filipino," said Nancy Werner suddenly. "Chris is Filipino.

So was the father." *The* father, Scilla noted, not his father. Faint but pronounced contempt. But Nancy was holding the boy as if she would bite anyone who came too close to him. Scilla settled back in her chair.

"You're Christopher's partner," she said.

"Right." Nancy Werner seemed pleased to have got to the heart of the matter so quickly. From her corner Anna nodded almost imperceptibly. That was why Scilla was here. She spoke the language.

Mike had pulled out his pad and was quietly taking notes. Anna cleared her throat, producing a sort of public gargle. Nancy Werner looked at her with alarm. Satisfied that she had everyone's attention, Anna began, "We've got reasons for figuring this is the same guy even though it's a female this time. Same getup—heels, nylons, petticoat. Wig. We got a preliminary report from the victim."

"Taken in the ambulance," said Nancy Werner.

"Yeah, taken in the ambulance," said Anna. "We take statements where we can get them. And furthermore, that statement is all we've got to go on till tomorrow, when hopefully we get some lab reports back and hopefully she's out from under the anesthesia and making sense again. And that statement isn't a whole lot because she lost consciousness about five minutes into the ride." She pulled a little spiral notepad out of the breast pocket of her uniform. "I got that statement right here, and believe me I'm holding on to it. Let me tell you one thing. She wanted to talk. She was very interested in having us lay our hands on this particular bastard."

Nancy Werner laid her cheek against the thick, shiny hair of the little boy. "Me too. I'm very interested."

"Look," said Scilla. "She fought back. She probably marked him in some ways." She looked at Anna again, and again Anna nodded. "So there's likely to be blood under her fingernails, maybe some skin, too. And because she fought back, she saw more than either of the other two victims."

"Under her fingernails," said Nancy Werner softly. Tears

102

were dropping one by one onto the head of the little boy. "You can send whole fingers to the lab." Nobody said anything. She blinked rapidly and took a deep breath. "She's very likely lost the use of her right hand. And she still got raped. She got raped by a homophobic maniac who probably has AIDS. So great. She fought back. I'm not putting that down. It's not insignificant. Anyway, I was the one who talked her into taking that self-defense class. I was worried about her working nights down there. They teach you to fight back. They don't guarantee it will work."

"We don't know he has AIDS," said Mike. No one looked at him.

"Homophobic now," said Anna. She had mastered the word; it rolled off her tongue as if she had been using it all her life. "I wasn't at all sure that was our angle before tonight," Anna continued. "Two guys, both of them gay, a rapist who called them faggots. But that might just have been part of the excitement for this guy, part of the humiliation. Like, I'm calling you a faggot because I'm making you one, see what I mean?" Scilla and Mike both nodded. Nancy Werner was staring at her in fascination. Anna snuffled and then wiped her nose with the back of her hand. Nobody looked away. "But then how come he got a girl this time? It doesn't fit."

"Her name—" Scilla began.

"You're telling me he couldn't tell?" Anna made a noise somewhere between her earlier snuffle and a snort.

"Well, presuming he was following her in the dark—"

"She's sure he wasn't following her from the club. She's absolutely sure. She says he was waiting by her car. He knew where her car was. Which means he knew a lot about her, which means he knew she's a girl, it isn't hard to tell, it wasn't something she was *hiding*. I mean, she's one of those topless dancers."

"But you think he knew she's gay," said Scilla softly.

"Lesbians are one of the lowest-risk groups for AIDS," said Nancy Werner suddenly.

"At the moment," Anna said. "It's just like in crime, we have low-risk groups and high-risk groups. But it's not like you can count on the statistics, and anyway statistics have a way of changing." She waved a pudgy hand at the far wall of the waiting room. "Solid citizen gets held up in the sanctity of his very own home, you get this outrage, like this doesn't happen, I'm in a very low-risk group. But it happens." She snuffled again. "People get to thinking they're immune. That's what it means to be a solid citizen. You're safe. You're sanctified. But you're not." She nodded emphatically, sat perfectly still for a moment looking at the floor between her feet, and then raised her head and squinted at Scilla. "So how'd he know she's gay?"

"There was that button," said Mike.

"That's not what the button means," said Anna. "I mean, maybe it was a lucky inference. But the other two weren't wearing buttons."

"*Did* he know she's gay?" Scilla asked.

"Oh yeah," said Anna. "Listen to this." She flipped open the small spiral notebook. "This is from Marvin Tirsch, who was with the first patrol car on the scene. Remind me to make a Xerox of this." She turned a page. "First of all, he raped her—" she glanced briefly at Nancy, "in the same place, okay?" Scilla looked at Mike, but he was writing busily. "Second, wait till you hear what he called her." Anna turned another page. "Here we are." She cleared her throat. " 'Faggot cunt.' " She looked up in triumph. "I ask you, is this guy confused or what?"

In the ensuing silence, Scilla wondered again why anyone ever assumed female cops would display greater sensitivity when dealing with rape cases. Then she looked at Nancy Werner and decided that maybe sensitivity wasn't the greatest of the virtues. Nancy was sitting bolt upright. All traces of fatigue had vanished. She was absently stroking the boy's back, but her mouth was set and her brown eyes glittered.

"Anything I can do," she said. "You just tell me what I can do to help."

Twelve

There were times when Scilla agreed with Chief Considine about keeping the press away from Anna. She and Mike had escorted Nancy Werner to her car, shouldering past the reporters massed outside the hospital entrance on Garfield and calling out "No comment" when microphones appeared in front of their faces. There was a nice photograph of them on the inside front page of the *Express,* Nancy hunched over the sleeping boy, who was all bare legs and fuzzy slippers, Mike at Nancy's right, in profile, and Scilla in the extreme foreground like one of the peasant observers in a painting of Christ performing a miracle, looking directly at the camera and appearing to ward it off with her forearm. After Scilla had read the front page, she cut out the photograph and attached it with pushpins to her kitchen bulletin board. She liked the way she came out in it, small but mean.

Anna had stayed behind in the intensive care waiting room and had emerged twenty minutes later to a tumultuous welcome from those reporters who had had the wit to stick around, including Rita Freeling, Alexander Radley, and a formidable young black woman named Leslie Sears from the CBS affiliate. Scilla arose from a moderately refreshing hour's sleep to catch the television interview, which seemed largely to be on the subject of what you can and cannot do with a semen sample.

"Put it this way," Anna was saying with the hulking intensity of a tackle discussing injuries he has just done to a quarterback. "Say you've got some fingerprints at the scene of the crime. Nice clear fingerprints. Only one hand could've made those fingerprints, that's why we dust for them. Everybody knows that. They get it from TV. Like that Cagney and Lacey." She indulged in a long, liquid sniff. Leslie Sears drew back a step. "Yeah, that Cagney and Lacey," said Anna, shaking her head. Scilla wondered whether the morning TV crowd was going to get Anna's entire Cagney and Lacey rap. Anna's animus was deep and abiding and had little to do with the portrayal of fingerprinting or any other technological aid to the solution of crimes. As far as Scilla could figure out, what Anna had against the program was that it showed women cops as complicated human beings with rich inner lives.

"So, fingerprints," said Anna. "So that's fine and dandy, but the big thing is if. *If* they match up with fingerprints you've got on file somewhere, then maybe you can apprehend the offender, that's the if. You with me so far?"

Leslie Sears, who knew a story when she was on one, nodded vehemently and said "Mm."

"Okay," said Anna. Scilla poured herself a second glass of grapefruit juice. "Say you've got a cartridge," said Anna. "Nice blobby cartridge, all smashed out of shape, you pulled it out of a body, it's why you've *got* a body. You can examine that cartridge and get impressions from a particular breechblock and a particular firing pin. Only one gun could have made those impressions. Lots of people know that, they get that from TV, too." She frowned for a moment but apparently decided against bringing up Cagney and Lacey again. "You still with me?"

"Mm," said Leslie Sears, looking rapt.

"Except you've got to have the gun or it doesn't matter diddly-squat what sorts of impressions are on that cartridge. You see what I'm getting at?"

The camera moved in on Anna's face. Scilla finished her

grapefruit juice without taking her eyes off the screen. "Okay, so you were asking me about genetic typing," Anna said. Scilla wondered how many viewers were now counting Anna's freckles. "Good question. They've probably got *that* on TV now, too, but it's still a good question. We've come a long way these last couple years when it comes to getting convictions on rape cases. You can get a lot out of a semen sample nowadays. However." The little eyes narrowed. "We're talking convictions here, court stuff. What you do when you've got your perpetrator. Like with fingerprints you've got to have the fingers. Like with cartridges you've got to have the gun. In this case—"

"So the police don't yet have a suspect," Leslie Sears interrupted suavely.

"You could put it that way," said Anna. Scilla thought about the headline that the print media people must have considered and rejected with regret: COPS HAVE NO DICK IN HAND.

"Can the AIDS virus be detected in a semen sample taken from a rape victim?" Leslie Sears went on, apparently unruffled.

"That's HIV you're thinking of," Anna assured her loftily. "That the human immunodeficiency virus. That's what they're looking for when they do what the layman generally calls your AIDS tests. And the answer is yes and no. Yes, you can theoretically get that information if the sample is fresh enough. No, we can't. We don't have the technology. Maybe we'll *get* the technology, but the way the budget is looking, you don't hold your breath."

That should have the mayor's telephone ringing all morning, Scilla thought with some satisfaction. She turned off the television as the morning anchor duo were making their ritual jokes about the weather and took her juice glass and cereal bowl to the sink. In the bedroom, her telephone began to ring.

She picked it up while she was shrugging into her raincoat. "Listen," said a voice she recognized as Missy's, although it was unusually hoarse even for Missy. Seven-thirty was early for the Old Downtown crowd. "I can't tell you where this comes from," Missy went on huskily, "but there was this weird john last night at the club, a big guy. Something about him smelled funny. The girls were steering clear of him, you know how you just get a feeling?" Missy paused. "No, of course you wouldn't know."

"I know," said Scilla. "Don't tell me I don't get feelings. This was at that topless place, Pete's?"

"That's what I'm telling you," said Missy. "He wanted Chris. Held out for her. She doesn't normally take guys that pushy but he kept saying he wanted her, he'd make it worth her while. So finally she did him. She was right back after three, four minutes. Said it was a snap. Said she'd barely unzipped him and he was coming all over her arm. She had to clean him up with bar napkins. But she was pretty up about the whole thing. Like he did make it worth her while."

"This was last night?"

"Last night. Maybe ten forty-five."

"So what did he look like?"

"She said big," said Missy. "Also white. I mean, Caucasian, nothing interesting. Darkish hair, short, thinning. Nearly bald on top."

Scilla stopped buckling the belt on her raincoat. "You're sure about that?"

"*She's* sure. What's the matter, you don't trust my sources?"

"I trust your sources," said Scilla. "I trust you. You know that. It's just that the hair is different than I expected, given one of my sources. I'll work with it. Go on."

"Think wig," said Missy portentously.

"I am," said Scilla. "I've been thinking wig a lot. Here it's wigs on wigs, though. I mean, it's getting weird."

"It wasn't weird from the beginning?"

"It was weird from the beginning," Scilla admitted. "Okay, give me the rest."

"Okay," said Missy. "All I've got left are clothes. He was

wearing jeans and a plaid shirt, but she didn't think he wore those things all the time, if you know what I mean. Anyway, that's it and it's all secondhand."

"How big?"

"She didn't do him. Chris did him."

"I mean, how *tall?* How big *around?* Feet and inches. Pounds. Come on."

"Hey," said Missy. "I wasn't there."

"You suppose your informant would cooperate with the police artist if we were to put together an Identi-Kit?"

"Nope," said Missy. "This informant has just informed. That's it. She's doing nothing else, and I promised she wouldn't if you get me, so I don't know her. It was dark."

Scilla sighed. "Right."

"But Chris will cooperate. You don't need this one, she's just backup. She's just looking to help you ask the right questions."

"Chris is under anesthesia right now," said Scilla.

"It's about time you got that bastard," said Missy. "You make sure someone's around all the time so she comes out of the anesthesia, know what I mean?"

"Anna's taking care of it."

"Well, Anna, sure," said Missy ambiguously. "You take care, too. And say hi to Mike. Tell him to come see me."

"Sure," said Scilla, who had no intention of doing anything of the kind. If asked, she would have said Missy was her source and her sources were her own, not for sharing even with a working partner. She was aware that her motives might be more complicated but she wasn't going to brood over possible complications.

Mike lived in Sunnyside, a neighborhood to the north of the university and the lake, which had sprung up all at once after the war like a crop of mushrooms after an autumn rain. Almost all the houses in Sunnyside had originally been built to one of five patterns and were variously split-level or ranch, two bedrooms or three, in a range of pastels with white trim. Years of home ownership had established more intrinsic differences. Garages had metamorphosed into bedrooms, and new garages swelled out from the side or back like malignant growths, to be transformed in their turn into master bedroom suites, utility-and-bath combinations, or family rooms. Colors grew autumnal or were bleached into shades called variously Cream, Buttermilk, Chalk, or Colonial White, and wrought-iron eagles appeared over doors. Mike's house was still its original pink. It had only one addition, a sunken master bedroom usurping what had been a single-car garage. Mike and Sally parked their Chevrolet on the street. They had bought the house in the early eighties from its original owners, who had retired to Palm Desert on the profit.

Mike appeared at the door as Scilla pulled the squeaking Plymouth, this week's draw from the motor pool, up to the curb. When she was driving she always picked him up on his porch. She supposed he watched from his picture window, jacket already on, pistol strapped neatly in place underneath it. She had never been inside his house. She never asked why, but reciprocated by keeping him out of her apartment, although this sometimes meant he had to stand for ten or fifteen minutes in her hallway, hands in pockets, whistling under his breath. She thought he was probably grateful for her attention to symmetry. It distracted from the reasons she wasn't supposed to be in his house, ever.

Mike slid into the passenger seat and slammed the door twice, the second time successfully. They both listened to the squeaks as she put in the clutch and pulled away from the curb.

"I think it's a belt somewhere," she said.

"I still think it's the brakes," he said. They had been having this discussion all week.

"They told me on Monday it wasn't the brakes," she said, signaling a right turn.

"I know that's what they *said.*"

She sighed and moved the Plymouth into the rush-hour

110

traffic on Bedford Boulevard. "You see channel seven this morning?"

"I was watching when she called me."

"Anna called."

"Yeah." Out of the corner of her eye she could see he was grinning. "Just when it was getting interesting."

"It didn't get very interesting."

"I didn't think they'd let it. Anyway, Anna says the girl's going to be better off than we thought. Medical science being what it is, they woke up this guy, this orthopedic surgeon, and he came in and actually just tied up two of her tendons. Flexor tendons. Just tied them back together." He shook his head.

"Yech," said Scilla.

"She'll probably lose the use of one of her fingers, the big finger, actually. I mean, she won't be able to bend it," said Mike.

Taking her right hand off the gearshift, Scilla indicated what might be the effect of losing the ability to bend your big finger.

"Right," said Mike.

"Maybe she'll be able to use it in court," said Scilla.

A cameraman and reporter from channel seven were outside Overlook, but they seemed content to track Scilla and Mike striding up the sidewalk and through the double front doors. Scilla wondered sometimes if Mike worked as hard as she did matching their strides.

Anna met them in the ninth floor elevator foyer. "About time," she said. "She's awake and alert. They let us at her at ten."

"Coffee," said Mike.

Anna held up a white paper bag. "Look what I got."

"Great!" said Mike insincerely.

"I'll stay here," said Scilla. Mike threw her an anguished look as Anna steered him toward the elevators, but she refused to meet his eyes.

Alone in the intensive care waiting room under the stoic regard of two new burly patrolmen, Scilla settled down in one

of the chrome and plastic armchairs and pulled out her notebook to do some stock taking. The hour's sleep had done
nothing for her grasp of a situation that seemed almost incom-
prehensibly diffuse, and all her detective's instincts were urging
her to group apparently discrete particulars under more general
rubrics. Flipping over the page covered with notes from her
telephone conversation with Missy, she arrived at a blank sheet
of paper and wrote at the top

LESBIAN!

She stared at the word for a minute, then wrote carefully after
it

= "faggot cunt"!

Then she gazed at the notebook for a long time, one leg
crossed over the other, foot swinging. Finally she wrote underneath

Chris Alvarez—AIDS pin
Alan Lindgren—*Advocate* staff
Bruce Levine—AIDS counselor

And below that

All three victims not only gay but involved in gay
issues.

Then underneath

(AIDS issues?)
(Central roster for involvement? Where?)
(Did Chris Alvarez know either Lindgren or
Levine?)

She starred the third item: something to find out at ten o'clock.
Then she wrote

Masculine name Christopher = significant?
If so, why?

When did he stop thinking she was male, if he ever
did think she was male?
Did it matter that she's female? If so, how?

Then, very fast, she wrote in very large letters

JOHN!
—Does she think he's rapist? If so, why?
—Can she describe?

And, after a moment's hesitation,

—Why would he pay her to jerk him off if he was
going to rape her?
(If he is the same.)

She drew a large box around this entire passage and starred it
in the right-hand margin. Recrossing her legs, she decided it
was time to abandon this line of questioning. General patterns
of rapist behavior were beginning to emerge from the crimino-
logical literature; motives were another thing entirely. You
might predict what a rapist was going to do on the basis of his
past performance, but you were still miles away from knowing
why he performed that way in the first place. She drew a heavy
line across the page and wrote below it

All evidence suggests that he picks out his victim
well ahead of time and knows his/her usual
movements well enough to stage an ambush.

She thought again and then wrote

(except maybe Lindgren?)

And then

(but probably Lindgren, too.)

Then very fast

How does he know that they're gay? How does he
pick out the ones to follow? How does he follow

them without them noticing? *When* does he follow them?

And finally

Who's next?

She was at the bottom of the page. She dropped the book to her lap and stared over it at the dull apricot wall of the waiting room. She was still in that position, albeit with her eyes closed, ten minutes later when Anna and Mike came back from the cafeteria and concluded, correctly, that she was asleep.

"That's what happens if you don't get your hot fat," Anna remarked, lowering herself into the adjoining chair. Scilla's eyes flew open. Mike thought he could detect vestiges of the infant startle reflex, a phenomenon he had observed in all three of his children, in the way her hands came clutching up to her chest. He wondered if she often woke up like that. Maybe she was one of those people who submerged completely in sleep, who lived another life at night, who returned dazed and tremulous every morning from a more vivid country they could never quite describe or recall. You'd want to introduce her to consciousness very gently, with light touches, soft words.

Thoroughly revived after her nap, Scilla noted that Mike was looking mopey again and resolved to speak to him about his caffeine intake. People who drank coffee thought they were becoming alert, but in fact what they were doing was killing off brain cells at the rate of hundreds of thousands per second. It wouldn't be fanaticism if she explained that to him. Surely he would want to know.

"If everybody's *with us,*" said Anna, "we can go in now." She looked up at the wall clock and then at the door to the ward, which was securely shut. "You coming?" she demanded. It still surprised Scilla that such a big woman could be so fast on her feet. She was already pounding on the door when they caught up to her, both of them rather embarrassed at the sudden effusion of noise and action. As if she were committed to kicking the door down, Mike thought as it swung open to reveal an outraged head nurse, who backed down the corridor as Anna came at her. "Police," Anna explained gruffly. The nurse flattened herself against the wall and they marched by in loud paramilitary single file, amazingly loud considering that both Mike and Scilla were wearing running shoes. When you needed the mystique of power you fantasized the boots. Tromp tromp, here come the fuzz. More as if they were going to arrest someone than question a victim, Mike thought, realizing that now, as so often, he was in the company of people who enjoyed throwing their weight around far more than he did.

They clumped along the corridor to the nurses' station, where Anna demanded, "Alvarez?" and got waved down the far left of three branching hallways. As they passed open doorways, doctors stood up and attendants faded into corners—in deference to the ultimate authority Anna was waving around like a truncheon, Mike acknowledged, although he didn't feel entirely part of that authority. Even the custodians of our mortality acquiesce to the armed might of the legal system. That was the appeal of the police force to most recruits, certainly to Anna, certainly to Scilla. But to him? Still clumping along behind the two women, he shook his head, prompting one small orderly, a recent arrival from Tijuana with a forged green card, to put down the bedpan he had been carrying and step noiselessly into a linen closet. That hadn't been the appeal. What had? He wasn't sure.

"Christopher Alvarez?" Improbably, the young woman was beckoning them in with a white gauze paw. "I'm Detective Lieutenant Anna Blessing." It was inevitable, Scilla told herself, that her commanding officer would now thrust her own hand at the prone figure. But Chris Alvarez hesitated only fractionally before pulling her left hand from under the covers and grasping Anna's.

"Boy, am I glad to see you guys," she said.

Mike started organizing chairs from the two other bedsides in the room. The other two beds were occupied, but their occupants seemed disinclined to pay attention to the interrogation. It was not entirely clear, in fact, that one of them was breathing. Anna took one sweeping look around the room and with magnificent disdain dismissed the other patients from consideration.

"There was a john." Scilla had pulled her chair up alongside Chris Alvarez's head. Mike had missed the nod that delegated power, but it was evident that Anna had assigned the roles. He moved his own chair in behind Scilla's and pulled out his notepad. It was the right decision, of course. Still, he often felt overlooked at moments like these, when Anna and Scilla combined forces. They might have consulted him. She might at least have turned around to look at him.

But Christopher Alvarez was speaking, no residual loginess from the anesthesia here, and he had to concentrate on getting it all down. "The asshole set me up," she was saying. "He got it both ways, got me to do it willingly, do it nice—" She stopped suddenly, and he wrote *willingly* and *nice* on his notepad and wondered where Scilla had got her tip. There was a short silence while Chris Alvarez contemplated her cast. Then she said, "I mean. We sometimes get extra money, table dancers. They sometimes tip us."

There was a noise like an ice jam breaking up. Chris Alvarez flinched. Neither Mike nor Scilla moved a muscle. Anna finished clearing her throat and said, "We're not interested in that. Prostitution isn't our thing. Hey"—and here she bared her teeth in a wolfish version of her Mrs. Claus smile—"I'm the one that gets flak because I'm such a good friend to prosses. You know about me?"

Chris had relaxed noticeably. Now she lifted herself on her left elbow and took a good look at Anna. "Yeah," she said. "You grabbed the Hacker. "You're one big lady." Mike noted that Scilla's shoulders were shaking very slightly. She'd be poker-faced, though, his partner. A pro, he thought, with a little surge of pride.

"Yeah, well, you don't believe me you can get your lawyer

down here, we'll get a D.A., and we'll do the whole bit, get it all on paper. We're perfectly willing to guarantee you immunity."

They all sat in silence for a moment, considering this pronouncement. Then Chris Alvarez said, "That you can't do."

"Prosecutorial immunity," said Scilla in a faint voice.

"There's all kinds of immunity," said Anna, so genially that Mike wondered for a split second if she had really grasped all the implications of this turn in the discussion. Then he caught himself. That was the one way he was ahead of Scilla: he understood more about Anna. She was about as subtle as a round of buckshot in the face, but she always knew exactly what she was doing.

"Sometimes you don't just have your immunity," Anna was saying. "Sometimes you have to get it. There are various ways you can get it."

In a clear, firm voice, Chris Alvarez insisted, "You can also lose it."

From the side, Mike could see something pass over Anna's face, too quickly to read. But all she said was "We'll cross that bridge when we come to it. If we come to it. Right now, I want you to tell this nice lady detective here all about this john she was so smart to find out about." Ahead of Mike, Scilla leaned forward. He lifted his pen.

"I've been thinking about it. Thinking and thinking." The lips pursed, relaxed, pursed again. An engaging face, Mike decided. Not beautiful, not even pretty, but full of something he instantly liked. Round, rather heavy-lidded, high cheekbones. A lot of Filipinos didn't look wholly Oriental, more Eurasian. But this woman was no Western wet dream, no Suzy Wong. Even flat on her back, everything about her was compact, condensed, geared toward action. He could see how she'd be a surprisingly good table dancer: good, and also surprising. It would be a kick for her, a riff on the kind of femininity purveyed in those places, an exercise, an athletic event, a game. He'd like to see her dance sometime.

"I mean, I couldn't think about much else. So I've got him, I think. I mean, I can see him. I can give you a fairly complete description."

He could have sworn they all breathed in and then out together. He settled down to transcribe the words exactly as they came out of Chris Alvarez's mouth.

Thirteen

"I didn't like him," said Christopher Alvarez. "I usually go by my gut feeling, not that you need, oh, a rapport with these guys. I mean, it's just hand over hand and a little moaning, you know what I mean?"

Mike concentrated on getting it all down. The chair to his left creaked as Anna settled back in it.

"This one was kind of, I don't know. Unsettling. Or unsettled. Not worried about what I was going to think about him exactly. Not that sort of, oh, eager-to-please thing you sometimes get, like my manhood's at stake here. Not that kind of investment thing. That I don't like either because you know they're going to want some kind of favor from you eventually to show it's not just business and they're not just anybody. You can get into some very funny scenes with that type. But he wasn't that type. He was something else."

Mike finished the sentence and waited. Ahead of him, Scilla was sitting very erect, the wings of her shoulder blades making soft protrusions in the white oxford cloth of her shirt and just touching the rungs of the straight chair. She was making no attempt to prod this witness. He sat in the quiet looking at the back of her neck, newly vulnerable above the white collar. She'd had her hair cut again. He wondered if she'd gone back to Hair Raid. It would be like her to be keeping an eye on the place on her own time and to be doing a spot check on the quality of speed freak haircutting. She was keeping it shorter than she used to. He approved: he liked looking at her neck and at her ears, small and rounded behind the little wisps of dark hair.

He especially liked watching her during moments like this one, when she was absorbed in the atmosphere her witness was generating, nostrils twitching as she tested the peculiar quality of the air. During moments like this she seemed to him to be exactly what he was not, a born detective. Not born, made, she would have insisted: these things weren't innate; look how she'd grown up, fixated on her father. Any cop strengths she had you could credit to the Oedipus complex, she'd said once, and then laughed. He was relieved that she had laughed. He had a vague idea what the Oedipus complex was, and he didn't like to think she had one. He knew about her father, of course; everybody knew about Pat Carmody, who walked with a cane now and was canonized despite some fuzzy edges to the story of how he got the hell knocked out of his kneecap. You didn't dwell on the fuzzy edges when you were telling cop stories, or hearing them. And here was Scilla, another cop; a better cop, he suspected. Saying good cops are made, not born. That was another of her articles of faith. She believed you learned things, inhaled them as you were growing up, the way she was inhaling the story Chris Alvarez was telling, story and silence both. He wasn't as sure. How would you ever know? Everyone was born, everyone grew up. Which made you what you are? Nature or nurture? Both? Neither? Which do you want it to be, she had asked him. Something you can change or something you can't? He admired her assurance that there were things you could change. He didn't think it would be easy.

"He was something else," said Chris Alvarez again. "I don't know what. It made me nervous, whatever it was. It made me very nervous. But I'd never run into somebody like this one so I couldn't point to anything specific. And he started talking money right away. Big bucks if you're a table dancer, forty dollars, double what I ordinarily get for a hand job on the best nights. And nothing else, just the hand. No special requests, not even a dance. Just that it had to be me. And of course I wondered, why me? But I wonder that a lot, why it matters whose hand, and basically you know there's no particular answer. It has to do with how you fit into their grid. Like what pattern they've got coming down over their dicks, what little square they've got the thing poking out of, that's why you really can't explain them in the long run. Which is what I was telling myself when I let myself get talked into it, when I was saying yes, sure, okay." She looked down at the gauze. "I should have gone with my gut feeling."

"What was your gut feeling?" Scilla spoke so softly that Mike wasn't sure at first that he had heard.

"Creep. Creep, jerk, nerd, psycho. Something in it for him I didn't understand, couldn't even deal with. I didn't want to know, if you want the truth." She was looking at Scilla now as if there were no one else in the room. "Do we know what was in it for him?"

In the silence Anna's chair creaked again. "No," said Scilla. "We don't know for sure. And even if we did, there are odds, probabilities. He couldn't guarantee infection. We have to wait this one out."

Christopher Alvarez nodded. "I keep wondering now why he wanted a hand job first. That seems like extra, if you know what I mean. And he wasn't young. I mean, you'd think he'd have worried about getting it up again so soon." Her eyes met Mike's for a minute and she shrugged. "Hey, these are the realities," she said.

"How old?"

"I'd say mid-forties to early fifties. He was in awfully good shape, though."

"How do you mean, awfully good shape?"

"Strong. He worked out, but he didn't strike me as the Nautilus type if you know what I mean. Not desk job and then an hour pumping iron in the health club then home to the wifey. I mean, yeah, home to the wifey but this guy was more outdoorsy. Not like he worked outdoors exactly but he was an outdoorsy kind of jock. Some tan already, sort of weathered around the skin. If you saw him, you'd know."

"Would you know him if you saw him?"

Chris Alvarez's mouth twisted. "Are you kidding? Sure I'd know him."

"It was the same guy that came at you in the parking lot?"

"Same guy. All that crap, that wig, those shoes, that femme getup, that didn't hide a thing. I knew who he was. You know what else? He knew I knew. And he didn't care."

Scilla leaned forward slightly and Mike found himself leaning with her, preserving the symmetry. "Why do you think he wore all those things then? I mean, if they didn't work as a disguise?"

She shook her head. "Not a disguise. Something sick. He hated something a whole lot. Me. He hated me."

"But he didn't know you."

"I know. It doesn't make sense. But he hated me. I could smell it, you know what I mean?"

He could feel Scilla letting her breath out slowly, and let himself breathe out with her. Exhale. Relax. O-kay. Okay, he thought. Let's get on top of this. But he wasn't sure where the top was. He didn't think Scilla knew either.

"Okay," she said. "Let's back up. You said something about the kind of man you thought he was. You said—" She paused. He flipped back a page. "Something about a wife."

"Home to the wifey," he supplied very softly.

"Home to the wifey," she repeated. "That struck me. Could you say some more about that?"

"Oh, you know. That middle-class thing. That straight thing."

Scilla had leaned just a little forward. "You're saying he's heterosexual?"

Chris Alvarez looked annoyed. They weren't tracking. "I'm not sure what that means in his case. I mean, is any of this sexual?" Mike was aware he was furrowing his brow, but then

Scilla couldn't see him. "All I know is he hated me a lot. Sexual preference—that doesn't seem to apply here. I mean, it's gone beyond *preferring.*"

Mike could hear Scilla letting out another slow breath. Things here to chew over. To talk over later, on the drive back to the precinct house. Let them go for the moment. Go for the physical stuff, stuff you can lay your hands on. "So he's outdoorsy, kind of a jock. How tall?"

"Tall. Maybe six-two, six-three. Big bones, too, thick arms, built up. Running to the belly these days, but most of it's still muscle. Broad shoulders. Barrel chest. Might weigh around two-hundred pounds. The kind of guy used to play football, you know the type?"

"Sure," said Scilla. "What's his face like?"

"Kind of a soft face, goes with the body if you get the body. Like he could get fat all of a sudden. Loose skin sliding down around the jaw, very soft little mouth. Pouting. Like a little kid. The mouth was one of the things that made me nervous."

"What else made you nervous?"

"The voice. It was a lot higher than you expected and kind of whispery. Like a voice you'd hear over the telephone, late at night, one of those calls you never want to get."

"You think it was his natural voice?"

Christopher Alvarez sat up against her pillows, the gauze hand twitching reflexively. "It's hard for me to call anything about this guy natural. He was too controlled, you know what I mean? He was thinking about everything. Even getting off, that was just part of it. Part of the hate. So I don't know about the voice. It could have been out of some slasher movie. That's the voice that goes with the chain saw, you know? Like, if you've ever thought kindness was possible you're going to have to think again. That voice." She looked in appeal at Scilla, who nodded.

"Eyes? Hair?"

"The eyes were another thing. Very pale eyes—light blue, I guess, or gray—I didn't get the sense of a color. More like no color. Like eyes that weren't for looking, or were for looking at nothing. At any rate, they weren't looking at me. They spooked me. But it's dark in Pete's and especially dark in the back booths. Nobody's *supposed* to see."

"What about hair?"

"Not much of it. Very short, what there was. He was almost completely bald on top."

Mike caught his breath but Scilla seemed unperturbed. The informant again, he thought. What about the shoulder-length dark hair that Mrs. Johannsen had seen, then? Cut off? But it didn't seem likely that the man described by Chris Alvarez would ever have had hair that long. Of course, all this presumed she had a fix on him, presumed there was something you could see or sniff or intuit that told you outdoorsy, jock, home to the wifey but probably not straight, consumed by hatred for Christopher Alvarez, topless dancer, single mother, lesbian, who didn't know him. Scilla seemed to be accepting the presumption. So was this a completely different man? Or was it the same man with another wig, a shoulder-length dark one? Or was that backward: was it the same man with a wig that was balding on top? Mike flipped over another page on his notepad. He didn't like the way the complications were bunching up on him. In any case, why? Why wigs and more wigs? Why taffeta, crinolines, nylons, high heels? Didn't all those things get in the way? If you were going to commit something risky like rape, like rape of adult, athletic men and women, why did you make it harder on yourself? But then, why commit rape? You never got to the bottom of those questions.

"What was he wearing?"

"Kind of generic jock clothes. It's hard to visualize them exactly. As if he had picked the opposite of that drag getup. A sweatshirt without anything written on it. Gray, I suppose. It made me think of locker rooms. Gray or maybe gray-blue pants, not quite sweats but cut like them. You know, the kind of pants you're supposed to relax in on the weekend? Running shoes. Nikes. I notice shoes. Gray and red. Broken in. Everything was very nondescript and very male. Like the army. Or like some sort of team sport. He was sweaty, too. I could smell it. Not anxious sweat, he wasn't anxious. Locker-room sweat."

"Anything else that might help us identify him? Scars? Moles? Tattoos? What about his nose?"

"Nothing special. Medium. Just a nose."

"Posture?"

"Kind of hunched over when he was standing there talking to me. But then I'm short. A lot of energy there, I thought, all of it cramped into that funny crouch he was doing over me. I didn't think energy at first, though. I thought rage. But that didn't seem to make any sense. Later I went back to thinking rage."

"Anything else?"

"Yeah," said Christopher Alvarez. "He had a tremendous dick. Not only long, thick. Not that I was, you know, impressed."

There was an abrupt screech from Anna's chair as Anna shifted her weight. "That's our boy," she announced with satisfaction. "Won't go into the Identi-Kit, though." Scilla was nodding, leaning forward toward the bed. "We'll send in Earl right away," Anna continued. "Earl, he's the guy with the overlays, all the noses and mouths and jawlines. You'd be surprised, there are only so many of those things, and he's got them. You tell him which, he'll put them together. We'll see if we can get a face to run in the papers tonight."

Chris Alvarez looked from Anna to Scilla and then smiled faintly. "Just the face?"

"Face, physical description, externals. The part about the, uh, dick goes out to the patrols, the prisons, the precincts. Identifying marks. Should go to the general public, but you know how it is."

Scilla hunched up her shoulders and then dropped them abruptly. Stretching, Mike decided. She had her own ways of relaxing, like a cat. "You have any idea how he knew you were gay?"

Chris Alvarez considered. "I don't hide it. I mean, the other girls know. I don't think Mr. Downing knows. Why should he? And the johns don't know, of course. Not that it would bother a lot of them if they did. I mean, sexual preference, what does it mean that I prefer anyone? They're the ones that do the preferring, that's why they pay."

"Your private life, what you wear, where you go. Do you belong to any organizations, for instance, where someone might be able to look you up, target you as a member of the gay community?"

Chris Alvarez shook her head. "No organizations. I'm not very political. Neither is Nancy. She's a house painter. I mean, we're out, I guess, but we don't hang out, if you know what I mean."

"What about the button you were wearing?"

She thought about it. "It's from ACT-UP, the AIDS activist organization. It's not exclusively a gay organization. I think about AIDS a lot in my job, but I haven't been an activist. I guess maybe I'm going to be an activist."

"Do you suppose he might have targeted you because of the button?"

"It's hard to say. I haven't worn it that much, only to and from work. I guess I wanted to say something about our work conditions, about the kinds of dangers we face." Her mouth twisted briefly. "I suppose I've said something."

Scilla nodded. "You've read about this rapist, I gather. Or seen coverage on TV?" Chris nodded. "You know there have been two previous victims. Can you think of any connection you might have with either of them?"

"We're all gay," she said promptly. "And he knew I was gay. Did he know the others were?" Scilla nodded. "That's the obvious connection. Did I know either of them? I don't think so. The names don't ring a bell. The faces don't ring a bell. This is a big town."

"Both of them were activists."

"Both of them were men," said Chris Alvarez. "I'm not an activist. Either."

"You said you were out. Just what does that mean?"

"Lots of people know we're a couple. We go to lesbian bars sometimes. Not a lot, we're not interested in picking anybody up. We know quite a few lesbian couples, have dinner with them, things like that."

"So if somebody were asking about you, it wouldn't be hard for him to find out you were lesbian." Chris Alvarez nodded. "But if someone were looking for a lesbian, how might he come up with you?"

"I don't know. A lot of people would seem more obvious."

Scilla raised both arms and pushed the little wisps of hair back behind her ears. Mike watched her shoulder blades flex like wings. "That's what I've been thinking," she said. "That's what we've got to work on."

He drove the Plymouth back to the precinct house while she went over his notes. It was going to be another long day, fading into the night, he told himself. He didn't even pretend to be sorry. All afternoon they would be working together on possible eyewitnesses now that they had a definite lead. Then the Identi-Kit drawing would come out in the *Herald,* and from around four, when the first papers hit the first porches and newsstands, until maybe eight or nine at night, at least one of them would have to be on hand in the precinct house to catch calls that might give them a lead to their rapist. There would be all sorts of calls, of course. You ran a picture like that, the whole city had a field day; every nut within fifty miles had just seen the guy, lived next door to the guy, had just been fired by the guy. But you worked through those identifications, tediously, scrupulously. Eventually, you got something that made more sense. Eventually, you got your bastard. When they got him, they would move. They would move together, he told himself; they were hot now; they would be doing what they did best, functioning as a real team. He liked thinking of them as a team. He liked referring to Scilla as his partner. That was what Scilla had called Nancy Werner: Chris Alvarez's partner. The word had connotations. Different meanings in different situations, he reminded himself.

By the time they got to the precinct house, Jane Lowry had ascertained from the business directory that Peter Charles Downing was the owner of Pete's Dockside and Pete's Olde Hinton Grill as well as Pete's Good Time. It appeared, however, that no one actually referred to him as Pete. "Mr. Downing is not in at present," said the woman who answered the telephone after the twelfth ring, and Mike identified Creedence Clearwater Revival in the background, with the bass turned up so far that he could feel it in his jawbone. "This is Detective Annunzio from the First Precinct, HMPD," he said, trying to imitate her repressive tones. It was hard, carrying your authority over that bass line. "I'd like to talk with him about a particular patron who came in last night."

"Mr. Downing don't remember particular patrons," said the woman promptly. "He doesn't mix much with the clientele. Plus, he's at the other places a lot. He's busy, Mr. Downing."

"I'd also like to talk with everyone else who was working last night," said Mike.

"I can give you Curt," said the woman, sounding a shade more forthcoming. "I wasn't here. I was off last night. It's about Chris, isn't it?"

Mike was about to affirm that it was about Chris, but the woman was shouting "Hey, Curt," so he waited, holding the receiver a little away from his ear. He could see Scilla eyeing him skeptically from across the detective room. He didn't have anything against the song; he kind of liked the song. It was just hard to set up an appointment to interview the entire staff when you had this background of rolling on the river.

They were on their way two minutes after he hung up, Scilla driving again, being a Type-A driver, something they had both learned about in patrol school. Type-A drivers have accidents,

he wanted to remind her, but he knew she didn't need reminding. It wasn't as if they were in a hurry, he told himself as she
pulled a sharp right onto the Harbor Freeway on-ramp below
the Market, goading the Plymouth into a cacophony of
squeals. Evidence that it was the brakes after all, he thought,
but he didn't want to tell her: you never knew how a Type A
would react to losing an argument. She liked to pretend this
was all a joke, something campy she did to scare him and shake
up his sex role stereotypes. That's what she told him when he
accused her of loving violence, her eyes narrowed with the
lashes standing up spiky and provocative, her lips pursed with
the effort of playing serious, playing ideologue. He knew her
better, though. She loved violence. It made her a better cop
than he was, and sometimes it scared the hell out of him.

Because it had no windows at all, Pete's Good Time was
shadowy and mysterious even at high noon. It smelled strongly
of stale beer. Most of the tables still had chairs sitting upside
down on top of them, but the bar was open and doing a fairly
lively business. Lunch crowd, Mike decided, counting twelve
men sitting or standing along an oak counter that had survived
from the days when the Old Downtown area was all there was
of Hinton and that had somehow escaped being sanded down
and varnished or replaced by something more ostentatiously
Olde. Pete's Good Time was not one of your renovated establishments. It was not one of your upscale restaurants, either,
and the lunch crowd seemed to be doing without anything the
normal legal secretary or gallery assistant would regard as lunch.
The only solid food in evidence was a bowl of beer nuts.

The only women in evidence were Scilla, hovering behind
him in the shadows by the door, and a very tall woman with
a great deal of blond hair who was leaning at one corner of the
bar alongside an elderly man who was taking advantage of the
lean to look down the front of her blouse. The woman wasn't
trying to obscure the view, but she wasn't encouraging the
man either. She was looking directly at Mike and when he
looked back she gave him a slow, appraising smile and straight-

ened up. The elderly man went back to his drink. The woman put her hands on her hips and continued smiling. She was wearing a very short skirt. Feeling slightly uncomfortable, Mike smiled back.

"Hey." Scilla was at his elbow. "We going to talk to this bartender or what?"

"Right," said Mike. He advanced on the bar. The woman arched her eyebrows at him. "Detective Michael Annunzio," he said gruffly. "I'm looking for Curt."

"You're looking at the wrong end of the bar," said the woman. At this distance, Mike could see that she was older than he had thought, probably ten years older than he was, but in good shape. Maybe she worked out on the Nautilus, he thought. At that moment she winked at him.

"Mike!"

Scilla was touching his elbow. He almost jumped. She hardly ever touched him. Turning away, he saw a tall, skeletal man standing with his arms crossed at the far end of the bar. "You must be Curt," he said, and then wondered if he was talking too loud. The men lined up at the counter were watching him appreciatively.

"Mary," said the bartender, "you take over here. We'll go back into the office." The tall woman brushed by Mike, grazing his arm just above where Scilla had touched it, and slipped behind the counter. She pushed her hair back from her forehead, looked directly at Mike, and smiled again. He turned away and followed the bartender and Scilla through a door that led into a dank, malodorous corridor. As he closed the door, Scilla leaned back and hissed, "You asshole."

"What did I do?" he hissed back, but he had an obscure sense of guilt, the way he often did when he realized he had once again eaten something that by Scilla's tenets was bound to have lasting consequences.

Curt led them through a door marked DO NOT ENTER, held it for them, and then closed it firmly. "I didn't see the guy," he announced, sliding behind an ancient oak desk and gesturing them toward two equally ancient oak armchairs. Mike sat down. Scilla pulled her notebook from the inside pocket of her raincoat, but remained standing.

"Who did?" Mike asked.

"The girls did. I stay behind the bar. The girls wait tables. I see the bar customers. They do the table customers." He grinned crookedly. "Do them, you know? Get their drinks. Dance. You know?"

"We know," said Scilla. Mike didn't think she sounded encouraging.

"Um," said Curt. "Well, Chris, ah, did this one. I didn't even hear about him till this morning when Lillian called Mary." He shrugged. "That's all. That's all she wrote."

"Who?" asked Mike. He could hear Scilla clearing her throat behind him. She was impatient with him, he could tell.

"That's just a saying," said Curt. "That's all she wrote. Like, that's all there is, there isn't any more. Got it?"

"You're telling me you don't have anything to tell me."

"That's right," said Curt, sounding relieved.

"Can you give us the addresses and telephone numbers of the dancers who were working last night?"

Curt looked uncomfortable. "I can't do that without asking Mr. Downing," he said. "Mr. Downing's not in until at least six tonight."

"Call him," said Mike. Curt stared at him. "Call him," Mike said again. Curt nodded and picked up the telephone. "He won't like this," he remarked to no one in particular.

"We'll take that chance," said Mike. He didn't stop to think about it; he just said it. In some situations throwing your weight around feels natural. Face it: sometimes throwing your weight around feels good. He stared without expression at Curt, who was saying something in a low voice into the receiver, until Curt hung up, pulled a battered Rolodex out of a drawer, and began transcribing names and numbers onto a piece of memo paper. He pushed the paper across the desk without saying anything.

"We appreciate it," said Mike. He had not tried to sound as if he appreciated it.

He could hear behind him that Scilla had closed her notebook and was putting it back into her raincoat pocket. A hardass team here, he thought, first with satisfaction and then with guilt. Was he playing heavy cop to make up for the fact that the woman out there, that Mary, had made him look like an idiot? He didn't like the idea very much, heavy cop as reflex. It sounded too much like what he saw around him every day. But then that's what cops were, he reminded himself. Heavy. Heavy by vocation. Probably heavy by temperament, too, most of them. Scilla was already out the door and bouncing down the corridor. Eager, he thought, wishing he felt more eager. She looked buoyant by contrast, like a little tugboat that precedes an unwieldy barge. He turned away from Curt and followed her, feeling ponderous, bulky, difficult to maneuver.

Fourteen

As the saying goes, rank has its privileges. The rank of lieutenant of detectives in the Hinton Metropolitan Police Department is below the rank of captain and in theory equivalent to the rank of desk lieutenant, but there are four desk lieutenants in a precinct and only one lieutenant of detectives. The desk lieutenants rotate the three eight-hour shifts so that at any time of the day or night, weekday or weekend, the precinct has someone on the first floor sitting in front of a blotter entering arrests, charges, tours of duty, sick calls, and so on. In contrast, the lieutenant of detectives works the eight-to-four shift on weekdays, although, of course, this lieutenant is on call all the time, a beeper tucked permanently in his, or in the case of Anna Blessing, her breast pocket. Or in the case of Anna Blessing, clipped on the belt, tucked into the inside pocket of an open, flapping uniform jacket, or even mingling fraternally with an assortment of doughnuts in a white waxed paper bag. There wasn't a lot of room in Anna's breast pocket for even the most high-tech and wafer-thin of beepers, scored in large quantities by Skuggy Norman in the course of one of his goodwill tours to Hinton's sister city Osaka.

Anna did keep the beeper with her at all times, but frequently in unorthodox locations. This was one of the privileges attached to her rank of lieutenant of detectives, one of many, most of them having to do with the fact that she was free to come and go as she pleased after she had checked into the second-floor detective room in the First Precinct station on Wettering Place and had gone over the residue of the twelve-to-eight shift with Jane Lowry. Desk lieutenants had to stay at their desks except to answer calls of nature, at which point they asked one of the clerical staff to cover. As Anna lumbered through the front office on her way to the back stairwell, the most direct route to her own office in the rear of the detective room, the desk lieutenant on duty, Johnny Costa, looked up from the meat loaf sandwich his wife, Alison, had packed for him and was seized with longing for the lasagna that was the Thursday special at the little home cooking place on lower University Way and with resentment at the privilege Anna possessed of eating where and when she pleased. The resentment was compounded by the knowledge that Anna would never willingly set foot in the little home cooking place. By Johnny's lights, Anna's girth was unearned.

Johnny Costa was not happy with his lunch. For one thing, he hated meat loaf, and he knew his wife Alison *knew* he hated meat loaf. This sandwich was her revenge for a discussion they had had Sunday on the subject of what you could afford on a desk lieutenant's salary unaugmented by the income from a part-time job, say, selling jewelry at Weidmer's out in the Maple Valley Mall. Johnny Costa didn't see why his wife couldn't go on doing what his own mother had done all the time Johnny was growing up, which was producing and raising little Costas. Alison maintained that now the five Costas were in school full-time, with two of them already in O'Dea, and Lucia set to enter next fall, there was every reason for her, Alison, to go to work the way Sally Annunzio had the moment Jennifer Annunzio had started first grade at Holy Names. O'Dea was soaking them, Alison pointed out, and if Johnny really thought it was worth the sacrifice to expose his children to all those men in black skirts who were named Father, it was certainly worth the sacrifice to get her out of the house and into the mall, where she could be of some use and, who knows, maybe meet some new people. It wasn't as if you were going to meet men in the jewelry department, after all, which was Sally Annunzio's chief complaint about the job, if the truth be known, and why she was trying to get herself transferred over to Men's Furnishings. Johnny had rejoined that he happened to know his *paisan'* Mike Annunzio wasn't happy with Sally in that job at Weidmer's. Alison had said that Mike's opinion wasn't the only opinion that mattered and that Jennifer couldn't have gone on at Holy Names without Sally in that job, and there were more words and the upshot was meat loaf in the lunch twice already this week, and Johnny Costa hated meat loaf. So he was inclined to resent the way Anna Blessing could come lumbering through the front office at 12:30 on her way from God knew where and on her way up the back stairwell to her office at the rear of the detective room, there doubtless to eat more of the things she picked up at places like Ogden's Tasti-Bake or the Dunkin' Donut shop on West Parker Street downtown, with its unsurpassed view of Pross Point. The least Anna could do with her privileges was eat decently, he thought.

Absorbed in God knows what thoughts of her own, Anna ambled past the desk with a desultory wave of her hand. Then she stopped and turned around. "That Marvin Tirsch," she said.

"Night shift," said Johnny Costa. The other things in his lunch bag were a hard-boiled egg and a little plastic bag of carrot sticks. Alison had pointed out on Sunday that not only was he spending too much money sending out for ham and turkey and Swiss cheese sandwiches with cole slaw and Thousand Island dressing at the delicatessen two blocks down Wettering Place, but he was putting on weight. Insult to injury, thought Johnny Costa, who had been one of the leanest and meanest of the patrol cops until he got himself promoted into the region of middle-aged spread. "Marvin'll be asleep now," he added unnecessarily.

"He did a good interview last night," said Anna. "Somebody should maybe tell him."

"I'll see that he's told," said Johnny Costa, thinking of all the insightful questions he had asked victims and witnesses during the years when he was on patrol and how no one had ever told him he was doing a good job. You got older, you lost a lot, he reflected. That was right and proper, that was how it was supposed to be, but sometimes there was this regret.

"You got any patrols coming in, I could use a ride downtown," said Anna.

Johnny looked at the hard-boiled egg. "I take it you checked your car back into the motor pool," he said. He hated the way Anna was always cadging rides off the patrols. It struck him as unprofessional, although it wasn't forbidden or even covered in the manual of HMPD operating procedures.

"Yeah, well it's tough parking down there," said Anna. Tough parking an unmarked detective car, Johnny filled in. A blue-and-white patrol car went anywhere it wanted. He'd be willing to lay odds that Anna wanted to eat doughnuts on West Parker. "Andy and Cyrus just booked a couple street salesmen," he conceded. "They're going back to the North Downtown area in maybe ten, fifteen minutes. Is that close enough for you?"

"Close enough," said Anna, and clumped away. Both of them knew that the bus transfer point on West Parker Street was the center of patrol activities for the North Downtown area. If you knew when your bus was due, you could sit waiting for it in the window of Dunkin' Donuts.

"Hey," called Johnny Costa suddenly, leaning back in his swivel chair to look at Anna's retreating back. "Listen. Anna."

She swung around slowly. "Yeah?"

"Listen." Johnny Costa was feeling a little desperate. "There's a place called Emilio's on West Parker just off the Old Market. Little hole-in-the-wall place. Just opened a couple months ago. The calzone is supposed to melt in your mouth. You should try it if you're down there."

Anna studied him with something approaching pity on her large, mottled face. "Thanks," she said, "but I got luncheon plans."

Jane Lowry was on the telephone when Anna came clumping up the stairwell. She held up one hand and Anna swerved from the direct line she was making for her own door, the only closable, lockable door in the detective room, and came to a reluctant halt. "Right," said Jane into the receiver. "Right. Got you." She hung up the telephone and sat back. "Calls are coming in," she said. "When are Scilla and Mike getting back here?"

"Late afternoon," said Anna. "Put Cogbill and Gannon on phones for now. There's gonna be so many calls you're not gonna be able to hear yourself think once Earl's picture hits the *Herald.*"

"Let me see," said Jane with proprietary interest. Anna removed a folded paper from her hip pocket and began unfolding it.

"This here's a Xerox," she explained. "We already got copies on fax going all over the state." The drawing was of a balding man with a soft mouth and eyes shaded in so lightly that they looked colorless. Jane studied it.

"You know," she said, "that could be my uncle Ralph."

"Think how many people are going to be saying things like that come this afternoon," said Anna.

"Well, it *could* be my uncle Ralph," said Jane. "He always did make me nervous."

"They *all* made *all* of them nervous," observed Anna morosely. "Maybe we better put more people on phones."

"I'll see who I can get," said Jane. "Assuming we get a pool of suspects, do we have medical evidence that can help us single him out?"

"Chris drew blood," said Anna. "She's one mean little girl. We have the semen sample, and given the noise this case is making, we can probably go for some fancy lab work, some of that genetic typing all the TV people are so big on. But we can't do that without a real suspect. We can't just round up all these tall balding guys, not even tall balding guys who can't account for their actions last Friday morning, last Monday night, and early this morning, and say okay, we're gonna take some blood. You know that. I'm afraid this is going to end up being a decoy operation."

"Great," said Jane without enthusiasm. "Who's the decoy?"

"I haven't figured that out yet. We don't know who the suspect is, either, remember. The big question is gonna be how he picks out his victims."

Jane sighed. "You got any ideas?"

"I'm thinking," said Anna. "I got a few people I might consult on this one." She spread her arms abruptly, pudgily cruciform. Jane watched the buttons straining on her shirt. Anna was capable of losing anything from one to three buttons every time she stretched, and Jane liked to keep track of them when she had the opportunity. In her own desk drawer was a small sewing kit and two cards of shirt buttons. Anna made a noise like a tractor starting up, which Jane interpreted as indicating gross physical satisfaction, and brought her arms back down to her sides. "Anyway, it's about time for lunch," she announced.

The patrol cars of the Hinton Metropolitan Police Department carry on their sides the letters *HMPD*. Many of Hinton's street people refer to these cars, and to the police force collectively, as Humpty, occasionally even rounding off the epithet with a terminal Dumpty. Jerrol Newman, certainly the flashiest street person on the West Parker Street transfer island during this noon hour, was making small talk with two girls who had cut study hall at North Central and were planning to spend the afternoon shoplifting at Woolworth's, when a squad car pulled up at the far end of the island.

"Anyway, you ladies could be doing much better than you are now doing, if you know what I mean," pronounced Jerrol Newman, sliding his liquid brown eyes sideways to see what the squad car was up to. "If I give you my number, would you honestly think about calling me? Just even if you want to *talk,* you can call me. In the meantime, you know, I'm gonna be moving on."

"Must you go?" crooned one of the girls. She was feeling very grown-up and sought-after and witty at this particular moment. The other girl was giggling.

Jerrol Newman flashed her an appreciative grin. "Actually, pretty lady, I must," he said. "You see down there? Well, that's Humpty Dumpty, boys and girls, and when Humpty comes along—oh dear God."

Anna Blessing was emerging slowly from the backseat, one blue serge leg at a time.

"What," said the second girl, "is that." She was not exactly asking a question. Anna had freed herself from the squad car and was moving down the traffic island toward them with all the insouciance of a tank. Her uniform jacket flapped loosely in the spring breeze. There was a long coffee stain going down the left side of her white oxford-cloth shirt.

"You ladies will excuse me I'm sure," said Jerrol Newman. Within ten seconds he was disappearing around the corner occupied by Lovely Lady Hair Specialties.

Two buses pulled up at the island. The girls eyed them dubiously. Anna was now shouldering through the line of people getting onto the first bus. "You girls hurry, you'll get back before lunch hour ends," she remarked as she pushed behind them. "Otherwise people might get ideas, know what I mean?"

"Oh, right," said the first girl. "We'd better hurry," she said to the second girl.

"Oh, right," said the second girl.

Dunkin' Donuts was moderately active during this part of the day, but most of the clientele bought takeout, and the people who liked to eat their bear claws and maple bars and butterhorns on the premises tended to be loners, who sat at the round stools bolted to the linoleum in front of the formica counter. Anna Blessing was a loner, too, but that fact had never stopped her from occupying one of the four booths. To be fair, she would have entirely enveloped one of the round stools.

"We've got some nice custard centers just out of the oven," said Alvin Nugent. He normally had one of the waitresses do the booths, but Anna was special, not only because she was a regular and enthusiastic customer.

"Some of those," Anna allowed. "Then some of those jelly ones." Alvin Nugent interpreted some to mean two and came back with a plate in one hand and a mug of milky coffee in the other. "So how's it going?" Anna asked.

"It's going," said Alvin Nugent. He put down the plate and the mug and wiped his hands on his apron. "I saw you on television this morning."

"Ygk," said Anna through a mouthful of custard.

"That was real interesting," continued Alvin Nugent. "I didn't know that about how you could look at the guy's, oh, you know—"

"Semen," said Anna.

"Come," said Alvin Nugent. "I didn't think you could even get it out of the girl."

"Or boy," said Anna.

"My, my." Alvin Nugent shook his silver head in wonder. "The things you do learn of a morning."

"Right in the middle of breakfast," said Anna, and tucked the last half of the custard doughnut into her mouth.

"Right before the weather report," Alvin Nugent confirmed. His light brown eyes were imbedded in little nests of wrinkles that radiated out to score his light brown cheeks. He looked like a highly intelligent turtle. "We're in for some rain pretty soon, you know what I'm saying?"

"Rain," said Anna thickly. "Pretty soon." She chewed energetically, swallowed, then took a large bite out of a second doughnut, bisecting the sphere of red jelly at its heart.

"No, you know what I'm *saying,*" Alvin Nugent insisted.

140

"You think there's going to be rapes in bad weather? That's what I'm wondering."

"Oh," said Anna. She swallowed. There were granular pink smudges at the corners of her mouth. "He does seem to have had a run of good weather," she observed.

"Those pretty clothes of his," continued Alvin Nugent. "You don't rape no one carrying no umbrella. You get all dressed up like that, you don't plan on getting wet."

Anna considered. "You think he's careful about picking his nights?"

"I think he's careful about picking everything."

"Like the people he rapes?"

"Um *hum.*" Alvin Nugent rocked back on his heels and surveyed his domain. Seven of the eight stools at the counter were filled. In the booth behind where Anna was sitting, two young couples smoked and giggled. "I know he's careful. So do you, big lady. These people are healthy and smart, so he has to catch them off their guard. That takes some planning. So he spots them early on and then follows. Maybe he follows for a few days, maybe a few nights. Must be some days, though, because he has to see them first, know what I mean?"

Anna had taken advantage of this disquisition to eat another custard doughnut. Now she disposed of half the mug of coffee and wiped her mouth with the back of her hand. "Oh yeah," she said with elaborate casualness. "What do you know?"

"I don't know. I got some ideas may be what you call ger*mane,* okay?"

"Okay."

Alvin Nugent took another look around the doughnut shop and leaned forward. "I am acquainted with some of the performers at Pig Alley. They comes in here sometimes after the show. Not that you'd know to look at them. That's my point."

"Um," said Anna approvingly. The club known as Pig Alley was a small First Avenue tavern whose ancient neon sign read PLACE PIGALLE. The tiny stage next to the bar had been home

141

to generations of female impersonators, the line stretching back to the murky dawn of Olde Hinton history.

"The main part that's hard is the makeup," Alvin Nugent said. "That takes time to get off, also you need stuff like cream. And you have to get rid of all that tissue. Even then, there's stuff left over on the face sometimes. You can tell. But this guy, we ain't heard about him wearing makeup, you notice? And the other stuff, that's a snap. I'm talking about big skirts, petticoats, *bouffant* wigs, the whole kit. That stuff they all wear down there, you know."

"You think he's one of the Pig Alley crowd?"

Alvin Nugent shook his head emphatically. "I don't think he's one of nobody. Nobody like that, at least. I think this little dress-up thing of his is a solo performance. Just him and the victim and the general public. But that crowd, they wear that stuff. It's what folks think when they think girl. I mean, when they think how girl can you get. That stuff, that's *very* girl."

"I get you," said Anna.

"Those folks, they can get rid of that stuff in, oh, half a minute. Those petticoat things, they look big but you can stuff them into a big bag, wad them down with, say, your shoes. Wig, the same thing. You don't take off the stockings and such, you just pull your pants over them. Shoes, not even socks if you're in a hurry. Same with the top, you just pull on a sweater or button up your jacket. And wa la. There you are."

"Straight," said Anna.

Alvin Nugent grinned in evident triumph. "Some of them ain't even gay," he announced. "I know some of these guys. Some are, but a lot are not. Figure that one out."

"Some things," said Anna gravely, "you don't figure."

"Too right, big lady. Too right. So here's what I'm saying. I'm saying it's easy to stop looking like somebody you could find real easy. That's the first thing. The second thing is, I know how I'd go about looking for a whole lot of individual homosexual people right in the privacy of their own homes."

Anna seemed fully concentrated on the last doughnut. This

142

time she bit carefully, almost daintily, into the rim, nicking a half-moon concavity out of the ovoid mass. She surveyed the effect with satisfaction.

"You want to know how?"

Anna held the doughnut up for inspection and nodded.

"The *Advocate.*"

Anna nodded again. She seemed pleased but not surprised.

"You follow the distributors," said Alvin. "Folks going out door to door. That's all."

"This seems possible," Anna conceded. "They take it out on Thursday mornings. Round about eleven. Different distributors do different areas." She took another tiny bite out of the doughnut and studied it again. "They use part-timers," she continued. "It's pretty amateur. People in vans, station wagons. You could hang around on South Street, nobody would notice. Even sit in your car with your engine idling. Then follow one of them. Spot where they deliver. Look for folks that take in the paper right away, folks that are home. Those are likely to be folks working nights. You want to find folks out on their own after dark, that's your first priority. That and being gay."

"You figured this one out already," said Alvin, looking pleased. "Maybe you already called the *Advocate* folks." Anna took another small bite out of the rim of her doughnut. "You figure to watch for him the next time they load up the *Advocate?* That's a whole week away now."

Anna set the doughnut down on the plate. "Not unless it rains," she said. "Otherwise that's too long to wait. He'll have somebody he's after already. We're too close now."

"You know what you're going to do."

With a sudden movement, Anna stuffed half the doughnut into her mouth.

Alvin Nugent smiled again. "I get you some more coffee," he said. "How about a couple of those chocolate old-fashioned now. I know you're big on chocolate."

143

Anna's little eyes were dreamy. "Maybe one," she allowed. "For dessert."

He turned away and then back. "Hey," he said. "How you going to catch him? You have to get him in the act, or just connect him with those clothes?"

"We have to get him," Anna said. "Period. If we get him, we've got the third victim, who says she'd know him if she saw him. But we haven't got him yet." She tucked the last piece of doughnut into her mouth.

"You figure someone is going to come forward with information?" Anna shrugged. "What if they don't? You going to put out one of those decoy people like last time? And who's that going to be?"

"Assuming we were going to play it like that," said Anna, "which I'm not for one moment assuming, but assuming that, just as an idea you understand, it would depend a lot on his next victim. As far as we can tell, he doesn't go by area, so it wouldn't make sense to post someone just out and about during the wee hours. He gets specific people in mind. Maybe he just picks them at random, but once he's on one, he follows. That we know."

"So you can't tell me who's going to be the decoy."

"Like I said, it depends," said Anna. "Jesus, how come everybody wants to know that?"

She emerged from the Dunkin' Donuts shop and stood blinking in the early afternoon sun, which shone equally on the just and the unjust of West Parker Street. There was no sign of the predicted rain and no patrol car in sight, in conformity with the popular wisdom of the area, which maintained that weather reports are always wrong and you can never find a cop when you need one. Finally she hitched up her voluminous blue serge pants and lumbered across the lane of traffic separating the sidewalk from the concrete island of the bus transfer point, apparently oblivious to the stir she was creating among its more street-wise occupants. After surveying the ragged line of people who remained, she climbed onto one of the buses running up Temple Hill. When she lowered herself onto the seat by the door reserved for the elderly and disabled, no one voiced any objections.

She got out halfway up the hill, on the corner of Simenon and East Parker, and ambled south on Simenon until she reached a four-story frame apartment house, still scruffily un-renovated but with a new sign over its entrance that said CHARDONNAY. She went up two flights of creaking stairs with surprising agility and was panting only slightly when Nancy Werner opened the door and showed her down a long en-trance hall into a high-ceilinged room full of light and foliage. As Nancy motioned her toward an overstuffed armchair, clearly the sturdiest piece of furniture in the room, Bruce Levine appeared between two large rubber plants flanking the kitchen door. He was carrying a plate on which were two chocolate doughnuts.

Anna did not mention her recent experience with the doughnuts of Alvin Nugent. Instead she smiled graciously and reached for the plate.

"We've got sources, too," said Bruce Levine.

"Mf," said Anna in apparent agreement. Nancy placed a little stack of paper napkins on the coffee table in front of Anna's chair.

"Lindgren couldn't come," said Bruce. "We talked to his partner. He isn't going out. Isn't talking to anybody. Until further notice. It took him that way."

Anna swallowed noisily. "Anything we need from him?"

Bruce shook his head. "I don't think so. Actually, what we can offer you isn't really information, it's just a point of view. But we have some ideas."

"Everyone has ideas," said Anna. "Have a doughnut."

Nancy shook her head as she lowered herself gingerly into the wicker chair across from Anna's. "We've eaten," she said. "Thanks. But it's not strictly true that we don't have any information. We have sources you don't have. Only we're not clear exactly what we're looking for. That's why we wanted to offer you some of our ideas. Bruce volunteers at the People with AIDS Storefront, you'll remember. He's got a lot of contacts. He *knows* a lot. More than the medical authorities."

"So-called," said Bruce. "But that's confidential and I'm going to have to be the judge of what's important enough to pass on to the police." He turned to Anna who nodded amiably. "All right then." He sat down in a second wicker chair, next to Nancy's. "We've been talking all morning," he said.

"I called Bruce right after I put Benjy to bed," Nancy explained. "I couldn't remember his name but I remembered the first victim worked nights in the emergency room right there at Overlook. It seemed important to put some of this together. From our side."

"As it turned out, I was on shift," said Bruce. "I came over here as soon as I punched out."

"So neither of you has had any sleep," said Anna.

Nancy frowned. "I couldn't sleep. This isn't all in a day's work for us. It isn't an exercise in abstract, oh, ratioc*ination*. We had to try to put things together. We're involved."

"Yeah, well, that could be a problem," said Anna. She reached for the other chocolate doughnut. "You got any other kinds?" she inquired carelessly.

"Boysenberry jelly and lemon custard," said Bruce.

"Nice," said Anna. "Sticky Fingers," she added.

"That's right," said Nancy. "The bakery," she said to Bruce, who was reaching for more napkins. She turned back to Anna, who had managed to consume the second doughnut while nobody was looking. "You can actually tell the bakery?" she asked.

"Those boysenberry jellies, those are a specialty," said Anna. "They only do them in Little Oslo. Regional." Bruce picked up the plate and started toward the kitchen. "I just want to remind you that being so involved might be a handicap," she continued. He nodded irritably and vanished through the door. She redirected her attention to Nancy. "Sometimes being outside means you don't jump to so many conclusions," she said. "You think more clearly. You don't get ideas and then go looking for evidence to back them up."

"Sometimes," said Nancy slowly, "you aren't really outside. Sometimes you just think you are."

Anna let out a little puff of breath. "Oh-*ho*. We have a theory, do we? We have *that* kind of idea."

Nancy leaned forward and put her hands on her knees. "First of all," she said, "we were both clear that we couldn't leave things up to the police."

"But you're talking to me."

"You rather than most pigs."

Bruce reappeared in the doorway. "Not that your track record is all that great," he remarked. "You were in on that Railroad Tavern bust back in seventy-one. Word has it you busted a little ass on that one, too. Back when you were a Detective Three."

Anna inclined her head. "I remember that bust," she said. "Big mess, that one was. Couple cops got hurt, too. Nobody thought fags would fight back." Bruce snorted. "Well, you guys really got it together around that one." She turned to Nancy. "Gals, too. That was the beginning in Hinton, wasn't it?"

"You want to take *credit* for gay mobilization?" Nancy demanded.

"Nah. I just meant times change. Speaking of which, you guys keep good records. Maybe you should come take charge of ours for a little while."

"Anytime you want," said Bruce. "They'd come out slightly different records, of course." Anna acknowledged the truth of this observation by inclining her head again. "And if we were conducting the investigation it would be a slightly different investigation," he continued. "Precisely because we're involved. But remember, you don't know yet who else is involved. So we thought we might conduct a slightly different investigation. More angles on this guy can't hurt, can they?"

Anna grinned suddenly. Her lips had turned a remarkable dark purple. "Why talk to me?"

Bruce shrugged. "Who else?"

"Go to the top?"

"You've got a reputation."

"Why not the detectives on the case? Why not Annunzio and Carmody?"

"We've got reasons."

"Ominous," pronounced Anna. She looked delighted. "Very ominous. I detect conflict of interest. I detect conspiracy theories. You guys prepared to substantiate any of this?"

Nancy shot a quick glance at Bruce. "There isn't anything to substantiate," she admitted. "You're going too fast. We didn't mean it's necessarily a cop. Only that it's the type."

"We started with the type," said Bruce. "Nancy talked to Chris after you interviewed her. We got the description. Jock type, Chris said. Middle-aged, probably late forties, early fifties. In good shape. Then those clothes. Chris kept saying they made her think of locker rooms. Gray athletic sweats, nothing on them, that makes me think of locker rooms, too. And Nancy tells me Chris is good on that sort of detail. She notices. She can place people."

"The type that used to play football," said Nancy. "She had this very strong impression, something about the way he was built, the way he moved. So we asked ourselves, what does that type go on to do after high school?"

"High school in the mid-, late-fifties," said Bruce. "Especially if he stayed in good shape. He might play on neighborhood teams, YMCA teams, that sort of thing. Or do something solo that takes him outside, running maybe. Or do somthing physical for a living, like construction. Or coaching."

"He might join the force," said Anna.

"Well, you can't rule that out," Nancy said. "A lot of them did. That's all we were concerned about. That's all I meant when I said sometimes you only think you're outside. That type might very well join the force."

"Actually, we thought of that right off," said Bruce. "Because a lot of them did. I mean if they're that age, late forties, early fifties. They didn't go on to college because they weren't big enough jocks to be recruited on those sports scholarships, so they joined the force, something else they could do that's physical, that keeps them rubbing up against all the other guys." Anna raised her eyebrows at him. "Oh, very reputable, all this male bonding," he added. "It's the era, you know. Boys together. So he could be on the force. Pretty high up by now if he joined out of high school."

Anna chewed thoughtfully for a moment. Then she said, "We've got some of those still, the older guys. One of my detectives now, Charlie Walinsky, he was some sort of football jock at North Central. He's a Detective First now."

"Also that guy who got shot a few years ago, Carmody," said Bruce. "Father of your detective, Scilla Carmody. I just thought I'd mention it."

Anna seemed to be enjoying the idea. "He was a quarterback when Walinsky was playing. Not a very bright quarterback, I understand. Anyway, not scholarship material. Just that habit of calling the plays. Get that ball and run."

"Not a team player?"

Anna eyed him skeptically. "Sometimes other people can tell you things. Sometimes you can tell things to other people. Sometimes not." She shrugged. "In police work you tend to play with the team. Whether you're a team player or not. Otherwise you never know who you're blocking."

"We're *talking* to you," said Bruce.

"I'm talking back. Carmody can't walk without a stick. They took off part of his kneecap. I've seen the x-rays. He's officially disabled. Believe me, he isn't prancing around in any high heels."

Bruce waved this information away in evident irritation. "I didn't mean him in particular. I didn't mean cops in particular.

I meant the type. That age group, that bunch. They hang around together. Especially if they were high school jocks together."

"You're assuming he's local."

"There's a certain amount of evidence that he's been here a while. He didn't just wander in, he knows too much about good places to rape people. More than that, he knows how to disappear. That's hard to do without connections, without a lot of folks who'd be glad to have him drop in. Very respectable folks, if you consider the odds on a stranger vanishing into those fortresses on the top of Temple Hill."

"That doesn't necessarily make him a home product," Anna insisted.

"It's a start," Bruce said. "Look, we were just thinking somebody could go over the high school yearbooks for that period. I mean, you could get them without any trouble. And you've got people you could put on the job."

Anna sighed gustily. "Look, during the fifties there were five public high schools in the Hinton metropolitan area alone, and they were all big. Plus O'Dea. Plus Hinton Academy. And you're not even looking at the suburbs. And all you can say is you're after a jock type. Not even the sport. Football maybe. But how about basketball, baseball, tennis, volleyball? I'll buy our witness on his build, even that he's a jock type, but how can you decide on which sport? Plus, when you're looking at high schools, you're looking for somebody thirty, thirty-five years ago. All we have now is an artist's rendering of how this guy looked last night in the dark to somebody who was giving him a hand job, and one of the most significant identifying marks we've got on him is that he's going bald. Plus, we're not sure how old the guy really is, so we're looking at a range of six or seven years, and maybe we're wrong about that. So we're getting all these yearbooks so we can look at pictures of several thousand high school boys. And you tell me I've got *people.*" She shook her head so violently that her jowls flapped. "I've got ten detectives, total, all three shifts. And you don't trust them anyway. Plus, I've got this picture running on the front page of tonight's *Herald,* which is enough to tie up everyone's telephone even if we didn't have other things we happened to be doing. Plus, we're trying to figure out the next victim, which takes a little time and manpower, too. So thanks for the lead, but I don't think I'm going to follow up on it. You folks have something else you think you can tell me?"

Nancy's face was pink. "Okay. Okay, so it's a long shot. I mean, we sympathize with the cops in their plight. I mean, you're understaffed, we feel for you. But we do have something else. Another angle. Another idea."

"Go ahead."

"Where did he get it?"

Anna appeared to be examining the doughnut for flaws. "Get what?"

Bruce drew an audible breath. "AIDS," he said. "What do you think this is all about? It's like we're not even supposed to say it. AIDS. Acquired immune deficiency syndrome."

Anna remained unmoved. "You can say it," she allowed. "I've got nothing against you saying it. Can you prove it, that's what I want to know."

"Since when does the burden of proof rest on the victim?"

"Victim of what, is what I'm asking. What I see you two doing here is making up this very complicated story about a jock who might be a police officer and has AIDS. But you don't even know the premise is true. We don't know he has AIDS."

"Assuming," said Nancy.

"It's a big assumption."

"You have to start somewhere."

"We have other places to start."

Bruce spread his hands in appeal. "Just listen for a minute. Let's not assume he has AIDS, okay? Let's assume it's just rape. A jock-type rapes guys, okay? Men *and* women. But so far always in the ass. Which suggests he's acting out certain . . . tendencies. They called it that, back in the fifties, early sixties.

Latency. The disease wasn't AIDS, it was homosexuality. You didn't tell people you had it. Usually it took you a long time to figure out that's what you were. Especially if you were a jock."

"You're saying he's gay," Anna observed.

"I'm saying he gets it up for men. That we know. *I* know."

"But that doesn't explain it," said Nancy. "It doesn't explain why rape. Why the rage. And Chris said he hated her. Her. For being lesbian. For being female."

"So we asked, why the hate?" said Bruce. "You're male, you're white, you're passing as heterosexual, so you feel superior to those others, those fringe elements. Okay. So you feel superior."

"And maybe you know you're not really heterosexual, so maybe you're not all that different from those fringe elements," said Nancy. "So you get scared and anxious and defensive. But do you take risks?"

"Crazy risks," said Bruce. "That drag, it's very strange stuff. Right on the edge. Prom queen gear, right out of his era if we've got his age at all right. And the heels, that's nuts. You're handicapped in those things even if you're very athletic. There's too much going on with all those clothes, too many signals pointing different ways, it's hard to read. But one thing you can definitely say is he's out to make an impression."

"We kept asking, why the acting out? And then, why the hate? And we kept coming up with one particular answer, which was that someone must have done something pretty awful to him." Nancy stopped suddenly and sat back in her chair. "That's all. That's why AIDS made sense."

Anna had been licking her fingers one by one with the composure of a large cat. "I don't suppose you think he got it from a dirty needle," she remarked.

"Come on," said Bruce. "He got it the way he's giving it out, allowing for variety in orifices. He's pretty mad at the person who gave it to him."

"Male or female? In your considered opinion."

152

Nancy smiled suddenly. "We have no basis for arguing one way or the other. It could be either. If it was a woman, that could have thrown him out of the closet, got him to where he's raping to give it back. Like he's been good, he's been repressed, and look what happened anyway."

"I don't follow," said Anna. "Why would he be raping gay men?"

"Figure she got it from somewhere," said Bruce. "Or our guy got it from a man. Wages of sin. He'd be raping as avenging angel, God's wrath. Either way it would explain the hate."

"It's one explanation," conceded Anna. "One story. So what am I supposed to do with it?"

Bruce sighed. "*Think* about it. I don't know. If you can't follow up the high school angle, may be you could keep your ears open for news about someone being worried because they might have given something to somebody."

"Like some disease," said Anna.

"Some disease," echoed Bruce. "It could just be some disease, some venereal disease, do you know that? It's a possibility. If you've got lesions, sores, damage of some sort, you're much more likely to get AIDS. Presuming you're in sexual contact with someone who has it."

"On the other hand, he could just create his own damage," murmured Nancy. "Violent penetration would do it."

Anna looked from Bruce to Nancy and then back to Bruce. "Seems to me you're the one who might hear about someone who's worried they might have given something to somebody. Being as you're working in the storefront counseling operation."

"The thought crossed my mind. In fact, I'm going in today to look through the files." Bruce picked up the empty plate. "I don't know what I'll find, and I don't know what might prove significant. And when I do know those things, I still don't know what I'll want to tell you. The information is confidential, after all. I'm not even sure what I *can* tell you."

Anna had heaved herself upright and was energetically

brushing crumbs from her uniform jacket. "Lots of decisions there," she observed. "Cheer up, maybe you won't find anything. Tell you what. I won't hold my breath, okay?"

"Don't hold your breath," said Bruce, who seemed curiously relieved by this piece of reassurance. "But if I do tell you something, can I count on you to act on it?"

Anna shrugged massively. "Depends on what it is." Her beeper went off. Nancy and Bruce both jumped. "Get some sleep," she advised them as she began patting her pockets in the attempt to locate it. "Got to go now," she added unnecessarily.

"If I tell you who the *rapist* is," said Bruce. "Whoever it turns out to be. Whatever profession he turns out to belong to. Can I count on you?"

"Oh yeah. Definitely." She reached out and took his hand. Her own hand was sticky. "You finger him, I'll catch him," she said with ferocious sincerity. "Deal."

Fifteen

The daytime dispatcher, Holly, swung her chair around and pulled back her earphones as Mike and Scilla bounced through the front door. "Have I got calls for you guys," she said. "You'd better get on upstairs. It's jingle-bell time. What's that you think you're doing?"

"A soft shoe," said Mike, pirouetting so that his jacket flapped open to reveal coy glimpses of his revolver in its shoulder holster.

"High spirits," Scilla explained. "We've been interviewing the topless."

"*In* their tops," Mike said. "No improper interviews from Annunzio and Carmody. No suggestiveness. No macho. Great bunch of women." Actually, the topless had been a disappointment, even discounting the fact that they had all kept their tops on. Besides Chris Alvarez, four girls had been working at Pete's Good Time the preceding evening. Scilla had assured him that "girls" was the accepted designation for people in such jobs, but Mike had a hard time applying the word to these irritable, evasive, and unglamorous women, less for Scilla's ideological reasons than because all of them were well over thirty, with one, the black woman named Lillian, admitting to forty-five years. The high spirits were due not to anything any of Chris's cohorts had told them when confronted in the privacy of their bed-sitting rooms and breakfast nooks, but to the effortless way

155

he and Scilla had fallen into their investigative routine as the pace of the investigation picked up. No good guys, no bad guys in this context, just alternating rounds of questions, what did you see, what did he look like, do you think you'd know him again if you saw him? It was predictable that the answers, over and over again, were Nothing, Don't know, Nope. None of these women had had their flexor tendons severed. Without that bit of negative stimulus, they were like most honest citizens, primarily concerned to stay uninvolved.

"Carmody and Annunzio," said Scilla. "Not Annunzio and Carmody. It doesn't sing."

"Alphabetically it's Annunzio and Carmody," said Mike.

"Alphabetically," said Scilla. "Soul of a pedant." She turned back to Holly. "Terrific women, right. Superwomen. Even with their tops on."

"Superwomen don't wear tops," said Mike. "You like that for a title? For one of those hard-boiled cop novels. What do you think?"

"Shows how much you read," said Scilla loftily. "Cops aren't hard-boiled. Only amateurs are hard-boiled. Private dicks in their little sleazy offices."

The switchboard buzzed. Holly adjusted her earphones and tapped a key. "Hinton Metropolitan Police Department," she said. "One moment." She tapped another key. "Hard-boiled what?" she asked.

"Detectives," said Scilla. "Tough talk from the olden days. Not what you think. Private dicks are a whole other thing from cops. They're amateurs, also solo. Cops, now, cops are more social. Cops occur in packs."

"Most often in pairs," said Mike.

"Prides of cops," said Scilla. "Coveys of cops. Also, cops tend to brood."

"About what?" Holly asked.

"Victimless crimes," said Scilla promptly.

"I could do with one of those now and then," said Mike. "Hey, I'd be willing to brood."

"You both go on upstairs," Holly told them. "Everybody in Hinton is calling about your creep."

"With his hard-boiled dick," said Scilla. "Come on, Mike." She pulled open the waist-high gate separating the main office from the waiting room relegated to the general public. Mike followed her past Holly's metal dispatch desk, which was marginally less seedy in appearance than most of the precinct furniture because of the high-tech computer terminal sitting on top of it and the two additional TV monitors on the shelf above, showing in ghoulish green-tinted chiaroscuro the insides of the two cells in the basement. She opened the door leading into the first-floor offices and held it until he had gone through. He didn't thank her. He had learned the hard way that thanking her neutralized the gesture and forced her back to finding something else to open for him. In her head she was keeping statistics on how many times they opened doors for each other. If she didn't have a slight chivalric edge on him, she got testy. He knew she was keeping statistics on a lot of things having to do with him, the number of times each of them got to be bad guy and interrogator, the number of neural synapses destroyed every day by his caffeine intake. When he thought about how conscious she was of the things he habitually took for granted, he was simultaneously exasperated and humbled.

"Things are hotting up for you guys," Johnny Costa remarked as they trooped by the duty desk. "The whole town has a line on your creep."

"Or somebody," said Scilla.

"Or somebody," said Mike.

"Lotta creeps out there," said Johnny Costa.

Anna emerged at the head of the stairs when they were halfway up. "I've got the phones covered for the moment," she told them. "You guys come into my office. We've got to talk about this weirdo." They fell obediently into line behind her and clumped past the row of green cubicles where the precinct's ten detectives conducted their business. In the second cubicle, a thickset man with very short red hair was talking

157

into a telephone. "Right," he was saying. "Now can you tell me if your husband was out of the house on Wednesday night?" He listened for a moment. "Well, if he was asleep in front of the television, he wasn't raping the Alvarez girl, was he?" he said. There was a squawk from the receiver. "No. No. Couldn't have been. No. Thanks for the tip." He hung up the telephone, which immediately began to ring. "Hope you catch this one soon," he said to Mike, and picked up the telephone. "Detective Gannon," he said. "Right. The AIDS rapes." He began making notes on the pad in front of him.

"We don't know it's AIDS yet," said Mike, but Anna was waving him into her office.

"Jesus, this is going to be a bastard to follow up," said Scilla after Anna had closed the door.

Anna was looking jolly again. "Offhand, I'd say we just ran a picture that could be of maybe two thousand guys up and down the coast here," she said as she slammed the door and waddled past them to squeeze between the arms of her desk chair. The desk chair squealed as she settled into it. Scilla and Mike stared stoically at the top of her desk, which was littered with computer printouts, pink While You Were Out slips, crumbs, and stray pages from the morning's *Express*, put to bed too early to have reported the latest rape. Anna went on. "Not all of them in Hinton, you understand. Spotted in the area. Give or take a hundred miles north or south, the mountains and the ocean being natural barriers to felonious types, as our solid citizens conceive of felonious types. He might be an itinerant, you know." They nodded without enthusiasm. Unsolicited calls from concerned citizens tended with monotonous regularity to advance the hypothesis of a wandering scapegoat. When you got a string of violent crimes, no one was eager to locate the culprit in our midst. Not one of us. A non-Hintonian. Preferably a non-American. At the very least, an easterner.

"But I got some people coming that might open up another avenue of inquiry," Anna continued. "So I want you guys to

talk with them when they get here, which should be immi-
nently." She smiled, and Mike thought of sharks. Fat sharks.
Scilla cleared her throat. "What people?"

A telephone began ringing loudly. Anna reached under a
piece of the *Express* sports page and pulled out a receiver.
"Yeah?" she grunted, and then "Send them up."

Good timing, Mike thought. You had to hand it to the Big
Lady; she had a feel for the cadences of an investigation. Sometimes he wondered if it weren't something more: if she weren't
somehow conducting the investigation like an orchestra, with
detectives, witnesses, victims, and finally even the criminal
scraping or piping to the flourishes of her baton. He didn't
think this impression denoted paranoia, more like wishful
thinking. He wanted Anna to be in charge. Or he wanted
someone to be in charge.

There was a knock at the door. "Come in," Anna called.
She turned to Mike. "We need more chairs."

He stood up while the two men and one woman filed into
the little office. Then he slipped out into the main detective
room. "Sorry," he said to Larry Mendoza, who was eating a
peanut butter sandwich while he filled out forms at the desk in
his cubicle. Mendoza only grunted when Mike picked up his
second chair.

He pulled two more chairs out of Hill and Walinsky's cubicle, currently uninhabited because Hill and Walinsky weren't
due to check in until four. It was awkward bumping along with
three chairs in tow, but he wanted to get back as soon as
possible. For the revelations. He needed to believe in Anna's
timing; there had to be revelations.

Everyone was standing around awkwardly like early arrivals
at a party. "Some of you have already met Detective Michael
Annunzio," Anna announced to the gathering as he carried the
chairs to the clear area at the right of her desk. "Mike, this is
William Teskey, managing editor of the *Advocate*. This here is
Alice Chancellor, who's the circulation director, and this is
Albert McBain, who's circulation assistant. Circulation mean-

159

ing how the papers get to people. Newsstands, but also individual people. The *Advocate*'s now delivering to subscribers. Sexual identity on your own front doormat. You see?"

"Oh," said Mike. The minute you saw it, it seemed glaringly obvious. Across the room, Scilla dropped gracelessly into the chair to the left of Anna's desk and wrinkled her nose at him. She hadn't figured it out, either, he interpreted. At least they were equal on that score.

"Alice here might have a line on our boy," continued Anna with menacing geniality. "At least she came up with some interesting ideas when I called her this morning."

Alice Chancellor was a plump woman with neatly bobbed gray hair and wire-rimmed glasses. She could have been somebody's grandmother, Mike thought, before he remembered Chris Alvarez's little boy and realized that maybe she *was* somebody's grandmother. Gay people seemed to have kids now and then. Eventually, you'd expect some of the kids to have kids. And what difference would it make to a kid if his grandmother was lesbian? You'd just have this grandma who lived with another old lady instead of with Grandpa. Like his own mother's mother, he thought suddenly. But she was widowed, and Tessa had been her best friend for forty years, he assured himself, turning his attention back to Alice Chancellor.

"I didn't see the car myself," she was saying. "I help with the loading down at our end, on South Street, but I don't go out with the delivery people, so I didn't hear about it till I asked around. We take the paper out around eleven-thirty on Thursday mornings. Newsstands and home deliveries all together. It makes sense because we split up the jobs by area, and we're not a big operation. Not yet, at least. Our carriers are part-timers, people who do other things most of the week and deliver the *Advocate* on Thursdays. They use their own vehicles, vans or station wagons. Two people per vehicle, one to drive, one to run in with the papers. Most of them are couples, I think. I mean in life, not just in work. I don't ask. I assume they're all

Advocate readers because we only advertise for carriers in our own classified section."

Anna had settled back into her chair and was beaming at Alice Chancellor as if she had just given birth to the woman. Mike wondered if she were about to bring out another bag of doughnuts. She had that look. But she only said, "How many vehicles?"

"Eight," said Alice Chancellor. "One to Victorian Hill and the south part of Little Oslo, up to Viking Boulevard. One to the rest of Little Oslo, Fairbridge, and then the rest of the Northeast up to the city limits in both directions." She looked around to see if anyone wanted an explanation of why only one delivery vehicle was necessary to service roughly one-third of metropolitan Hinton. No one looked puzzled. Little Oslo was the Scandinavian ghetto. Fairbridge, directly across the canal connecting Oslo Bay with Lake Dickson, was an old neighborhood composed in the main of squat brick apartment houses and turn-of-the-century bungalows, many of them rehabilitated and refurbished by a variety of people in a variety of living arrangements. Scilla lived in Fairbridge, in a one-bedroom apartment two blocks up the hill from the canal. Presumably most of the *Advocate* deliveries were in this area. The neighborhood unpicturesquely characterized as the Northeast, a long stretch of flatland gridded into neat blocks by identical featureless streets with numbers that began in the 50s and ranged into the 200s, was covered with tract houses, most of them built since the war and designed for young couples intent on producing the baby boom. The families were commensurately older now, many of them boomers with children of their own, but they were still, in the main, families as the postwar generation had defined the phenomenon: two parents, at least at the outset, plus offspring. Any potential *Advocate* readers in this part of the city would probably be buying the paper at a newsstand downtown and smuggling it home inside a copy of the *Herald*.

"Three for Temple Hill," continued Alice Chancellor. Again to no one's surprise. "Divided into West Slope up to

Mason Avenue, West Slope from Mason to Temple Way, and East Slope from Temple down to the Inlet Bridge. Then one for the University District and Lakeview, one for the Central area including Emory Hill and the North Downtown, and one for the South Downtown including the Old Town and the whole South End." Nobody asked about the South End either, traditionally a working-class area around the packing and processing plants that spewed industrial waste into the lower reaches of Nanteco Bay. Anything you said about gays in the Northeast went double for gays in the South End. Temple Hill, now; Temple Hill was another story.

Scilla had been taking the notes. Now she placed her pad carefully on her navy blue twill knees and observed, "Chris Alvarez lives on Simenon Street, so that's your first Temple Hill area, below Mason Avenue. Alan Lindgren's in one of those warehouse renovations in the Old Town, so that's your South End delivery people. Bruce Levine's in the Central district, another delivery area. So we can hypothesize that the rapist follows a different vehicle every week."

"Lindgren's also on the masthead," said William Teskey. Everyone turned to look at him, a slight, blond man in a tweed suit with a neat mustache. "Alice and I talked about this coming over here," he continued, "and we were thinking that the rapist might have picked out Alan as his first person to follow or might just have been after an *Advocate* staffer. After all, we're as conspicuous a group of gays as you're going to find in this city. Then he stumbled across our home-delivery service and realized he could branch out. We're discreet about deliveries but we're not exactly clandestine. If you knew when we were loading, you could wander down to South Street and just hang around watching us. It's a busy area weekdays and we haven't been particularly paranoid about who sees us."

The young man who had been introduced as Albert McBain cleared his throat. "It's not paranoia when they're really out to get you," he intoned in the voice of a postulant reciting his creed. Anna Blessing grinned balefully at him. "Old sixties saying," he explained to the room at large.

"So's Off the Pig," said Anna.

"Yeah, well, it's a little different here," William Teskey interposed. Mike thought that if Albert McBain had been sitting any closer he would have got a smart kick in the shins. A diplomatic kick, not a kick born of conviction. He wouldn't have put it past William Teskey to have been one of those people marching around shouting Off the Pig, back in his palmier days. Maybe with reason. There was the Railroad Tavern incident, after all. Back in those palmy days, before the advent of a kinder, gentler HMPD. Before organized gays had acquired a modicum of political clout, at any rate. For whatever reason, they were on the same side now, uneasy as the alliance might feel. You took your allies where you found them, he concluded. It's not paranoia when they're really out to get you.

"So paranoia aside, did any of your distributors spot any, ah, suspicious characters?" Scilla was having trouble with her terminology, Mike gathered. Understandably: it's hard to know what to call a menace when in the mind of much of the general public it's the menacee who is by definition a suspicious character.

Alice Chancellor nodded vigorously, her gray bangs bouncing. "Paranoia isn't aside," she said. "That's the point. If Sharon and Carla hadn't decided they were being overly suspicious, we'd have known about this car right from the start."

Scilla was suddenly sitting very straight. The transformation was instantaneous: one moment she was slumped back looking fatigued and beaten, the next she was bolt upright and quivering like a taut string. "What car?"

"A blue Ford Taurus wagon. This year or last. State plates beginning with A, maybe AV or AY."

"Hinton plates," Mike murmured. The state Department of Transportation coded personal-vehicle license plates to the owner's place of residence. The metropolitan areas with the largest populations got the earliest letters of the alphabet. As residents of by far the largest city in the state, Hintonians were accorded plates on which the first letter was *A*. The other letters were less referential, having to do mainly with when you registered your car or truck.

"When was this?" Scilla demanded.

"Two weeks ago yesterday. Two Thursdays before." There was a moment of silence. Mike was certain that everybody in the room was thinking about Bruce Levine, who had been raped one week and thirteen hours later. Finally Scilla asked, "Sharon and Carla do the Central district?"

Alice Chancellor nodded. "Central, Emory Hill, North Downtown."

"And how long was this car behind them?"

"They went directly up the hill into the Central district. They drove up on Sherwood. Started with the three-hundred block, that's two major apartment complexes. Then one smaller building, two deliveries, on the four-hundred block. Then the five-hundred block, where they make deliveries in five separate buildings. Lots of hospital personnel in that neighborhood."

"Male nurses and such," Anna observed.

"And such," Alice Chancellor said. "Anyway, they lost him somewhere on the five-hundred block. First they were relieved, then they decided he wasn't really following them. Just paranoia."

"Five-fourteen," said Scilla. "That's Bruce's building."

"Looks like it," said Anna. She was grinning again. Mike wished she wouldn't.

"Was the car spotted by anyone else?" he asked.

"That's what we've been trying to find out. And the answer is yes, although I had to lean pretty hard on Sam and Douggie before they came up with anything."

"I thought we'd got rid of Sam and Douggie," William Teskey murmured from his corner.

"Sam and Douggie do lower Temple Hill," said Scilla. It

wasn't a question, just a request for confirmation. Simenon Street, where Chris and Nancy lived, ran parallel to the freeway on lower Temple Hill.

"This was last Thursday. A week ago yesterday," said Mike.

"Right on both counts. Blue Ford Taurus wagon. State plates, blue and white. No notion of the letters or numbers."

Scilla leaned forward, pen poised over her notebook. "Did you tell them you were looking for this particular car? This blue Ford Taurus wagon?"

Alice Chancellor smiled suddenly. "These guys are space cadets. They've probably heard of Fords. And blue they'd recognize. But identify the make of a car?—listen, these two mostly sit around getting stoned and talking about old movies. I think Douggie has some kind of retail sales job but basically they're just kids, you know? Cars aren't what they *do,* is what they'll tell you. Don't ask about the van they use Thursdays; it belongs to one of their fathers. What I asked them was whether they thought anyone was following them yesterday. And that's the way of putting the question that finally got a rise out of them. Anyone suspicious?—oh my, no. Any sense of foreboding or menace from the folks out there on the street? Why, what could be foreboding or menacing on just a beautiful April day? But anyone *following* them, why yes, of course. They thought he was kind of cute. For an old guy."

"They saw him," said Scilla.

"Him, yes. The car, a little bit. They conceded, when pressed, that he did seem to be driving *in* something. But him, oh, yes. Nice mouth, they said. Turned-up nose, Sam has a thing about noses. Claims they indicate—oh, you know that one. Cute nose, said Sam. Funny eyes, though. Wearing a sort of baseball cap with a visor. White. Something written across the front."

The room was very quiet. Scilla leaned forward. "What?"

"Couldn't read it. They tried. They also debated having Douggie go back and just ask him what he had across his cap.

Kind of a get-acquainted gesture. But they got cold feet. Something about the eyes, they said."

"Have they seen the picture we ran in the *Herald* today?"

"Oh yeah. Anna came down with that police artist and showed them a copy. Not their guy, they said. No way. Then the police artist penciled in a baseball cap. That's him, they chorused. Amazing transformation."

Mike cleared his throat. "It's just *called* a baseball cap," he said. "It isn't just something baseball players wear. Painters wear them a lot." He wasn't altogether sure why, but he felt as if his record as catcher for the Loyola Eagles was being impugned.

Ignoring him, Scilla asked, "Do we have any stuff from the South Downtown and South End delivery team about Lindgren?"

Alice Chancellor looked at William Teskey, who said, "Alan doesn't have the *Advocate* delivered. He doesn't have to. He's a full-time employee. Also, he lives with me."

There was a moment of pained silence. Then Anna said, "Which all just goes to support our theory that the rapist started by following Lindgren. But Lindgren's schedule is erratic. He comes and goes pretty much when he pleases, day and night. And that turns out to be pretty much true of the whole *Advocate* staff."

"We work when there's work to be done," William Teskey confirmed. "Wednesday from about noon on, everybody's on hand. But that would be hard to figure from outside. It's easier to see when we send the paper out."

"Especially if you only have certain times when you can watch," added Anna.

"Do we know that?" Mike asked.

Anna shifted her gaze to him. He sat still under her scrutiny, feeling only a little as though he were being assessed as possible dinner by some large and tenacious predator. Finally she said, "We have to go on the odds. He rapes at night and on different nights, Thursday, Tuesday, Thursday again. That might mean he works some nights but not Tuesday and Thursday. But it's more likely to mean he works days."

"Like most people," said Scilla.

"Like most people," said Anna. "Not cops. Not *Advocate* staff, although I wouldn't rule out most newspaper people on that score; lots of them have to put in regular hours. And not emergency room night nurses or table dancers."

"Except for Lindgren, he's picked people who work nights," said Mike. "He probably had to follow Lindgren around a lot before he got his moment."

"When Alan was not only out alone but also in one place for a long time," added William Teskey. "He was in that parking lot for over an hour. He had his tripod set up there—"

"Long enough so the rapist could nip back and put on his little outfit," said Scilla to the room at large. Mike found himself watching her hands as if they could tell him the truth about the whole investigation. She was holding them close to her body now, with the palms up and fingers spread. They were surprisingly delicate hands considering all the guns they had gripped, all the triggers they had squeezed. The pen had rolled off her knees to the floor, but she didn't seem to have noticed.

He leaned toward her across the open space of linoleum in front of Anna's desk. "How could he tell?" he asked. "How did he figure out which gay people worked nights?"

Scilla pursed her lips and contemplated the floor. Anna looked from her to Mike, then observed, "You'll notice he picked people who lived in big buildings where several papers were delivered. That way he could keep an eye on several prospective victims at once." She looked at Scilla expectantly.

Scilla was nodding, impatient with herself for not having worked it out on the spot. "Sure. To see who was home. To see who was around during the day to take in the paper. Those are the people likely to work nights. So now we've figured out his method, the next question is who he's singled out for the next attack." She thought for a moment. "Maybe that's jump-

ing to conclusions, though. He might not have followed anyone yesterday, especially since last night was when he went to
Pete's Good Time and attacked Chris Alvarez. He'd have to be
pretty well organized if he were casing out one victim while he
was setting up to rape another one. I mean, that takes planning.
He'd need something like an appointment calendar to keep all
his rapes straight."

Mike shook his head. "But we already know he's well
organized. That's one of the things that bothers me most, all
that planning. Not only does he stalk his victims well in advance of the night he rapes them, but he targets his next victim
before he attacks the one he's following. Look, he followed the
delivery people to Chris's house around noon of the day he
raped Levine."

"That's the pattern," said Alice Chancellor. "And you're
right. Another delivery team spotted him yesterday. The mid–
Temple Hill people, Denise and Jody. Blue Ford Taurus
wagon. They'd stop and he'd stop. They'd start up and he'd
start up. Went on for four or five blocks, they told me. After
I'd *asked,* of course. No sense getting paranoid about these
things."

Scilla was nodding emphatically. When Mike caught her
eye, she grinned at him. His point. He turned back to Alice
Chancellor. "Did they get a license number?"

Alice shrugged. "State plate, ADP, they thought. Or maybe
AB something. They were sure about the A."

There was another silence.

"They lost him where?" Scilla prodded.

"They aren't sure. Somewhere on Temple Way, they're
pretty certain, but Denise says she didn't see him after the
thirteen-hundred block, while Jody's maintaining he turned up
again on the sixteen-hundred block. But that might just mean
he crossed their path on the way back."

"To wherever he goes," said Scilla. "He always hits the first
part of the delivery. Does that mean he has to get back soon
after noon?"

"It could mean he's worried about being spotted if he tails the delivery vehicles too long," Mike suggested.

Scilla had started making notes again. Mike admired her capacity to write as she talked. "Yeah, that makes sense. But still, we've got him waiting on South Street, tailing one delivery team up to the area of their route, then flaking off after a few blocks, probably to park and check the apartments that are actually getting the *Advocate* in a given building. How long does that take him?"

"I see what you mean," said Mike. "Maybe an hour, eleven-thirty to twelve-thirty, something like that."

"Something like a noon hour," said Scilla. She turned to Alice Chancellor. "Can we talk to these two people, this Denise and Jody?"

Anna shifted her weight. The chair squealed. "They're expecting you at four-thirty," she said. "They do carpentry, a little wiring, a little painting. That's what they do. In baseball caps, for all I know. But they're cutting off early today to talk to you guys. And then you get to check out their route. Early, if you know what I mean."

"Wait a minute," said Mike. "You don't think this guy is going to try it again so soon? There were twelve days between the first and the second rape, and two days between the second and the third. He just raped Chris Alvarez last night."

Anna looked from his face to Scilla's. "He's been biding his time," she agreed. "Waiting for the right opportunity, then getting dressed up so he can do it right. And you have to admit he's had a lovely run of luck. Those sweet opportunities, lone figure on a stretch of asphalt. And a lovely run of weather."

William Teskey had been watching her closely. "Unseasonable, really," he observed. "Remember last April? *Any* April before this one?"

"Greenhouse effect," Albert McBain contributed.

Teskey pointedly ignored him. "They're calling it a drought. Nice for us now, but we're going to have a water shortage this summer if we don't get some rain pretty soon.

Heavy rain. That's what we usually have in April. Up into May, in fact. Some people call it the monsoon season."

Anna had been nodding vigorously. Now she addressed the room at large. "Not pleasant to be out in. Not this fine drizzle, kinda *steam*-room effect, not what you'd call exhilarating. Not conducive to outdoor activities even if you had an umbrella, which you wouldn't, you know, needing both hands. I like monsoon, who thought up monsoon?"

Nobody answered her. After a pause, Alice Chancellor remarked, "It's coming. Late tonight, early tomorrow. You can feel it. The barometer's falling."

Anna was smiling again. "That's what all the weather folks are telling us. Remarkable agreement on all channels. Tonight's likely to be the last nice weather we have for quite a while. The last optimum outdoor assault conditions, if you're thinking that way. Not that our rapist isn't capable of biding his time, as we know. But it's worth taking into consideration, predicted showers. Predicted deluge."

"Okay," said Scilla. "Okay. But we've got to remember, too, that there's a picture of him running in tonight's *Herald*. Our phones are ringing off the walls. The whole town's on the lookout for him. He'd be insane to try it again so soon."

A dull silence succeeded this pronouncement. Scilla shook her head as if she were trying to clear it. "I mean more insane. That's an enormous risk."

"He seems to be into taking risks," Anna observed.

"So much?" Scilla insisted. "So soon? He's just increasing the odds against him. Sooner or later, we're bound to catch him."

"Better sooner," piped Albert McBain, who had maintained a sphinxlike silence since being rebuked by his employer. "I mean, *really*," he continued, glaring at Anna. "You can't just let the man go on killing off members of the gay community until he manages to trip over his own feet."

Anna flashed him a sharky grin. "It's not killing till somebody dies," she said. "Let's not everybody jump the gun on

170

this one. But no, we can't just let him go on. I also think this bastard gets off on risk. I mean just literally, physically. It helps him get it up, you follow me?" It was a tribute to her authority that everyone in the room nodded soberly. "He's flirting with getting caught, is how I see it," she continued. "Like in the old days, flirting. Bouffant hair, bouffant skirts, teetery high heels, nylons. Real girly. Real femme. And he's a performer, that's another thing we know from those costumes of his. Now he's got a great big audience."

"You're saying he wants to get caught," murmured Scilla.

"I don't think it's that simple. Catch, get caught, take, get taken, rape, get raped. I think it's all mixed up with him, one side and the other. Sex. Violence."

"Gender," supplied Scilla.

"Oh sure, gender," said Anna dismissively. "This is all gender, that's where we started. But it's all wound up with hate."

"It tends to be," said Scilla.

"Not necessarily," said Mike.

"And of course the weather's changing," said Anna. "And while it's not likely that he'd try something tonight, he knows and we know that he's not going to have a chance again for quite a while, assuming what we're going into is the monsoon season." She beamed at William Teskey. "Burglaries go way down when it rains like that, did you know?"

Albert McBain looked indignant. "How about rapes?" he demanded.

Anna flapped her hand languidly. "Harder to plot. Being that there's fewer rapes in general than burglaries in general. I suspect they go indoors. Of course, this guy might go indoors, too."

"Harder in that getup," Scilla pointed out.

"Definitely harder," Anna allowed. "Harder climbing up the fire escape in spikes. Harder knocking at the door and saying Hey there, mind if I come in and dry out my crinoline? But we don't know he'll keep to the outfit. We don't know much at this point, so we have to deal with what we've got."

She looked almost kindly. "So I figure you've got twenty minutes before those dyke painters get home."

Mike closed his eyes. The concerted wincing in the room felt like a shock wave. "I'm keeping Gannon and Cogbill on the phones," Anna continued. "Mendoza's already following up a list we got from the Department of Transportation, trying to track down that Ford Taurus. As soon as Hill and Walinsky get here, I'm sending them out to interview people around Bruce Levine's and Chris Alvarez's apartments, pushing for a better description of the guy or a better look at the license plate on his car. You guys have to find who the next victim's gonna be."

"So you think it could be tonight?" Mike was already standing, wondering if it was going to be cold enough to warrant a sweater, wondering if in that case he should buckle his gun on over the sweater. Extra time. Extra hassle.

"It could be tonight," said Anna.

"The victim could already be at his job," said Scilla. "Presuming he works nights. He or she."

"In which case you look for him or her at his or her job," said Anna. "You guys better hurry up."

They stopped in their cubicle while Scilla called her parents' house. "Mom's birthday," she whispered to Mike, who was buckling his shoulder holster over his sweater. "She'll be disappointed that I'm not coming to dinner, but she's used to cops' hours." He turned away as she began to speak breathlessly into the receiver. She sounded about ten years old, he thought. Give us a mother, we all revert.

"It could be big, Mom," she was saying. "You saw the picture in the *Herald,* right? Well, it looks like things are breaking. Anna's got almost everybody working on it right now. With luck it could all be over tonight." Without luck it would go on for weeks, he thought. Months. Remember the Hacker. He sneaked a look at her. She was nodding as she listened. "Dad always worries," she was saying. "It's like a reflex. He forgets I am a detective." Her eyebrows twisted

172

briefly. "Well, I am *not* his little girl," she said. "Okay, you take care, too," she said. "I'll call you tomorrow. And happy birthday." She hung up. He pretended to be engrossed in retying his tie. She touched his elbow. "You don't think I said too much, do you?"

"I wasn't listening," he said.

"It's not like they're civilians," she said. He didn't comment. She was buttoning a wine-colored vest over her oxford cloth shirt. In her subdued way, she looked rather glamorous, he thought, buttoning his own jacket.

"So what do you think about the idea that this guy gets off on risks?" he asked her.

"I don't know," she said. "I'll bet Anna's been reading something. Some cop psychology thing. I sometimes wonder if she isn't going off the deep end. Look at what she eats."

Although he didn't say so, Mike didn't think Anna had been reading anything in particular. He also thought she was right, although he wasn't about to explain why. He thought she was right because she was talking about the things that scared him most about himself. You could get off on risk. On violence and the threat of retaliatory violence. On hate. You might even choose to be a cop for those reasons. Although this stuff about getting it up, about being physically turned on by those things, couldn't have been anything Anna knew about firsthand. It was a matter of imagining again, he decided. Specifically, it was a matter of imagining what it would be like to be someone else. The thought made him feel a little sick. He didn't want to imagine being this bastard. That was Anna's strength, when you got right down to it. She just went ahead and put herself in the guy's place without even worrying about whether it would be such a horrible place, such a *seductively* horrible place, that you couldn't get back out of it.

"I'm not sure it pays to even try to understand creeps like this one," said Scilla, who was now shrugging back into her tweed jacket. He picked up his own raincoat. "I mean, it's not like you'd want to get to know him," she said. "It's not like you're going to play baseball with him or something."

"More like football," he said, feeling unjustifiably irked. Periodically she liked to ride him about his athletic scholarship. Catcher, she'd say; sounds like cop material to me. That wasn't the way catching worked in baseball, he wanted to tell her. Catchers were generally the nicest guys on the team. They just squatted there and took it. But when he thought about saying this, he heard himself the way she would hear him. It sounded perverse when he imagined her hearing it. As if catchers were women. Not that there weren't fine women playing baseball nowadays, he assured himself hastily, and then felt a little confused and a little relieved because that wasn't really the point at all.

Sixteen

"There goes the neighborhood," said Scilla.

They had pulled the Plymouth over to the curb and were contemplating the tree-lined expanse of Temple Way dwindling into the distance like an exercise in perspective. The house Scilla had indicated needed paint, but that fact alone would have testified to nothing more than decaying gentility if there had not been other telltale signs: two bicycles chained to the railing of the porch, mismatched curtains, some of them looking as if they had come off beds, rock music pulsing from somewhere behind the dark bay window of the first floor, even though it was only five-thirty and the golden light of an unseasonably warm early spring slanted across vivid green lawns and the chromatic explosions of azalea bushes. On this block, the house looked like a bag lady among an assembly of Urban League matrons. Mike's police sense was alert for trouble.

"Group house," observed Scilla.

"Students?"

"Probably not. Too far from the university."

"Oh." He wanted to ask who, if not students, but of course that was what they were there to find out. Someone in this house subscribed to the *Advocate*. Or maybe everyone in this house: he didn't know how these things worked. The address was 1224 Temple Way, and it was the first delivery that Denise and Jody made from their creaking Volkswagen bus after they had driven it, lurching and juddering, up the leisurely curves of Eastern Star Drive to the crest of Temple Hill, where Scilla had spent too much of last Wednesday afternoon gathering no information. For three blocks on both sides of the Masonic Temple, the mansions loomed eccentric and inviolate, their stones expertly repointed, their windows authentically re-glazed, their gables, turrets, and cupolas structurally certified by the architectural gurus of the Historic Hinton Commission. But as you moved down Temple Way, a certain diminution set in. Part of the reason for this was historic, too. The mansions themselves became progressively smaller and less ostentatious, family residences built for a burgher class clinging tenaciously to the outward and visible signs of respectability despite the glamorous example set by the nouveau and generally outré rich of Hinton's first boom—the whaling captains, the outfitters who fitted out would-be prospectors heading for the Alaska gold fields, some of the prospectors themselves, returned to build Gothic or baroque castles based on hallucinations cherished and elaborated during long nights in frozen canvas tents, the innkeepers, barkeepers, brothel keepers, and infamous initiators of the China trade, who helped introduce opium to the Chinese and the Chinese to the rigors of American railway construction. Such flashy entrepreneurs had built the first mansions, setting the tone. The more mainstream merchants of Hinton found all this display a little dubious, not out of any concern with the ethics of accumulation behind the grandiose structures but because they had always found it unwise to call too much attention to yourself. They had scaled down, es-chewing ornament, evading grandiosity. Ironically, the hulking and pretentious mansions had proved more enduringly popular, having been most recently snapped up for rehabilita-tion during the boom of the last decade. The more decorous houses languished, too big and drafty for the current middle class, too subdued for the Historic Hinton Commission, which had terminated the Temple Hill Historic District at the 1100 block of Temple Way. From here on you had some houses owned by single families, some rented by single families, and some that had subdivided like amoebas into near-apartments in tacit defiance of the zoning code. And among the rentals you also had an increasing number of group houses.

Group houses made sense, Mike told himself, given the convenience of the location to the jobs and amenities of Temple Hill and downtown, given the rising number of single professionals in Hinton, given the rising cost of housing. If you granted that there were decent people willing to live like that. Not all of them were drug dealers, he told himself. Not all of them were engaging in white slavery with runaway teenage girls. Not all of them were homosexuals. Although these probably were, he reminded himself, or some of them had to be because there was this subscription to the *Advocate,* which was why he and Scilla were here, and the fact that the residents were homosexuals made them victims, not criminals, not lumped in the same thought with drug dealers and white slavers. There were times, he told himself, when the things you took for granted being a cop got in the way of being a cop.

"Okay, so he was definitely on this block," Scilla said. Denise and Jody had been explicit on that point. As they had reached the crest of the hill, they had remarked on the blue station wagon that had not passed them despite the huffing crawl they had slowed to going up the Drive. That was what they needed, they had told each other. A big new wagon with lots of power. New, yeah. One of those Ford Tauruses or Mercury Sables, hey, they looked at these things all the time. They could do deliveries with a wagon, plenty of room for papers even if the number of subscribers on this route doubled. What they couldn't do was put all their painting stuff in it, the ladders and scaffolding they carried around. Even if they could afford one of those cars. Which of course they couldn't, they could barely afford to keep this old hulk going. But they had talked about it anyway, Jody driving, Denise jumping out and running into the buildings, and the wagon, Ford Taurus, Mercury Sable, whatever, had lazed along behind them, yeah blue, oh that medium blue they come in, and they had started wondering a little but then he had turned off on Poe Street, no, he didn't pull in, he turned *off* because they'd watched, so then they stopped wondering, figured he'd found what he was looking for, oh shit that sounded weird now, looking back. Except Denise saw him again on the 1500 block. Yeah, same car, same guy. No, it wasn't the license number, it was the guy they noticed. Middle-aged, she thought. She didn't *know* why. She hadn't mentioned him to Jody because what was the point? He wasn't anybody, she'd thought. Just a guy in the neighborhood looking for a place to park. State plates, probably city plates, you know those A plates? A something, she really didn't want to commit to anything further. Jody had thought AB, AD, something like that. Or could have been AP. Hell, it could have been just about anything, they weren't looking at the plates all that hard. That's about it.

That's all she wrote, Mike supplied mentally, although Scilla was asking the questions and he was writing.

So now the two of them had three blocks of Temple Way to cover, twenty-six subscribers, most of them on the 1500 block where you started getting into the apartment houses. Three blocks if you presumed the rapist was only going where he saw Denise going and not, say, wandering into buildings at random later on, just to see if any *Advocates* were lying on any welcome mats. Presuming he stuck with buildings he had actually seen Denise go into, they had twenty-six possible points of delivery with God knew how many possible victims living at each point. And God knew how many of them worked nights. And God knew how many of the ones working nights would be around to say where it was they were working, because by now of course it was already night. Already night and well into the shift of a waiter or bartender or usher or actor or parking attendant or night watchman or exotic dancer or emergency room nurse. And they were after a bastard the whole town was looking for, a bastard who got off on risk. And the weather was changing. So maybe time was of the essence. And then again, maybe it wasn't. Maybe they were going to scurry around in a panic for nothing, the bastard lying low, taking his time, letting the monsoon blow itself out, waiting for the impetus to die down. Then bango, caught you napping, public outcry, letters to the editor, marches to take back the night or the street or the parking lot, justifications, explanations, purges. So you scurried around on the theory that time was of the essence and hoping that subsequent events wouldn't send you scurrying in an entirely different direction. You couldn't predict.

"Where do you want to start, this end or the other end?" Scilla was drumming her fingers on the top of the steering wheel. He realized he had been staring despondently at the group house. It was more her sort of thing, he told himself.

"Let's flip," he said.

"Right. Heads means I start up here, tails means you do." He nodded. She spun a quarter across the dash, and as it shot toward the floor and the unreachable wasteland underneath their seats he caught it and slapped it against his thigh. When he lifted his hand, the quarter lay against his khaki pants, tail side up. Do it again, he thought.

"So this one's your baby," she said, flapping her hand languidly at the group house. "Probably not where he got his newest victim. Too hard to zero in on one person when they share a space. But we've got to ask. Then you can hit the three houses on the next block. Then go down to the fifteen-hundred block and start at this end, the north end. I'll be working from the other end toward you. We'll check in at ten-minute intervals or when one of us gets a lead on something that looks like our bastard." She looked at him until he realized he was supposed to pull the walkie-talkies out of the glove compartment. He was feeling disoriented, he realized. Another long day, this one. What did it feel like working regular hours, getting off and being through for the day? How would he ever know? He pulled out the oblong black boxes and handed one to her. She pulled up the aerial, pressed a button, and lifted the unit to a point about three inches from her lips. "Testing," she murmured, and her voice, metallically doubled, emanated from the black oblong in the palm of his hand as well as from her mouth.

He pressed his own button. "Testing."

"Works," she said. The door creaked as he pushed it open and climbed slowly out of the car. "Good luck," she said. He slammed the door and she pulled away from the curb.

A handwritten sign taped to the door of 1224 Temple Way read DOORBELL BROKEN—POUND HARD. He pounded. Nothing happened. He doubted whether anyone would have heard him if he had kicked the door down, given the volume of the music, but he pounded again, very hard, before he tried the knob. It turned. He stepped into an entrance hall lit by a single bare bulb. The music was much louder. He closed the door behind him.

Standing there under the very bright light, he felt a little like someone in a fairy tale presented with a choice between three options. There were, in fact, three closed doors confronting him, one on his right, one straight ahead, and one on his left. He straightened his sports jacket, patting first the breast pocket holding his beeper and walkie-talkie, then the Smith & Wesson nestled snugly underneath in its shoulder holster. He pulled his raincoat shut but did not button it. Detectives learn not to button their raincoats when their pistols might be needed. Detectives are rarely sure that their pistols will not be needed. He looked around the brightly lit box he was in and wondered for a moment whether his entire fate hung on his selection of a door. He suppressed the thought the moment he realized he was having it. This was a routine investigation, after all. He wasn't walking into the lair of some known felon or some cache of prohibited substances. At least, felons and prohibited substances weren't what he was after here.

In the end, it was a foregone conclusion that he would pound on, then open, the door on his right. The music was coming from there.

Except for the last sunlight of the afternoon filtering through the closed curtains of the bay window, the room was dark. Dark and throbbing: the volume of the music was so intense that he was not so much hearing the drums and bass as feeling them surge against his temples and the soles of his feet. He stood for a moment in the doorway trying to identify the shapes looming out of the shadows, acutely aware of being framed in a rectangle of light, the most visible thing in the room to anyone waiting inside. He was tolerably sure that someone was inside. In the dark, waiting, keeping still, but there: sentient, intelligent. Or else why the music?

At that instant the music stopped and a reedy voice inquired, "Do I know you?"

Mike stepped into the room and to the left, so that he was no longer framed in the bright light of the entrance hall. The movement brought his shoulder into grazing contact with something much taller than he was, and as his senses registered the presence, his right hand moved smoothly across his body and under the lapel of his jacket. The whole process was reflexive and barely conscious, so that at one moment he was stepping forward and sideways, the next moment he was frozen in a crouching half-turn with the Smith & Wesson securely gripped in both hands and pointed at a gigantic stereophonic speaker. He realized that the thing was a speaker a split second after he realized that it was inanimate and rectangular, because suddenly the music came on again in full, deafening force, causing him to jump but not to squeeze the trigger. He straightened up slowly, snapped on the safety, and lowered the revolver. He did not put it back in his shoulder holster. He was not sure he was out of danger. He was not sure of anything.

Except, he told himself, that nothing was moving in that room unless you counted sound waves. As his eyes adjusted to the dusk, he noted the winking lights of the turntable and tuner on the floor under the bay window and a massive shadow that was probably a couch directly across from the door. It was most likely that the voice had come from the couch. He turned, stepped across the doorframe with the Smith & Wesson cradled against his body so that it would not appear in silhouette, skidded slightly on an area rug, regained his balance, and moved more gingerly to the corner, where he located a power switch and pushed it. The room again fell silent. Lights, he thought, but he could not locate a lamp, despite the fact that his eyes had largely adjusted to the dimness. For some reason it seemed inappropriate to pull the heavy curtains away from the bay window. Anyway, the daylight was going fast. Okay, he thought, no lights. O-*kay,* Scilla's self-defense mantra, cleansing breath, taking control here. "Detective Michael Annunzio, Third Precinct, Hinton Metropolitan Police Department," he said into the shadows. He was supposed to pull out his shield to confirm the identification but confirmation didn't seem to the point in this obscure setting. Besides, he was still holding the Smith & Wesson.

"How you doing?" The voice was steady but very soft, as if muted by distance.

"I'd like to ask you a few questions." Formula. I'd like. A few questions. The impression you wanted to give was that this was a contract between consenting adults, one citizen requesting aid from another citizen, fair and free and no coercion. No? You wouldn't like? Then you have the right to have a lawyer present.

There was a slight rustle from the couch, the briefest brushing of one object against another. Mike moved to the foot and looked down. At first he saw just a shape, long and furrowed under dark covers. Then the hands, pale and gaunt and large-knuckled, loosely clasped, immobile. And then, as the darkness congealed into discernible forms, the eyes, dark, too, underscored by great scooping crescents of shadow, barely visible under heavy lids. But there, open. And looking at him. "Ask," said the voice, thin and high and palpably uninterested in what Detective Michael Annunzio was doing in this room of this house on this lovely afternoon in early spring.

Mike swallowed. "What's your name?"

"Dave."

"Dave what?"

The fingers spread, then relaxed. What can I tell you? "Delgado."

"Dave Delgado," said Mike. He was uncomfortably aware of the gun in his hand and the eyes looking up at him. This is insane, he thought, and slowly moved the gun up into Delgado's field of vision, slid it slowly into the shoulder holster, and pulled his lapel back into place. Delgado's eyes noted the action without acknowledging anything in particular. Maybe there was nothing to acknowledge. Maybe a drawn pistol was no threat to someone in the condition Dave Delgado was in. Or maybe armed detectives in your living room at dusk were just something the Dave Delgados of this world had learned to expect. What kind of world was it that this Dave Delgado inhabited? Mike didn't want to know. Especially not when the inhabitant had a name like Delgado.

He reached slowly into the inside pocket of his raincoat and pulled out his notebook and a stubby pencil. He opened the notebook to somewhere around the middle. No matter which side he'd started from, he was likely to have hit a blank page. "You live here, Dave?" he asked. Dumb question. No, sir, just dropped in for a nap. But necessary to get confirmation. So conversational cop tone. No reason, really. Just wondering.

"That's right."

"For how long?"

People often objected at this point, but Delgado only turned his right hand over on the blanket so that it lay palm up. The fingers curled inward like a baby's. "Eleven months. A year ago April thirtieth."

"Who else lives here?"

"Here?"

"In this house."

A crease appeared between Delgado's eyebrows. How old? Forty? Fifty? You couldn't tell in this light. Maybe it would be hard to tell in any light.

"Four of us. Me. Peter Livingston. Edward MacPherson. Tom Sylvester. We signed the lease together. Back in April."

"It's a year-long lease?"

"Yeah."

Mike put his pad back in the inside pocket of his raincoat. "What are you going to do then?"

The lips pursed for a long exhalation. Cleansing breath. O-*kay*. "We can't try this one again. We can't all show up to sign. The landlord might think that was funny. We can't risk anything looking funny." A long pause. "Tom'll get the next place. Tom's all right still. I mean, he looks all right. He tested positive over two years ago, but we don't know that means anything. I mean, it *could*. But I didn't test positive till last July, so who knows, man. Tom's working, too. We're getting by."

"He work days or nights?"

"Days. Tom's a lawyer. For the city, man. Nobody knows down at his office. Nobody knows anything, if you get me." The crease between the eyes reappeared. "Hey."

"No reason why they should," said Mike.

"Right, man." The face relaxed so suddenly that Mike wondered whether Delgado had lost consciousness. But after an interval, the lids lifted again and the eyes were again looking up at him.

"So you're alone here now?" Mike asked.

"I think Peter's in his room. That's upstairs. He still gets around some but he sleeps a lot. Karposi's is what he's got. Tom and Ed went to the clinic."

"At Overlook?"

"No, man. The AIDS Task Force Clinic. It's in a storefront off Mason Avenue."

Mike nodded, although it seemed unlikely that Delgado could see him. "You know Bruce Levine? He does medical counseling there."

The eyes opened fully for the first time. "Sure I know Bruce. You know Bruce?"

"Yeah," Mike said. It seemed inadequate. "He's a great guy," Mike said.

"You know Bruce," said Dave Delgado. "That's really something."

"Yeah," said Mike. "Anybody in this house work nights?"

"Nobody in this house *works* except for Tom," said Dave Delgado. "Come on."

"You ever see anybody hanging around here?" asked Mike. "Tall guy, balding, maybe wearing a baseball cap."

"Around where?" Delgado's eyes had closed again. "Anyone hanging around this *living room* I probably wouldn't notice most of the time. Unless they offered to help take me to the bathroom."

"You want to go to the bathroom?"

The lips pursed again, but more in amusement this time. "No, man. Don't need to. Thanks."

"Any time," said Mike, and then felt idiotic. Not any time. When would he see this man again? Probably never, especially given Delgado's probable life span. Probably Delgado wasn't worrying a lot about where he was going to live after next month. "Thanks for talking with me," said Mike. "Sure," said Delgado.

Mike turned toward the door, then turned back. "Delgado's an Italian name," he said.

"Yeah," said Delgado distantly.

"I'm Italian," said Mike.

"Hey," said Delgado without interest.

"You from around here?"

"Victorian Hill High. Class of eighty-five."

"No kidding," said Mike. Delgado did not reply. It seemed unlikely that he was kidding.

"I'm older than you are," said Mike. "By about eight years." Delgado received this information in silence.

The room was almost completely dark now. At any moment Scilla would be calling on the walkie-talkie, her amplified voice tinny against his chest. She would wonder why he was still here. She had said the victim had probably been chosen from the apartment houses, not the group houses. It would be hard to single somebody out in a group home. A solitary apartment dweller would be the rapist's best bet.

"Play any baseball?" Mike said into the darkness.

Delgado's voice was very faint. "Not now, man."

"Ever? Did you ever play baseball?"

There was a long silence. Then the voice, sounding very far away. "Just CYO teams."

"Hey," said Mike. "Me too." He wanted to ask Delgado what position he played, back in his Catholic Youth days, and whether the recruiters had come around from Loyola to watch and congratulate him on his grades and talk about how he would be the first person in his family ever to go to college. But he didn't think Delgado wanted to talk about baseball. He didn't think Delgado wanted to talk about much of anything.

"Good talking to you," said Mike. Delgado said nothing.

The evening had advanced to the point where the cars on Temple Way all had their headlights on. Mike stood on the sidewalk in front of 1224 swinging his arms back and forth and watching the traffic. Still rush hour in Hinton on a balmy Friday night. Still balmy, even with the barometer falling. Still time to take your bicycle out to the lakefront park, to play a little baseball, throw a Frisbee around, take a little walk to clear your head, sort things out. Still time to hang around in a parking lot waiting for your next victim to emerge from wherever he or she worked. Still time for an outdoor rape. After that, you'd have to stay inside, wait out the monsoon. You wouldn't want to be rained on while you had somebody by the throat, that wouldn't be any fun. You wanted lovely weather. Lovely weather we were having. Unseasonable. Not for long. Mike shook his head abruptly. All the more reason not to waste time finding out who the next victim was and where he or she worked. On to the 1300 block, he told himself, setting off down the sidewalk.

The buzzer went off in his breast pocket before he had even

186

reached the corner. He stopped, pulled out the walkie-talkie, pulled up the aerial. "Annunzio," he said. A man walking past him paused in mid-stride, then went on hurriedly.

"Sorry to have waited so long before calling, Mike, but I'm pretty sure I've got the next victim. Not pretty sure. Really sure. I'm coming to pick you up now. Where are you?"

Mike looked up at the street sign. "Corner of Temple and Sowall."

"You're kidding. You spent all that time in one house?"

Mike looked around. Two teenagers across the street had stopped and were watching him with interest. "Yeah," he said into the walkie-talkie.

"You can tell me in the car."

"Right," said Mike.

But when the Plymouth pulled up to the curb three minutes later, Scilla was doing the talking. "It was that last building, fifteen thirty-eight," she began as Mike was fastening his seat belt. "I mean, the first building I went to, but there were eight *Advocate* subscribers in that place and I hit five of them before I got my lead. And the man himself wasn't home. One of his neighbors came out and talked to me. Friendly guy." Mike raised his eyebrows. "Gay," said Scilla reprovingly. "Definitely gay. He said it was practically a gay building. And he saw our bastard. Saw him, Mike. Tall, baseball cap. Right in that hall-way. This guy's home all the time doing something with software, and he gets lonesome. So he checks the hall now and then in case he can just happen to run into somebody to talk to. Any time he hears a sound, Ralph's out there taking out garbage or something."

"Ralph's the victim?"

"Ralph's the *neighbor*," said Scilla. "The *victim's* name is Avron Odabashian." Mike studied her profile as she negotiated a sharp left onto Sherwood. She didn't seem to be joking. "I've written it down, Mike," she said, braking for a fraction of a second as a small dog shot out into the street ahead of them. They cleared the dog with maybe three inches to spare.

"That's his name. It's an Armenian name. He goes by Ron."

"He's Armenian," said Mike.

"Obviously."

"If you hit something, we're going to have to stop and talk to the owners," said Mike. Scilla braked again, slowing their progress down the west side of Temple Hill by four or five miles per hour. Below them, the lights of the thruway, the downtown, the Harbor Freeway, and the waterfront twinkled like stars in the night sky. Beyond the lights, Nanteco Bay lay like a black hole. "Where are we going?" Mike asked.

"Waterfront. North waterfront. Pier eighty-eight."

"He works on the docks?"

"He works at Malvolio." Mike shrugged. "He's some sort of cook. It's a restaurant. Very in. Opened last year and won the Readers' Poll in the *Weekly Reader* for Best Food, Sixty Dollars and Over."

They had resumed their original speed or perhaps they had now exceeded their original speed. Scilla didn't reckon with gravity when she went downhill, Mike decided. He wanted to grab the dashboard, but that would have been disloyal. "Sixty dollars for what?"

"One dinner," said Scilla grimly. "That includes wine, coffee, and dessert, of course."

"Of course?"

"Don't ask me. I don't go there."

"I don't go there," said Mike, unnecessarily. "Sixty dollars. Jesus."

"I know," said Scilla. They had reached the intersection of Sherwood and Ninth Avenue, and she had seized on the occasion of a yellow light to make a squealing right turn. Mike braced himself with his right elbow until the car straightened out. He realized Scilla was watching him out of the corner of her eye.

"Want to go there?" she asked.

★   ★   ★

As they careened past car dealerships, hairdressing supply companies, and lighting-fixture wholesalers, accelerating occasionally for yellow lights glimpsed in mid-block, she explained that there was really only one way they could enter a restaurant like Malvolio on a Friday night without calling attention to themselves. "We're not exactly dressed for it, but I think we'll pass," she said, looking dubiously at his khakis. "Like a date," she concluded. "I'm sure Anna will be good for it. It's a stakeout, right? We can't very well sit in the dining room and send out for a pizza."

Mike told himself that whether or not this was a stakeout, it was enough like a date that he would be wise not to tell Sally where he and Scilla had eaten. He could avoid telling Sally only if Anna decreed that a meal at Malvolio was a legitimate investigative expense. Otherwise it would end up a glaring entry on his American Express bill and there would be hell, as well as American Express, to pay when Sally got hold of it. It was a big risk to run for dinner at an overpriced yuppie establishment with a woman who didn't even like the way he dressed. He reflected that on all the dates he'd ever had, except the ones involving baseball, the girl had worn a skirt. He understood times had changed, but that didn't really explain why his khakis were more problematic than Scilla's navy-blue pants. Maybe he was the one who was supposed to be wearing a skirt?

"He might be watching, after all," Scilla continued, executing a neat left turn just shy of an oncoming city bus and shooting them down Hillerman Street toward another yellow light. "Hold on," she cautioned, and they flashed through the intersection while the light turned red and the cars to their left and right began to honk. "It's not just that he might be watching," she amended. "If he's targeted this kid for tonight, this Ron Odabashian, he'll definitely be watching. He might even be in there having dinner right now. That's his pattern, or that's what he did with Chris Alvarez."

Mike didn't think she meant that the rapist would go into the kitchen and ask Ron Odabashian for a hand job. She had to be thinking on a more abstract level, he decided. First patron, then assailant. "Odabashian's a kid?" he asked. "Twenty-two or twenty-three years old. That's what Ralph told me. Started out in high school as part-time dishwasher at Ole's Kettle of Fish. Works hard. This kitchen thing at Malvolio is evidently a big step up for him."

They were going downhill again, preparatory to hitting the level blocks under the Harbor Freeway that would take them to the waterfront. Scilla was still using the brake sparingly. Mike cleared his throat. "Why Malvolio?" he inquired.

She gripped the steering wheel with such rapt intensity that her knuckles were white in the bursts of illumination from passing streetlamps. Another yellow light: he could tell without even looking. "I don't know," she admitted as they sped through the intersection with headlights coming at them from both directions. "I think it's one of the owners."

They seemed to be slowing down. He hoped so, or they would be driving right out onto the pier. "I mean, why not Malvolio*'s?*" he persisted. "Why don't they put in the apostrophe-*s?*"

She shook her head. "They don't. They just don't. It's some sort of yuppie thing. It means the place is expensive. I don't know why." He nodded to himself. He admired her for admitting she didn't know. She liked to know things.

Now she swung abruptly right, onto the Shore Drive, and he saw at the end of the block a blue neon sign that said MALVOLIO VALET PARKING with an arrow pointing right again. One up on Sullivan Lots, he told himself, with a little shudder because he was not at all sure that Anna would be good for this one either. Valet parking was something he knew about only because it encouraged the young people generally employed as valets to covet other people's BMWs and Mercedes. As the medieval churchmen had warned, it was a short step from covetise to flat-out theft, the latter not only a sin but also, at least in the case of those BMWs and Mercedes, a felony, and so several times over the past four years of his career as a

190

detective Mike had visited restaurants in the wake of a missing European touring sedan to interview managers about the mechanics of valet parking. One thing he had learned was that valet parking cost a lot, even before you tipped the valet for having brought back your car instead of driving it to Montreal.

The valet who took over their Plymouth showed no sign of coveting it and seemed rather more inclined to bash it into one of the concrete pillars supporting the Harbor Freeway, but Mike didn't consider that his problem. He was more interested to observe that all of a sudden Scilla seemed to be having no problems of any kind. In the spirit of their cover as a dating couple she had taken his arm, or so she whispered to him, her lips so close to his ear that he could feel the spurts of breath occasioned by individual syllables, as they strolled, cozily linked, across the Shore Drive on a crosswalk presided over by a WALK sign. A doorman stood under the awning and opened the glass door without evident disdain for their raincoats or their running shoes. Immediately inside, a dazzlingly pretty young woman deprived them of the raincoats and a tall man in tails and the whitest shirt Mike had ever seen informed them that there would be a forty-five minute wait for a table but that they would be welcomed warmly in the bar if they cared to while away the time there. At that point Scilla squeezed his arm so hard that he had to bite his lip to avoid wincing and said, "I'll just make a phone call. Order me a club soda, will you, honey?" before disappearing into the cloakroom after the dazzlingly pretty young woman. The tall man gazed after her in consternation but rallied to bestow a menu on Mike and wave him through heavy velvet curtains into the bar, which turned out to be heavily carpeted, heavily cushioned, and lit by brass lamps with green glass shades. Mike, who had been expecting varnished wood and hanging ferns, wondered if the decor was supposed to be one of those historic reconstructions, capturing the authentic flavor of Olde Hinton. Olde Hinton had been distinguished less for its restraint than for the variety and sumptuousness of its brothels. For the second time since he had left

191

the precinct house that afternoon, he found himself squinting into shadows. On this occasion his vision adjusted to the point where he could ascertain that the motto of Malvolio seemed to be "Some Have Greatness Thrust Upon Them." The words were inscribed in large letters on the cover of the menu and at the head of every one of the thick vellum pages. They sounded like bragging to Mike, but then, maybe bragging was the new high-class thing in keeping with the cathouse theme. How would he know?

He had begun to register the smells seeping in through the velvet curtains and the entertain the suspicion that he was about to have an extremely good meal, extremely good even if he couldn't keep the words Sixty Dollars from passing back and forth across his mind like the slogan on an airplane banner over the university stadium the afternoon of the big grudge match football game, extremely good even though he tended to be put off by a restaurant having such a high opinion of itself that it claimed to have greatness thrust upon it. The club soda arrived along with his own glass of 7UP. The cocktail waitress said it was on his check, which Mike interpreted to mean on Anna. At some point in his assessment of the smells, he had come to the conclusion that Anna would take responsibility for this dining experience and that his own responsibility was to enjoy it. While keeping his eyes open for the rapist, of course. He wondered belatedly if there was anything on the menu that Scilla could eat. He wasn't sure, in part because Scilla's dietary laws seemed to change at least once a week and in part because he couldn't see well enough to read the menu.

Scilla was not thinking about eating, although she was strolling past any number of people engaged in the act. She had discovered that reaching the women's room involved negotiating a whole series of small dining rooms designed to make Malvolio seem charming and even intimate to the several hundred patrons who could be seated within it at any one time. The lounges—the cloakroom woman had been distressed at Scilla's own word, *bathrooms*—lay beyond the dining area. So did the kitchen, Scilla reasoned. It even seemed likely that the lounges and the kitchen were close to each other, inasmuch as both involved plumbing, although Malvolio did not strike her as the sort of place where you had to be careful about flushing when somebody was trying to wash the lettuce. On the other hand, Malvolio did strike her as the sort of place where it mattered a lot where you were seated. The interlocking-rooms layout meant that the closer you were to the front door, the farther you were from the kitchen, and the more likely you were to be eating a meal that had cooled considerably since it had left the hands of the touted chef. The waiters servicing these outer reaches had a long way to go with food, although they were commensurately closer to the bar than the waiters servicing the inner reaches. They did move very fast, she had to admit. Twice she had almost collided with one of them, presumably one who was compelled to sprint most of the distance from the warm center of this establishment to his own Siberian station. Question of rank, she supposed. She had interviewed enough serving people to know that certain dining areas in any restaurants were highly preferred and went to the staff with most seniority or pull. More to the point, certain restaurants were highly preferred, because the size of your tip varied directly with the size of the bill. No accident that Malvolio employed waiters instead of waitresses, she reminded herself, just as one pushed past her calling, "Behind you, love."

"I'm not your love," she said to his back, but it occurred to her that she might travel faster in his wake. It was the same waiter as before, she noticed. The very fast waiter, probably from the outermost room. He had the manic efficiency of the newcomer. She kept one speedwalking stride behind him and followed.

They sped through two more rooms before rounding a bend cunningly draped with more velvet curtains and arriving without warning in a vast, noisy, and brightly illuminated space where, clearly, the reputation of Malvolio had its origin. As her waiter continued at top speed toward a long steel counter where a long line of filled plates lay waiting, Scilla bore right and found herself in a region of giant steel pots, many of them exuding the odors that Mike, some nine linked dining rooms and a set of velvet curtains away, was savoring as he sipped his 7UP and wondered what was taking her so long. Scilla had been downwind of the same smells since at least the third dining room, but her attitude toward them was more dubious. Sauces, was what she suspected, although she was willing, even eager, to be proved wrong. In her experience, things smelling like that turned out to involve substances like egg yolk, dairy products, and even animal fats. Standing on tiptoe to look into the top of a gargantuan double boiler, she decided she was glad she had taken things into her own hands and gone directly in search of Ron Odabashian. If she and Mike had hung around waiting for the place to clear out a bit before advancing on the kitchen, they would almost certainly have been forced to order something.

She was interrupted in these meditations and in her examination of a glutinous yellow substance in the top part of the double broiler when she was seized by her oxford cloth collar and pulled violently backward. Using the momentum of the pull, the force of gravity, and a kick against the front of the stove, she engineered her landing to put the bulk of her weight on the point of her left elbow, which was planted comfortably in the cushiony stomach of the person who had grabbed her. As this person let out a wheezing shriek reminiscent of certain New Year's Eve party favors, she reached around with her right hand, shoved two fingers into two nostrils, and jerked sideways. This time the shriek was completely vocalized, terminating in a gagging sob that probably carried through four or five of the dining rooms. Someone else had grabbed her arm. Relinquishing the nostrils, she grabbed in turn, squeezed hard on an inadequately developed bicep, heard the gasp as the grip on her own arm loosened, slid her hand down to just below an elbow, jumped to her feet, and twisted. Not hard: no sense breaking anything until she had this scene sorted out. The second person screamed somewhere in the tenor range, no serious damage. She pushed him back and pulled out her wallet. Flipping it open, she held her shield up above her head, turning it in a slow circle so that it was displayed to the entire kitchen, like the head of Medusa. The effect was similar. If no one turned to stone, everyone became very still, even the tall man in tails who had greeted them on their arrival and who had just come swinging around the corner with his fists up in approved pugilist position. Quite an audience, Scilla thought, turning slowly, watching the faces that encircled her. Cooks, undercooks, dishwashers, waiters. No women. Spot the inter- loper. "Priscilla Carmody, Detective Three, Third Precinct, Hinton Metropolitan Police Department," she said in her clear, carrying voice. "We need your help in an ongoing investigation. We have reason to believe one of the kitchen staff here may be in danger."

A gratifying murmur arose from the assembly. Gratifying until you realized the hazards of putting on this kind of public performance. She turned to the tall man in the tails. "You'd better get out there and assure anybody who asks that there's been a minor accident in the kitchen. Everything's under con- trol now. Not to worry. And listen." No need to tell them that, really. They were listening. "I don't want to alarm anybody, but there's just a chance that the man we're after may be among the customers. Right now. So let's not act as though anything unusual's going on, okay?"

The tall man had come forward to examine her shield. She stood still while he scrutinized it, feeling a little like a dog being sniffed by another dog. Finally he stepped back and nodded. "I assume you're acting with the authority of your commanding officer," he said.

"Lieutenant Anna Blessing, Third Precinct," said Scilla. "Call her." The man nodded and turned on his heel.

"Oh, *her*," murmured the man whose arm she had twisted. He looked cross but not incapacitated. Focusing on his face for the first time, she recognized the waiter she had followed into the kitchen. "The Pig Lady," he explained to the assembled staff. "What are you, the girls' Dirty Harry?"

"You attacked me," replied Scilla with dignity, but she was beginning to rethink her entrance into the kitchen. The aim had been to insinuate herself inconspicuously, after all. She had allowed herself to be deflected by the sauces, with the consequence that at this moment the entire business of the restaurant had effectively come to a standstill. "Don't you have customers out there?" she asked.

The mention of customers galvanized the waiting staff, who began picking up plates and rushing out. Within a minute, the number of people standing around Scilla was substantially diminished. The person on whom she had fallen moaned softly, and she directed her attention to him for the first time. He was a large, soft man with greasy black hair and a complexion that suggested to her that he ate the sorts of things she had seen steaming in the large pots. Not necessarily a suspicious character, but definitely someone to keep her eye on. His nose was not bleeding, she noticed. She had done a nice job, very few marks showing.

"Monsieur Clement, our chef," said a reverent voice.

Scilla decided all this high drama was getting out of hand. "Which one of you is Ron Odabashian?" she asked.

There was some scuffling toward the back of the circle around her and then a young man came forward, wiping his hands on a towel. Through all the commotion he had been tearing romaine leaves, she gathered, at least judging from the shreds of lettuce clinging to his cook's apron. She approved: in times of crisis, the cool heads carry on as usual. Not a bad-looking kid, either, although not her type. As he came to a halt in front of her, she tilted her head back and looked him over. It was a signal that their luck was turning she told herself. The height was perfect and so was the hair: color, cut, dead on. The build was very close, broad shoulders, narrow hips. The mouth was wrong, too wide, and the chin was more prominent, but those differences wouldn't be important in the dark. The walk would take some work: He had the springy stride of a young athlete. But it could be imitated, she assured herself. She would do the coaching. "Ron Odabashian," she said aloud.

"That's me."

She nodded. The kitchen could go back to its business now. She would call Anna back and tell her where to send reinforcements. They had their game plan. They had their decoy.

Ron Odabashian was looking uneasy. Well he might, she supposed. It's not pleasant learning you've been tapped to be in the next act of a deadly drama. But it's better to be tapped than to be on stage. Especially when there's a stunt man in the wings waiting to take over the risky bit.

Suddenly she smiled at him. "Anyone ever tell you you look Italian?" she asked.

Seventeen

Night in the detective room of the Third Precinct house was not all that different from day; if anything, a little brighter, with the light radiating green-tinged from ancient fluorescent ceiling fixtures rather than from the long, filthy windows overlooking the HMPD Restricted Parking Area. Anna Blessing's door was ajar so that Detectives Gannon and Cogbill, who were resigned to spending most of their shift fielding calls from concerned citizens who thought they had information about the so-called AIDS rapist, could see Anna moodily picking her nose in the middle of a collection of Big Mac boxes. Jim Gannon counted three of these boxes from where he was sitting in his own cubicle with the telephone receiver held approximately three inches from his ear.

"The way I see it, he's got to be a Virgo," a voice was saying out of the telephone receiver.

Jim had spent a great deal of time this evening contemplating the Big Mac boxes. They were beginning to get on his nerves. Anna customarily wadded up the white paper bags the doughnuts came in and flung them at her wastebasket, but she let the Big Mac boxes sit. Jim Gannon didn't think this conservation of Big Mac boxes indicated a concern with recycling. It seemed more due to the fact that Big Mac boxes are not aerodynamically engineered to be flung anywhere in particular. Jane Lowry dealt with the Big Mac boxes in the morning. For all Jim Gannon knew, she recycled them.

"Virgos are into heavy violence trips," the voice coming out of the receiver observed. "Especially with a water sign ascendant."

"Shit," said Anna Blessing. In the cubicle across from the one Jim Gannon was occupying, his partner, Henry Cogbill, hung up the telephone and looked nervously toward Anna's doorway. It was frequently impossible to tell whether Anna was summoning you or whether she was addressing, say, her wastebasket. You had to keep an eye out for other indicators. Henry Cogbill's telephone began to ring again so Henry picked it up.

"You know any Virgos?" the voice continued conversationally across the space between the telephone receiver and Jim Gannon's ear. "Bet you do, being in law enforcement and all."

"I'm a Virgo," said Jim Gannon, although he didn't know what he was. Blood type O positive was about all he could remember.

"You see?" said the voice.

"Hanging around where?" Henry Cogbill was saying. He didn't sound impressed. All suspicious characters were spotted hanging around somewhere.

"When one of you has a moment," Anna called out her door. Jim Gannon put his ear back against the receiver, thanked his caller, who was in mid-sentence about constellations and their effects on career choices, and hung up. His telephone immediately began ringing again. Ignoring it, he got up and went into Anna's office.

"We got complications," Anna greeted him. Jim Gannon noted that the three Big Mac boxes he had seen from his cubicle were the only Big Mac boxes visible on Anna's desk. Which was a relief, he guessed. Three Big Mac boxes were still within the bounds of probability. Four Big Macs, five Big Macs, and you were into some pretty weird eating patterns. Jim Gannon himself had on occasion eaten three Big Macs in one

sitting. On the other hand, he had never eaten a dozen doughnuts in one sitting.

"What kind of complications?" he asked. The far corner of
Anna's desktop was occupied by a pile of large, lavishly bound
books. The top one had a black leather cover with a drawing
deeply etched into its padded surface The drawing was of a
complacent-looking young woman dressed to go to a formal
dance and holding a shield aloft. On the shield was a smaller
drawing that he recognized as the university clock tower.
Under this picture were the words AEGIS '61. They conveyed
little to Jim Gannon. Rearing back slightly, he could see that
the words on the spine of the volume immediately below were
AEGIS '60. You never knew what Anna would be reading, he
decided, turning his attention to the thick pile of computer
printouts that she was staring at morosely.

Anna tapped the top printout with a pudgy index finger.
"This here vehicle, this Ford something or other."

"Taurus," said Jim Gannon, who was an avid, envious
reader of automobile magazines.

"Yeah. Taurus. Whole new model a few years ago. Very
popular item in the Hinton Metropolitan Area."

"I know," said Jim Gannon. He drove a Ford but it was ten
years old.

"So you figure, Taurus wagon, blue, state plates starting
with A, everybody agrees on that, maybe AV, AY, ADP, AB.
Well, okay. A something. You've narrowed it down to maybe,
oh, six hundred cars? Because nobody can tell the difference
between years, it wasn't *significant* back in Detroit or Tokyo or
wherever they're making this particular hot item, this Ford
Taurus. But okay. So here we've got this Department of
Transportation printout and there's Tony Hill slogging around
to the various addresses of people who happen to own this
particular kind of vehicle, Ford Taurus wagon, blue. It's a lot
of people but a finite number, you get me?"

"Yeah," said Jim Gannon warily. He had a feeling he knew
where this was going.

200

"Yeah. So maybe Tony can get it down to maybe forty, fifty suspects just by dropping in on the folks owning this here kind of vehicle, this very popular Ford Taurus, and looking them over to see who's male and middle-aged and very tall and maybe can't account for his actions certain evenings. This is all a start. Very positive in a low-key kind of a way. And then some alert fellow at the Department of Transportation comes up with an idea and suddenly I've got this *other* printout. She thumped a second pile of pages. Jim Gannon guessed it was about half as fat as the first pile.

"Mercury Sable," he said.

"You *knew* that."

He felt unaccountably guilty. "I thought everybody knew that."

Anna shook her head. "What I want to know," she said with venom, "is how come given free enterprise these Ford and Mercury people have to come up with the exact same car. This is freedom of choice?"

Jim Gannon cleared his throat uneasily. "They're the same company," he said.

"That's what I mean," said Anna. "The Berlin Wall came down for this?"

"Right," said Jim Gannon. He didn't want to spend any more time than he had to on the bad side of Anna Blessing.

"So you see where that puts us," said Anna, who seemed mollified. "Tony's been visiting these Ford Taurus owners all afternoon, at least those he can find at home, and now it's Friday night and he's supposed to start on Mercury Sable owners?"

"You want to put more people on it." It sounded better to Jim Gannon than answering phone calls from people who thought they had information on the guy in the picture on the front page of the *Herald*.

Anna sighed gustily. "I don't have that many people, and right now everybody on this shift is working on this one case anyway. I've sent Hill and Walinsky down to help with that decoy setup Annunzio and Carmody have going on the water-front, but that's kind of a long shot and I'd rather get the guy on this end, get a probable identity and then put a tail on him, know what I mean?"

Jim did know. Ever since Laurie Brangwen got slashed in the operation that finally caught the Hooker Hacker, the HMPD brass, not to mention the rank and file, had been nervous about decoy strategies. It was one thing to acknowledge that cops sometimes got hurt in the line of duty, like Pat Carmody, Scilla's dad, who had his kneecap smashed in a shoot-out and now regularly hobbled into benevolent-association fund-raising dinners where he could be displayed as a war veteran. It was quite another thing to send cops into situations where the whole point was to get hurt, or to get as close to hurt as was necessary to establish somebody as a hurter. That got weird. That was like asking for it. Jim Gannon was just as glad that his newest would-be victim, this Armenian kid, wasn't beefy and redhaired and freckled. Because in that case he, Jim Gannon, would have been down there right now, in the kitchen of that chichi restaurant, learning how to walk different. And even with Hill and Walinsky on the spot somewhere and two patrol units lurking in the area and Scilla Carmody trotting along behind looking inoffensive and not at all like some sort of female Karate Kid, he wouldn't have felt all that good about walking different, walking Odabashian style, whatever that was, into the shadows under the Harbor Freeway where the Odabashian car was waiting, nowhere near the chichi valet lot that served the customers of that chichi restaurant. Knowing maybe, just maybe, some very large nut case with a wig and a garter belt and a nice, sharp knife was going to loom up out of the darkness and grab him. What if nobody could get there in time? And what did it mean, in time? He had liked Laurie Brangwen. Everyone had liked Laurie Brangwen. They all spoke of her in the past tense, although she was very much alive at her mother's house. She didn't want to see any of them, was why. He supposed that was why.

"But I'm not going to get a probable identity on the bastard for at least a week if I've only got his car to go on," Anna continued. "Which leaves us with this decoy setup and I'm not any too happy about that. What if he does plan to hit Odabashian tonight? What if something goes wrong and he gets away? Then we're stuck with a couple hundred-some big blue station wagons in the Greater Hinton area and evidence a jury is likely to call circumstantial if Chris Alvarez can't make a hundred percent positive I.D."

Jim Gannon shook his head soberly, staying on the good side of Anna Blessing. "What you need," he said, "is a break."

Anna began stacking the Big Mac boxes on the upper left-hand corner of her desktop. "I deserve a break," she said. After a moment's reflection she amended, "I deserve a break *today*." Jim Gannon remembered this as a McDonald's slogan from some years back. Abandoning the Big Mac tower she had constructed, she reached across the desk for the volume entitled *AEGIS '61*. "Like this," she said, sliding it across to him. "Yearbooks from the university. A break, I'd hoped. One of those hunches that wasn't. Somebody picked up on the idea that our guy was a jock, maybe a football type, and suggested we should look at high school yearbooks. But since that would have given us a hell of a lot of pictures of high school kids, I asked myself, where do you go if you're looking for a real show-off, somebody into big-time performance? So I thought, where except the U?"

"The Hinton Bombers," said Jim Gannon.

"Come on. They weren't even here until seventy-three. We didn't *have* a pro-football team till seventy-three."

"Still don't," Jim Gannon observed, stolidly echoing popular opinion.

"That's my point. Everybody bitches about the Bombers. The Trojans, on the other hand, they're a going concern. You say University football, you're talking thirty thousand people in the stadium, TV, write-ups nationwide. And all those big guys dressed up as bigger guys. Big heads, big shoulders, big asses. A little shadow dabbed on underneath the eyes. You see?"

"Huh," said Jim Gannon, noncommittal.

"Oh yeah," said Anna "I mean, you want to get looked at dressing up funny, that's the place to get looked at."

"Dressing up like a man," Jim Gannon objected. "The guy we're after dresses up like a woman."

"*Very* man," said Anna. "I don't know. It doesn't seem all that different to me."

It seemed very different to Jim Gannon, who had loved the helmet and padding that he got to wear as starting center at South Central, but he knew when to keep his mouth shut. He said instead, "That would make this guy a college graduate."

Anna nodded approval. "College graduate ex-jock. Smaller pool. At least for that generation. What did those guys do when they left college?"

"Went pro."

"Maybe. Some. Not a whole lot. Anyway, what would he do after that? Presuming he was local?"

It all seemed pretty hypothetical to Jim Gannon. "Run a bar?" he suggested. "Or some other kind of business. Sell cars. Sell mattresses. Sell sports equipment."

"Become a sportscaster," Anna contributed.

"Teach P.E.," said Gannon. "Coach."

"A lot of them coach," Anna affirmed.

Jim Gannon shifted his weight to the other foot, one of a number of techniques he had learned for avoiding drowsiness when he was on foot patrol, and wondered where this was going. "The problem is," he ventured, "you have to be good."

Anna nodded again. "That's the problem, all right. They're *all* good. Anyone who made the team, offense, defense, starting lineup, even second string, was damned good. They recruited those boys from all over the state, after all. Nowadays, they recruit them from all over the country. So you look at the team for a given year, you're looking at fifty, sixty jocks maybe twenty-one or twenty-two years old. Plus in the pictures they're all wearing helmets and bent over or leaning back in those hunk poses, looking mean at the camera. You find me a soft mouth. You find me anything looks like the middle-aged guy we got in our Identi-Kit."

"What I meant," said Jim Gannon, "is it isn't enough to be a jock and like dressing up for the crowd. You have to be good, too. You have to be one of the best players in the state for your age group to play for the Trojans. Nothing we have on this guy says he's a *great* jock, you see what I mean? On the other hand, if you really want to dress up and get looked at, there are a lot of other things you could do."

Anna's mouth drooped. She looked like a very large baby, he thought. Then he wondered how he could have had the temerity to poke holes in her pet theory. She was clearly into this football thing, he told himself irritably. She wasn't what you'd call feminine, not likely, but occasionally you got a bias you had to say went with being a woman. Lots of women hated football. Probably because it was one sport they just couldn't play, he reasoned; there were some things women couldn't do, and just as well, or there would be more women around looking like Anna. Not all women hated football, of course. Not by a long shot. "Cheerleaders," he said aloud.

"Huh?"

"*Male* cheerleaders," said Jim Gannon, with the sudden certitude of someone who had just been addressed by a burning bush. "The U always has two or three of those along with the girls. They jump around like fools, those guys."

Anna lowered her big head and peered at him. "You think?"

Jim Gannon considered. "Well," he said finally, "they tend to be little guys. Wiry, anyway. But maybe there are exceptions." He thought about it some more. "You have to admit they're problematic," he said. "In a gender sort of way," he said.

Anna received this remark in silence, but she had begun

flipping through the pages of *AEGIS '61*. "Cheerleaders," she muttered.

"The *type*," said Jim Gannon.

Anna had reached a double-page photograph of a number of very pretty young women in very short skirts. Three of them were seated horseback-style on the shoulders of three very clean-cut young men. "Those were the days," she murmured, more to herself than to Jim Gannon.

Jim Gannon agreed fervently but he did not say so. He knew Anna was capable of saying all sorts of things she didn't mean, for reasons that generally eluded him.

"Well, these guys all look like Van Johnson," she concluded. "Maybe some other year. But I don't see what you mean about the type. They don't look like football jocks at all." She began flipping pages again.

"I didn't mean the physical type exactly," said Jim Gannon

"You mean—oh lordy!" She was glaring down at a page of black-and-white photographs with such ferocity that he felt compelled to edge around the desk until he was standing beside her chair. For a long time they gazed at the pictures. The top two showed the same pretty young women wearing football jerseys with padding that stuck out like coat hangers, and peering winsomely out of cavernous football helmets. The four photographs below showed a number of large young men in Kewpie-doll makeup, corkscrew curls, and very short skirts. None of the young men had shaved their legs.

At last Jim Gannon said, "It's not what you think."

Anna seemed vastly amused. "Oh yeah? What do I think?"

"It's not . . . what it looks like, you know what I mean? It's just the awards dinner."

"What does it look like?"

It struck him that he had better not answer this question. "It's a kind of tradition," he continued, feeling vaguely responsible for the whole disreputable scene spread out on the page in front of them. "The cheerleaders and the team do this little act, skit. They sing the fight song." Anna was blinking amiably.

"*Everybody's* there," he explained. "It's like a roast or something."

"Who's there?"

"All the team and the coaches and, oh, the president of the university and those guys who sit on the board that runs it and a lot of downtown guys—"

"Just guys?"

"No. Their wives and girlfriends. And all those cheerleaders. The female ones. It's in all the papers. Hell, it's on the TV news usually. It's all in good fun. They always do it."

Anna screwed up her little mouth for a moment, as if she were unsure what to do with it next. Then she said, "You mean to tell me that every year the whole football team dresses up in these little outfits?"

"And vice versa," insisted Jim Gannon.

"I'm not interested in vice versa. I'm interested in the football team."

"Not the whole team. Just a few of them. Five or six."

"Aha," said Anna.

"It's not like that. The guys in this . . . skit, this show thing, they're the really, oh, fun-loving ones. The zany ones. It doesn't mean they're—"

"Okay, they're not," said Anna with massive tolerance. "So granting they're not, do we know any of these guys here, the fun-loving, zany ones? What I'm trying to find out is, did any of them come home to roost?"

It seemed like a reasonable question. Jim Gannon began reading aloud the tiny print beneath the first photograph. "Jerry Winterberg. Jeffrey Elias. Robert Riley. Roger Martin Brozowsky. Alan Bodine." He looked up. "Bodine's got that big Honda dealership in Constantine. You've seen him, he does commercials sometimes—you know, big guy gets into little Civic—"

"Big mouth," Anna interrupted. There were limits to what you could take from your commanding officer, Gannon thought, until he saw that she was staring hard at the picture.

"Chris was very clear about the mouth," she said. "Little, she said. Soft, she said. This guy's got a mouth like a frog."

Gannon accepted the judgment. "I think Elias might be in business downtown somewhere. The name is real familiar."

"Which one is he?" They leaned together over the yearbook. Finally Anna sighed and observed, "That's no turned-up nose, that's a beak."

"Could've got a nose job."

She shook her head. "Let's not get carried away here. I'd say there's not much to interest us in sixty-one. But we've got six more years right here. Let's check out that, um, roast thing you say goes on every year." She reached for the second *AEGIS*.

"Sixty," Jim Gannon read.

"Good year," said Anna Blessing. "Let's see, where's sports? Oh yeah."

"Didn't they go to the Rose Bowl in sixty?"

"You bet. Roses up the *ass* here. Didn't win, I take it." She found her page and leaned back, ignoring the frenzied creaks of her chair. "Oh, hey now, you see roses are a sort of motif this year, you see? Look at how all these guys have big bunches of them. Sort of a Miss America thing in drag. And look here, see in this next picture, all the other guys are holding their pom-poms like *petals* around this central sweetie, like in those movie musicals back in the thirties with the chorus waving things and spreading their legs?" She fell silent. Jim Gannon peered at the central figure. "Isn't he cute," she murmured. "There's your soft little mouth, all right. This one's got it down, don't you think? Look at those eyelashes."

Jim was reading the captions. "I think that one is Edward Hunter. The name rings a bell, too. Ed Hunter?"

"Here he is again," Anna said. "In this picture he's the one who kicks highest. Cute panties."

"Ted Hunter?" muttered Jim Gannon.

"Try Whitey."

"Whitey Hunter." He stood up straight. "Whitey Hunter? Big Whitey? The coach?"

"That's him all right. The coach." They examined the photographs again. "Strange how I didn't recognize him. You can't miss Whitey from the sports page. If it's O'Dea, he's in the picture somewhere. Once you know it's him, it's perfectly obvious. He hasn't changed all that much."

Gannon shook his head. "I wouldn't have believed Whitey could look like that."

"Makeup can do wonders," pronounced Anna with satisfaction. "Not to mention the right hairdo. So you think he's our boy?"

"I don't see it."

"O'Dea's where you've got your kids, haven't you, Gannon?"

"Two of them," Gannon admitted. Even as he spoke, he was rethinking the decision. If Michelle and Jim Junior were in public school, he and Judy could definitely handle payments on a new car. There was a lot to be said for the public schools, even in Greater Hinton.

"Okay," allowed Anna. "Okay. This is a very long shot. Or a somewhat long shot. But you know why you didn't think of him, don't you? This guy's like a cop camp follower. You can count on him to show up at all those functions, those Policeman's Balls, those fund-raisers, those testimonial dinners. Jeeze, yeah, that face, how did we miss it? He's everywhere, Whitey, a very *public* man. Great performer. And a local boy."

"That doesn't mean—" began Jim Gannon, but he thought better of it and shrugged.

Anna's eyes were almost closed. "Lots of cop kids in O'Dea. Lots of cop kids on Whitey's teams. Whitey's the cop's coach, know what I mean? You know how many of you guys swear by Whitey? You know how many cops turn out to help him with those teams, be boosters, provide moral support? Like poor old Pat Carmody." Her face was dreamily somnolent. "Poor old gimpy Pat Carmody. Men's men, know what I mean, Gannon? Lots of punching arms and little talks about stay away from women, they sap your vitality, all that standard stuff. Could be, too, that there's lots of dropping in on the boys at home after dinner, chats with the parents, just happened to be in the neighborhood. Any old parents. Could be cops, some of them. Any old neighborhood."

"Temple Hill," said Gannon.

"Temple Hill, for instance." Anna's smile had broadened until her little eyes were almost lost in the folds of her cheeks. "Nobody told us that Whitey dropped by, but then Whitey isn't anybody's idea of a suspicious character. Happily married, you know. Coaches are. To a man, happily married. I mean, married to a *woman,* let's not get perverse here. I mean they're all happily married, all of them, married. Happily."

"It's still a long shot."

"True," murmured Anna. "Wonder what he drives." She picked up the stack of printouts listing Mercury Sable owners, riffled through the pages, found one, and said "Nope." Then she picked up the stack of printouts for Ford Taurus owners. "Yep," she said, flipping a page back. Gannon leaned over her shoulder.

"Edward V. Hunter," he read. "121 164th Avenue Northeast. ADP 677. Blue."

Anna smiled blandly up at him. "What do you think?"

Definitely public school, he told himself. The kids would be fine. After all, he had gone to public school. Judy had gone to public school. "Why would he do a thing like that?" he asked.

"Damned if I know. Mad, probably. Wonder who at." She was already dialing. "Yeah, Bruce Levine, please. Yeah, he's there. Look in back." She was still looking up at Gannon. "Your kids on any of those O'Dea teams?"

"Michelle is. Jim Junior's only a freshman. But Michelle's a big deal in volleyball." She looked benignly interested. "Her coach is named Sister Amy," he finished lamely.

"Got the sisters in there with the fathers now, have they?"

And the great Whitey Hunters, he said to himself. Judy would have a fit.

"Don't suppose you see any mothers around that place?"

He shrugged. "They're in the convents. Except there don't seem to be many convents anymore." Michelle had recently gone with the team to have tea and muffins in Sister Amy's apartment. It didn't seem right, somehow, to have a sister all on her own in an apartment, but Michelle had had a good time.

"Bruce. Lieutenant Blessing. Listen, I need a favor." The receiver buzzed with indignation. "Yeah, I know you're at work. Yeah, I know you don't have to tell me anything. You want to know what I'm asking?" More buzzing. Gannon had heard all about Levine from Mike Annunzio, who still couldn't figure out why all this back talk had served to endear the man to Scilla Carmody. Some female thing, he thought, watching Anna grin wolfishly into the receiver. "Okay, now this doesn't commit you to anything," she said. "Just say no, Bruce. That's perfectly okay with the HMPD. But what I'm interested in is whether anyone's mentioned a guy named Edward or Whitey Hunter. You got that? Hunter. Like the guys with the guns. Yeah. Or knives, right." There was a long pause. "No. It's your conscience, Bruce. I'm just asking you to check the records, think about it, decide whether you want us to *catch* this man. Or not, Bruce. You understand?" She listened with apparent rapture. "That's fine, Bruce. Anything you decide, we understand. We're just doing our job, Bruce. Right, Bruce." She listened for a moment. "Hey, no problem, Bruce. Call me Anna. Yeah. Good luck, Bruce." She hung up and swung around in her desk chair, which emitted a sharp squeal. "You want to drop in on Whitey?" she said to Gannon.

"Sure," said Gannon, who was watching Henry Cogbill pick up his ringing telephone again. "I'd like that," said Gannon.

Eighteen

"I think you have to roll more on your foot," Scilla said. Her eyebrows were twisted to the point where she looked as if she were suffering from cramps. But it was really all right, Mike reassured himself. She always looked like this when she was analyzing something. His own eyebrows twitched in sympathy.

Scilla noted the twitch and pointedly looked away. She wished he wouldn't look so pained when he was trying to pay attention. "You hit ground with your heel all right," she continued. "But then you have to follow through, rock forward to the point where you're finally kind of pushing off with your toe. Like a diver. Do it again, Ron."

Ron Odabashian walked springily down the aisle between the dishwashers' sinks and the drying racks. The two dishwashers watched him critically. So did Mike, who was having a hard time walking like a twenty-two-year-old squash player. Never mind gay, it was the squash that was throwing him. What kind of game was that for an Armenian kid from View Ridge? Odabashian had said he'd even lettered in squash at Nathan Hale. A fast game, he explained to Mike. You had to be on the ball like *that*. When he said *that* he bounced forward and sideways, ending up in a half-crouch that looked like something you'd be afraid of running into in the jungles of Vietnam, if you weren't fantasizing a squash racket in Odabashian's right hand. Mike wondered if maybe it wouldn't be better just to use Odabashian as the decoy. The kid was quick, and those moves of his were scary if you didn't know what they were.

The problem was that this rapist might very well know what they were. Anna had filled them in on this rapist after the pugilistic maître d' had called to confirm that Scilla was who she said she was and Mike had been summoned from the bar into the nether reaches of Malvolio's mammoth kitchen. Now that they had a good idea who the rapist was, they had to reckon with the fact that he might well recognize a squash lunge when it came at him, even if O'Dea didn't have a squash team. Or not yet. According to Odabashian, squash was the coming thing on the high school sports circuit. Whitey kept up with those trends: everybody knew that. Especially Mike knew that. Mike had played baseball with a lot of the O'Dea product at Loyola. The baseball team was nowhere near as implicated in Whitey as the football team, which had been about half Whitey's boys, but there was still a creditable O'Dea representation on the diamond when Mike was playing, three or four guys, all of them fanatically loyal to their old high school coach, even by baseball standards. Mike shuddered. He didn't like it, didn't like one bit the idea that it was Whitey Hunter who might be coming at him in a few hours dressed up as James Dean's Saturday night date. It felt too close to home, perverse in a far more intimate way than he had envisioned.

He looked warily at Scilla, who was leaning against the far end of one of the drying racks studying Ron Odabashian's walk as Odabashian walked toward her. What must she be feeling? Ever since her father had retired from the force, he had been hanging around with Whitey Hunter. The guy was practically her uncle.

She looked up and caught his gaze. This time she didn't look away. Instead, she smiled. He smiled back.

"Hey," she called down the aisle. "It's not on yet. Chances are, Gannon will find him at home watching TV. Then we all can go over to the precinct house and ask him embarrassing questions for a couple hours. Like where he got that *cute* skirt."

He glanced involuntarily at the telephone on the wall by her shoulder. It had an array of buttons on it, two of them lit up. All the calls to the restaurant came through one line and were routed from the manager's office off the cloakroom to the various extensions: maître d', wine steward, bar, front kitchen, back kitchen. If enough people happened to call Malvolio to make a reservation for tonight or—more likely now—tomorrow night; or to ask what the dinner, salad, and dessert specials were or were going to be; or to ask when the dining room closed or when the bar closed; or just to shoot the breeze with one of the bar, dining room, or kitchen staff. . . . Well, if any of those things happened, Ann Blessing, sitting at her littered desk like a huge spider at the center of her web, her own telephone linking her not only with all the other telephones in the world but with Fidelia, the four-to-midnight dispatcher, and through Fidelia all the prowl cars in operation out of the Third Precinct, would not be able to reach them here at the back kitchen extension. She would have to beep them, and they would have to intervene somewhere, to clear a line so they could call her back. It all seemed fairly arbitrary to Mike. It was disquieting to think that in a highly technologized society, law enforcement communications were still so primitive.

"Hey, Bash!" The voice came from somewhere in the populous middle of the food preparation area. Ron Odabashian stopped in mid-bounce and looked inquiringly at Scilla, who shrugged. "Hey," the voice wailed. "What goes in the chef's besides romaine and capers and sun-dried tomatoes and croutons and, oh shit, Stilton? What's Stilton, man?"

"Cheese," Ron Odabashian shouted over the rattling of silver from the dishwashers' sinks. "You also need arugula and fennel. And the Caesar dressing, but no egg."

"Oh, *man!*" The voice had slid up half an octave.

Odabashian looked at Scilla. "I'm going to have to go show him," he said. "Sorry."

"That's okay," said Scilla. It was another piece of bad luck that the intended victim on this balmy spring night would turn out to be the salad chef. Big salads were outselling everything else on the menu at Malvolio. She didn't think they looked so bad, either. If you watched very closely what went into them, you could probably get away with having one. She would have to mention that to Mike. Neither of them had eaten since noon, and right now, almost ten o'clock by her own watch, he was looking green again.

The telephone began to ring. She looked around, but no one in the vicinity seemed disposed to answer it. She picked it up. "Back kitchen."

"So what are you, the scullery maid?"

"I don't even know what a scullery is," said Scilla with dignity.

A wheezing cackle prompted her to hold the receiver away from her ear. "It's a back kitchen. If this were a *real* detective story, now, you'd be belowstairs questioning the servants."

Scilla surveyed her surroundings warily. In the distant reaches of the kitchen, Monsieur Clement, apparently recovered, was waving his hands at one of the younger cooks. He caught her eye and looked away. Sooner or later they were going to have to talk about this. "Since when do you read that kind of crap?" she asked.

"I read all kinds of crap," responded Anna Blessing with great good humor. "Just not your kind of crap. Not nutrition crap. Puts me off my feed." The silence stretched weighty and portentous while Scilla tried to think of tactful ways to suggest that Anna might benefit from being off her feed. She reflected that Anna was always setting her up like this.

"I wanted to let you know," said Anna suddenly, "that Bruce just gave us some information that tends to confirm the identification."

"Whitey," said Scilla.

"Whitey. It's still circumstantial, but yeah, the name Hunter pulled some interesting things out of the People with AIDS

215

computer files. Bruce can put two and two together, so he decided to call me back. You ever hear of Ann Hunter?"

"Sure. Annie. I've met her a couple of times, although generally Whitey shows up on his own. She used to be some sort of beauty queen. Sigma Chi Sweetheart. Something like that. Still looks good."

"She used to be a cheerleader," said Anna.

"Yeah. So?"

"She's got it."

Scilla blinked and looked around. The kitchen appeared to be in an advanced stage of disintegration. She supposed this was business as usual on a big night. "Got AIDS?"

"No symptoms at last report. But she's HIV positive. Left town in December, right before Christmas, prime battering season and old Whitey's got a vicious temper. He's beat her up before. She didn't think she'd get out of there alive if he found out she'd been cheating on him, so she left for points south, no forwarding address. But in February she called the storefront long distance, spoke to a counselor, not Bruce. She didn't know what to do. She didn't want to be around when Whitey found out, but she thought he ought to know."

"Who told him?"

"Another People with AIDS counselor. Guy named Joe Negron, although he didn't give his name. From time to time, the storefront feels responsible for letting somebody know they might be contaminated. Their policy is to keep the call anonymous. Just 'We have reason to believe that you might want to take the AIDS test.' Pretty weird coming out of the blue like that, but they're afraid of irrational responses. Retaliation even. Nobody loves the bearer of bad news."

"They just suggested that he have the test?"

"Right. Then hung up."

"Whitey wouldn't like that," said Scilla. "Whitey wouldn't like that at all."

"We don't know if he had the test. Or what the results were. And that kind of information is hard to get, as you know."

"It's still circumstantial."

"We're still on for tonight," Anna confirmed. "By the way, Gannon drew a blank. Whitey's not home right now."

Scilla drew herself up a bit straighter and glanced at Mike. He was bouncing down the aisle toward her, his forehead furrowed with the effort of imitating Ron Odabashian. "Somehow I didn't think he would be," she said.

"Nope. Gannon drove out there with a patrol unit. Decided to do without the sirens, in the spirit of sneaking up. Turned out he didn't have to bother. House dark, car gone. Neighbors said Whitey had gone out around seven. Not unusual, according to the neighbors. Goes out a lot of nights, especially recently."

"Do we know where the car is?"

"Yep."

More silence. "Do I have to guess?" asked Scilla.

"Malvolio valet parking lot. We're not touching it, of course. Hill and Walinsky located it about ten minutes ago. The parking attendant says it came in maybe forty-five minutes before that."

"So he's here," said Scilla.

"You bet," said Anna. "Got there maybe nine-oh-five, nine-ten. So he's in there, and barring unforeseen *ruses* on his part, he's having dinner. I gave a description to the maître d'. You guys better lie low. He might just pop into the kitchen to give his compliments to the chef."

"Or the salad chef."

"I would've said Whitey was a meat-and-potatoes man, but I wouldn't put it past him."

"Thanks," said Scilla faintly.

"Any time. I'll stay in touch, okay?"

"Please," said Scilla, and hung up.

When she turned around, Mike was at her elbow. "He's here," she said. "We've got to let Ron go back to making salads. We can't let anything look unusual."

Mike looked blank. "You mean here. In the restaurant."

"That's what I said," said Scilla. "And we, technically, aren't. I think we'd better go into one of the storage rooms."

They spent an uncomfortable forty minutes in the shadow of immense cans of crushed tomatoes, chicken broth, and evaporated milk. Somewhere along the way, one of the dishwashers appeared with two dinner salads, and Scilla ate hers without even asking what was in it. Mike spent some time wondering if there would be ensuing courses and had just decided there weren't when Ron Odabashian showed up with several hard-boiled eggs, a bowl of grated cheese, and half a loaf of French bread. "Kitchen's closing," he explained in an undertone. "I don't think anybody'll miss this stuff but you'd better eat it quick." Mike nodded and bit into the French bread. It was slightly stale. He could have used some butter, but that might be the sort of thing somebody would miss. Odabashian watched him for a moment and then turned to Scilla. "There's a call for you."

Scilla peered around the door of the storage closet, noted enough frenetic activity to cover her presence from any casual blunderer into restaurant kitchens, and slipped across to the wall telephone. "Yes?"

"He's gone."

"What do you mean, gone?"

"Paid his bill, left. Gave his stub to the parking guy, got the car, tipped the guy a dollar, drove away."

"You let him go?"

"The parking guy almost didn't. A dollar's not a tip by his lights, it's an insult. Or so he told Walinsky. Speaking of Walinsky, your dad called."

From somebody else this would have been a non sequitur. "Called who?"

"Charlie Walinsky. As soon as Charlie came on shift this afternoon. They're all tight, those guys. Wanted to know where you were."

"Where *I* was?"

"*Worried* about you," said Anna. "Seeing as you weren't

coming home for Mom's birthday because you were on a stakeout. You told him that, huh?"

Scilla swallowed. "I told Mom," she said.

"No secrets in your family," observed Anna. "Pat also knew what case you were on. Or put two and two together. Didn't approve at *all,* having you involved with the deviant and generally antifamily elements in this here investigation. Fag stuff, he told Charlie. No place for an impressionable young woman. God knows what you'd catch."

"Oh shit," murmured Scilla. "Do you think he knows about Whitey?"

"Name didn't come up. Pat just thought maybe you should stay on the sidelines on this one. Specially given the, um, *eccentric* nature of the leadership in these perilous times. Not like in the old days. Men were men. Word to the wise to an old pal. Meaning Charlie Walinsky. Not meaning me."

"Charlie told you?"

"Charlie told me about five minutes ago. Pat said he should keep quiet. Took Charlie awhile to sort things out with his conscience. Divided loyalties. Comrades in arms. Boys together. Male bonding versus the law. I may have to do something about Charlie. On the other hand, he did decide to play by the rules."

"Unlike Dad," said Scilla faintly. "Does he know where I am?"

"He knows," said Anna. "But your dad isn't exactly operative these days. Hardly in shape to do a Chuck Norris, even to protect his little girl during this general breakdown of traditional values. His little girl being a prime instance of said breakdown, you understand. Following in Daddy's footsteps, on one hand. Being unwomanly, on the other hand. On the same hand, actually. What's a man's man to do? You don't mind me talking to you like this, do you?"

Scilla took a deep breath. "Like what?" she demanded. "You think I shouldn't know this? If Dad's going to screw up the case, I'm better off warned, aren't I?"

"Glad you think so. I don't think he'll screw up the case. I took the liberty of calling him just now. Told him if he interfered there'd be charges this time. He's a civilian now. Nobody's going to stand behind him. I told him specifically not to try and reach the criminal. The rapist."

"What did he say?"

"He said he didn't know who the criminal was. Or where."

"What else?"

"You're a smart kid. He said he wasn't going to interfere in a fag thing. He said I shouldn't either. He said the HMPD is well out of this one."

Scilla let out a breath. O-*kay*. "I see," she said. "You think he'll do something?"

"I hope not."

"Great," said Scilla. "Great. I'll keep this in mind. Thanks, Anna."

"Don't mention it. Can we get back to Whitey now?"

"Sure thing," said Scilla grimly. "Let's get back to Whitey."

"Whitey drove off with Gannon tailing him. That's where we are with Whitey. We'll just have to watch what he does now."

"What do you think?"

The receiver rattled at Scilla's end. Satisfaction, Scilla interpreted. On the other hand, it could just as well mean fatigue. It's hard to evaluate a sigh when you don't have any of the visual cues.

"I think we've got an okay setup. No sense blowing it now. Look, we've got Gannon on his tail, Walinsky and Hill on Odabashian's car, two patrols pulled in behind a warehouse off of Grover maybe two and a half blocks from Odabashian's car, and you following Mike. If we pull him in now, the whole thing rests on Chris Alvarez's evidence. Another thing. He didn't go near the kitchen tonight."

"He didn't?" All she could think of was Mike sitting glumly on the floor wresting bites out of the French bread.

"Nope. Ate, paid, got his coat, walked out. The only thing

noteworthy about him was that he was all by himself. That's why the maître d' knew who I was talking about. But no compliments to the chef, nothing. On his best behavior."

"You think he knew we were watching him?"

"It might have crossed his mind," said Anna. "Even if your dad didn't tell him, he knows we're getting close. Lots of attention being paid to the so-called AIDS rapist tonight."

"You think he'll move anyway?"

"I've told Gannon to stay *way* back. Figure Whitey's looking for a tail, act accordingly. We do know he's after Odabashian. He's not likely to have figured out that we know. So our best hope is to keep him in sight but to concentrate our attention on Odabashian's car. That way we're coming at him two ways. Three ways counting you."

"And Mike?"

"Call it four ways, then. He'll have his pistol—tell him to carry it in his pocket and keep his hand in his pocket. Odabashian's got pockets, doesn't he?"

"About twelve of them." On his off hours, Ron Odabashian favored a black leather motorcycle jacket with a great deal of brass hardware. Mike had already tried it on. He didn't look half bad in it, Scilla had to admit. Not a nice boy, and hardly Catholic at all, except in an ambiguous Sal Mineo sort of way.

"Well, make sure he knows which one he's put the pistol in," said Anna. "We know this guy's got a knife and isn't hesitant to use it."

"How am I supposed to follow him?"

Anna's snort was unmistakable. "Be a girl. Be *out* of it. Be oblivious to everything."

"I don't know any girls who act like that at one in the morning," said Scilla.

"Come on. Be a *drunk* girl."

"Chances are somebody will try to rape me."

"Lucky us," said Anna. "We've got enough people on this one to catch a couple, three rapists."

"I don't like it," said Scilla. "It could get confusing."

"I'll leave it to you," said Anna with massive forebearance. "You be whatever you want to be. Just don't be sinister. And don't let Mike out of your sight, even for a moment. Okay?"

After she had hung up, Scilla turned around and surveyed the kitchen. Toward the front, several of the cooks were hosing down the floor. Bits of green and orange debris were skittering down the aisle, driven by the spray toward the big floor drains. The method made a lot of sense, made for efficient cleanup, Scilla thought, although it didn't make you feel any more like paying sixty dollars for a dinner.

She walked carefully over to where Ron Odabashian was sloshing lettuce around in a deep steel sink. "You usually get out of here about one?"

Odabashian had stripped to a T-shirt that had the sleeves rolled up almost to his armpits. If he stuck a cigarette pack in one sleeve, the image would be perfect, Scilla thought, but of course he didn't smoke. Of course he didn't. Bright boy, aiming for a long life barring unforeseen circumstances. "On weekends, yeah," he said. "I do all the salad prep the night before because on Saturdays and Sundays we get a big salad crowd for brunch. I don't work brunch but I'm supposed to set it up for the guy that does. All the salads are ultimately my responsibility."

She nodded. "You usually leave by yourself?"

"Always. The only people around by that time are the dishwashers—they go till maybe three, depending on how much stuff there is—and the bar staff. The bar doesn't close until two on weeknights, so the bartender and one of the cocktail waitresses close down the building."

"Are you ever afraid of walking alone?"

Odabashian straightened up and contemplated the segmented leaves of Bibb lettuce that he had laid out to dry on an ingenious arrangement of wire racks. "Sure. I mean, reasonably afraid. I look around a lot. I keep to the pier side of the Shore Drive until I get to the parking lot I usually use. That lot's not real handy to any of the restaurants around here, so it's easy to find space there at night. I told you which one. Three blocks down. A Sullivan lot."

Scilla nodded again. She had relayed the information to Anna, who had relayed it to Hill and Walinsky, who had located Odabashian's car, a hulking beige Buick with damage to the door on the driver's side, and in turn had passed on word to the two patrols who were assigned to back up the decoy operation. Hill and Walinsky's car-pool car, another Buick as it happened, was now parked on the other side of the same lot. Walinsky, who had been driving, had gotten out, locked the door, and strolled over to put money in the numbered slot. He had then crossed the Shore Drive and wandered down the sidewalk like a tourist taking in the sights. Half an hour later and far more circumspectly, he returned to the area via Grover. He was now settled behind some fragrant trash cans belonging to a luncheonette. From that vantage, he had a clear view of Odabashian's car. Hill had remained in the back of the motor-pool Buick, covered by a blanket.

All these arrangements had been relayed to Anna by the first patrol unit, which was maintaining radio contact with both detectives. Anna had relayed them to Scilla when Scilla had first called in to report that she and Mike had penetrated the Malvolio kitchen. As it were, penetrated, Scilla reflected ruefully. Her mode of getting in had been quite a bit like rape.

"We'd like you to stay here while the decoy setup is in place," she said to Odabashian. "It shouldn't be long. Mike will walk to your car, and if he isn't assaulted he'll just get in and drive back here. If the bastard does put in an appearance, we'll get back to you as soon as we handle him." Now there was a euphemism, she thought. Handle him. Manhandle him. But it struck the right note. It created the impression that the HMPD was in control.

"Fine with me," said Odabashian. "I don't mind waiting. Anyway, I want my jacket back."

Mike was still sitting on the floor of the storage closet when she got back. "It's okay to come out now," she told him. "At least for a while. He's driven off somewhere. Anna's got a tail on him." It didn't seem the right time to mention her father.

He rolled his eyes up to look at her. "She thinks he's coming back." It wasn't a question.

"She thinks he might. Don't worry, there are all sorts of people sitting around Odabashian's car waiting for the fun and games to start. Anyway, you've got me." He ought to be moving around more, she decided. All this sitting just bred anxieties. He was still looking green despite his dinner. "Let's work some more on that walk," she said. He got reluctantly to his feet.

The telephone rang at about the point where she had decided she had done all she could. Mike had the bounce down all right, but it wasn't an exuberant bounce. He was too rigid, she told him, but telling him didn't seem to help. If there were such a thing as a hysterical bounce, Mike would be doing it, she thought. He looked as though he were being jerked up at every step by some malign puppet master. Probably he'd do better at a glide, she thought; he might do a really sexy glide, especially in that motorcycle jacket. It was a pity, really, that Odabashian went in for visibly high spirits.

"Better get back under cover," Anna greeted her. "We lost him."

"What do you mean, we lost him?"

"Gannon lost him. Up on Emory Hill, right around O'Dea."

"He went to O'Dea?"

"Nope. He *didn't* go to O'Dea. Gannon figured on psyching out the criminal mind, figured Whitey would return to the scene of the scrimmage, some dumb thing like that. Whitey didn't. We don't know where he went. Maybe to pick up his glad rags, is what we're inclined to think. Gannon guessed he was keeping them somewhere at O'Dea. Bad guess."

"So he might be back here."

"He might be heading back. It's only been seven minutes

since he threw Gannon. You said you've got windows back in that kitchen?"

"Right," said Scilla. "Not very big ones, but someone could still see in."

"Okay, so he might be back for a look. Let's try to keep up appearances."

"Right." Scilla hung up and turned to Mike. "Back into the closet," she said. One of the dishwashers giggled.

They sat in silence for the most part as the kitchen quieted down and emptied out. There wasn't a lot to talk about. They knew what they were doing, how they would handle the various contingencies that might arise. They had already made those decisions. Still, Mike told himself, his state of mind wasn't quite what he had anticipated. He had been in a lot of stakeouts, and there was no reason why this particular wait should be any different from any of the others. But in fact he was finding it hard to concentrate—even, in a peculiar way, to be *present* right now, in this kitchen, for this operation. He kept thinking about things that didn't have anything to do with this case, about Dave Delgado lying on the couch in that dark living room, about Sally lying in their bed in their dark bedroom with no idea where he was or when he was coming back, about his maternal grandmother, who had lived with another old lady and died when he was ten years old. These thoughts not only kept him from maintaining a conversation but also made him feel guilty that he wasn't keeping his end up. For some reason, tonight he felt that he was obliged to be entertaining. Something about being a decoy. Something about being marked as a victim.

It was almost a relief when Odabashian appeared at the door in his leather jacket with a muffler pulled up around his face. "It's not that cold outside," he explained, "but this is the only bright light you'll be in, so you should probably keep your head sort of ducked until you get to the door." He turned to Scilla. "He should turn out the lights as he leaves. If you give him maybe half a minute's head start you can probably get out without anyone noticing the door's been opened again." She nodded. Smart kid, this Odabashian. If he ever got sick of lettuce, he might think about a career in law enforcement. She resolved to mention the possibility to him after this was all over.

"The door locks automatically?" Mike was zipping up the jacket. The resemblance was amazing, Scilla thought.

"Nobody can get in. She can get out, though."

"Okay." Mike had wrapped the muffler around his jaw. He looked at Scilla.

She felt suddenly awkward. "Okay," she said.

"I'm off."

"Wait a minute." She reached out and pulled the muffler up over his nose. "Better," she said. "Look, you're going to be all right, you know."

"I know," he said through the muffler.

"I'm going to be right behind you."

"I know."

She had a strong urge to adjust something else on his Odabashian outfit, but there was nothing left to adjust. Come on, Scilla, she told herself, you want to fix his *tie?* Smooth his *hair?* She wanted, she realized, to kiss him good-bye.

"Break a leg," she said. He nodded and turned away. She heard the door open and then shut as she began buttoning her raincoat.

Nineteen

The moment he had switched off the kitchen lights and closed the door behind him, he felt certain that someone was waiting in the darkness. Here, on the pier, in back of the restaurant. Not the ideal site for a leisurely sexual assault, but possible given this rapist's track record, his known appetite for risk. So what? he demanded of himself and the night, hesitating on the creaking boards, sniffing the salt air, listening. Scilla was behind the door. Scilla with her karate skills. Versus Whitey Hunter with his athletic skills, his weight, his strength, his knife. No. Wait. Remember the pistol. He slipped his right hand into the bottom pocket of Ron Odabashian's jacket. His palm touched the stock of his Smith & Wesson. Remember the pocket, he told himself. Too many pockets in this damned jacket. With his fingers around the stock, he listened again. No noises except the murmur of waves and the muted *shush* of cars passing on the Shore Drive. Move, he told himself, and started down the narrow walkway between the side of the restaurant and the water. It occurred to him that if someone were watching, listening, he should be trying to look like Odabashian. Or sound like Odabashian. Bounce, he told himself. He had never felt less like bouncing.

Scilla stood in the dark kitchen with her raincoat buttoned and a flowered silk scarf, borrowed from one of the cocktail waitresses, tied over her hair and under her chin, watching the luminous second hand sweep slowly past the luminous numbers on the dark dial of her wristwatch. When an interminable minute had gone by, she added another ten seconds as a penance for impatience. Then she turned the doorknob very slowly, feeling the latch ease back, willing it not to click. Mike would be in front of the restaurant by now, starting down the long, carpeted entrance to the pier under the awning. When she rounded the corner she would probably get a glimpse of him on the sidewalk, under the street lamp, before the Drive made a leisurely curve around the next inlet with its cluster of dark buildings. He would be out of sight for perhaps a minute after that point, until she in her turn rounded the curve, but he would be on a sidewalk regularly mottled with patches of light, alongside traffic going up and down the Shore Drive. Until he crossed the Drive to go into the shadows under the freeway, they had decided she could keep her distance.

"Stay here!"

After the first long hiss, the whisper was barely audible, but he had her wrist, the right one, her good one. A strong enough grip to cause a bruise; strong enough, too, to use against him, countergrab, twist back, slide kick sweeping away both feet. She didn't move. Instead she made her voice conversational. Nonconfrontational.

"Hello, Dad."

The grip on her wrist relaxed, but he didn't let her go. Wasn't about to let her go, she realized. And what was she going to do about that? Okay, she thought, and then thought it again, breathing out. O-kay.

"If you want, you can tip me right over," he remarked just as conversationally. You learn that conversational tone early. It's working copspeak. You learn how to provoke, too, but you know that sometimes it's best to avoid provocation. "You don't need any complicated karate, Scilla," he continued reasonably. "Any little thing, the knee will give, you'll be on your way. So you just listen to me a second."

She thought of pulling back his thumb, breaking his grip.

Thought better. He still had it in the upper body and he squeezed things, rubber balls, spring grips. She would have to use the knee, and that would be cowardice by his lights. Hers too. Taking advantage of a disability. "I don't have a second, Dad," she told him, hoping there wasn't too much fervor in her voice. Emotion encouraged them, felt like resistance, gave them something to fight. "There's a rapist out there," she told him. "I'm following somebody he might be after."

His fingers dug into her lower arm. Bruises, Dad, she thought. She didn't say anything. Even with one arm fully occupied bracing the cane, even unsteady as he was on those three pins, he could inflict pain, given the fact of no resistance. Her nonresistance was a fact, for both of them. Fathers have the right. "It's none of our business, Scilla." His voice had sunk back to a near-whisper. "It's a deviate thing. You think you know them, but you don't. You think they're like us." In the long pause that followed she heard water slapping against pilings, a lone horn sounding out on the Drive, high to low, Doppler effect. "You know them for years and find out you don't know anything," he whispered. "Scilla, they're not like us. We don't understand anything about them. Let them do it to each other. It's what's supposed to happen. We shouldn't interfere."

She had to sound calm now. Rational. "He's a rapist, Dad," she said. "It's not that he's gay." The hand tightened on her wrist. "He's gay, Dad," she repeated firmly. "But that's not why we're after him. This is sexual assault. This is a violent crime. He's forcing himself on people. Innocent people."

The words came spitting out. "Innocent faggots!"

"Innocent people," she insisted. She could see him clearly now. All she had to do was kick, and he would topple.

"They're not innocent. They're faggots. They're admitted faggots."

It seemed to take far too long to go through the things she might have said and he would certainly have rejected, to reach at last the one that might work with him. "The man I'm following," she told him, trying not to rush the words, trying not to think of time slipping by and Mike turning right at the foot of the ramp to proceed as planned down the sidewalk, confident that she was behind him, as planned. "He's not gay. This is a decoy setup. That's Mike out there. He's all alone out there. There's nobody backing him up now."

For a moment his grip relaxed. Then it tightened again and she could hear him take a shuddering breath. She told herself not to tense, to keep her head, to think this is a man with his hand on me, just a man, any man.

When he spoke, she had the eerie sense that they were at the dinner table again, head and right-hand girl, family silent and attentive. Debating issues. Engaging in discussion. Hammering out the ground rules of their relationship, doting father, contentious daughter. He had resumed the conversational tone. "I don't want you mixed up in this, Scilla."

She could see his face now, close to her own. Teeth bared. Father knows best. He was smiling.

She kicked. He shouted going down, the sound carrying out over the water, down the pier, doubtless to Mike, who wouldn't know what to make of it. Not a word, just a bark, monosyllabic, clipped, glottal to alveolar. She refused to believe that it was a word. There might have been more, but she was running now down the slippery boards alongside the building, water to her left and no guardrail, rubber soles drumming, no one to hear but Pat Carmody rising slowly on one elbow to look after her.

Mike was directly under the second streetlamp when the shout stopped him cold. He felt again for his pistol but did not draw it. He had drawn it without cause already this afternoon. He was still Ron Odabashian, he told himself. He was fully visible now from the street, even if the curve of the Drive hid the Sullivan lot under the freeway overpass where Odabashian had parked his car. For the next three blocks he would be stepping from pool of light to pool of light, with only a few feet of relative shadow between them. Unless he was sure Scilla was in danger, he was responsible for maintaining his cover. And how could Scilla be in danger, he asked himself. That was a man's voice. Probably not even from this pier; sound carried strangely on the waterfront. He whirled back and started walking again, hands jammed deep in the pockets of the jacket. I'm Ron Odabashian, he told himself. I'm leaving work at the usual time, after a busy Friday night. I'm tired. I'm used to obscenities coming from God knows where this time of night. All I want is to get home and go to bed. Anyway, it's still warm outside. Even if the stars are disappearing, even if the wind is picking up, there's a new moon. I'm feeling good about things. I'm twenty-two years old. I'm gay. I play squash. He didn't have to tell himself to bounce. Suddenly he was bouncing.

He bounced down the sidewalk out of the yellow light and into shadow. A car sped by trailing a burst of guitar and contrite male voice, country western, great night for cruising. A second car slowed as it passed. Great night for cruising, he told himself, remembering who he was and looking pointedly away. Could they tell? Was it the bounce? Or was it just that any man alone on the street this time of night might be available? Like any woman on the street this time of night, he reminded himself. Might be vulnerable, attackable. Might be prey. He moved to the inside of the sidewalk as he entered the circle of light from the next streetlamp.

She rounded the corner of the restaurant and slowed to a cautious walk as she passed in front of the lit-up Malvolio sign. A cautious walk was in character, never mind her father writhing on the pier in back and liable to shout again, never mind shout what. In character for a lone woman, bundled up although it wasn't cold, bundled against visibility. A cocktail waitress or cashier, unluckily stuck with closing, negotiating the distance between job and car in the dangerous wee hours. Scarf over head, head down in collar. Rapid, purposeful steps. Mike was nowhere to be seen. Past the curve of the Drive, of course, in the shadow of those buildings close in on the next pier, aquarium and snack bar and tourist shop of some kind, shells and glass floats and dried starfish for the folks back home. Moving right along, springy, athletic strides, imitation Odabashian. She picked up her own pace as she started down the carpeted walkway to the sidewalk. Not drunk, not likely, just a working woman making a beeline for her car. Like Chris Alvarez, she thought suddenly, and thought then of her pistol, still holstered under layers of raincoat, jacket, vest. You're slipping, Scilla, she rebuked herself. Dad threw you off. She repressed the corollary, that she had thrown him off. Thrown. Literally. Off. She didn't want to be at war with all the fathers. It was bad enough knowing the man out there in the weird costume was Whitey Hunter, Dad's cohort, Dad's sidekick. Sidekick. She had used a side kick, easiest way to unsettle a standing attacker, easiest way to humiliate the handicapped. She shook her head in irritation. Concentrate on Whitey. She tried to remember if he had ever done martial arts. She didn't think so. He would have said so, she thought. In some context somewhere. Dinner table. Over beer on the deck, Mom pouring, favorite daughter home from college, beer in hand, posturing, excited, telling them about women's rights. Indulgent laughter. Mom going back into the kitchen. She shook her head again. Whitey might have done some boxing. Plus, he had strength and weight going for him. She could reach the pistol now if she wanted, but it would look funny to anyone watching. She didn't want to do anything that would look funny. She wanted to do things that would signal she was leaving work, that she just wanted to be left alone.

He didn't look behind him. He didn't look around. He knew that even if no one was watching, the curve of the Drive here with its pile of dark buildings put them out of sight of each other. He had to trust that Scilla was back there somewhere, having counted off her minute and opened the door again. If things were going according to plan, she would be beginning the curve now, her raincoat drawn close around her, her head shrouded in the silk scarf. Within a minute she would be looking at his back as he bounced along, hands in Ron Odabashian's pockets. In a minute he would know that if he looked back he would see her, he thought, just as he saw the figure that seemed a parody of Scilla, a Scilla larger than life, scarved, unsteady on shoes that weren't Reebocks, lurching across his path to the curb, looming up alongside him, bumping him so that he stumbled sideways, found himself falling sideways and then being dragged backward onto a walkway alongside those dark buildings, curio shop, snack bar; good idea, he thought, it's another pier. A hand over his mouth now, a big hand. The other hand between his legs, even as he was dragged past a grimy side window draped in fishnet and into the deepening shadows beyond. A much better place than the parking lot, he thought, weirdly clearheaded. Not at all public. Who would be haunting the aquarium and its side attractions at this hour of the morning? He felt the pressure of the ballooning skirt on the backs of his legs, heard the rustle of crinolines. The voice was so close to his ear that it seemed to be coming from inside his head. "Don't make a sound, faggot."

No sound, he agreed. Not very likely under the circumstances but maybe this meant Whitey would take the hand away, put it to use elsewhere, don't think about elsewhere. Think about how Scilla is coming, how it could be soon, could be almost now, about how one shout might alert her to where he was, why he wasn't bouncing ahead of her in the pools of light made by the streetlamps of the Shore Drive. He drew in a shaky breath as the hand fell away. Then he felt it on the left side under his jaw, very cold, very sharp. Ready to slice the artery, slide in a leisurely manner through the windpipe, slice the second artery on the follow-through. Excellent use of his weight, of gravity. Coaches know a lot about the human body.

"We're going to walk backward together now. You and me. Easy now."

Like some folk dance of Balkan idiots, the kind of dance they made you do in P.E., clasp your partner between the legs, around the jawline, move backward. He stepped on Whitey's foot and wanted to apologize. Grotesque way to travel. Gets you where you're going, though. Almost everything does if you keep at it. In a moment they would be behind the buildings, on the open pier, surrounded on three sides by water. Dark back there. Where was Scilla?

She was on the sidewalk now, negotiating the pools of light, keeping close to the Drive, huddled into her collar and the silk scarf, frail protection from the passing cars. Girl on the street alone. Nice girl, easy mark, not some Ninja cripple kicker, not some raving feminist soldier of fortune who would attack her own father in the artificial kneecap. Nice girl. Somebody honked very close behind her. She drew up her shoulders, picked up speed. Not interested. Don't hurt me. She couldn't think of her father; she had other things to think about. They would put him in the ambulance and take him to the emergency room. Eventually. She was rounding the corner now, bearing down on the aquarium, the snack bar, the curio shop. No Mike in sight. That was wrong. This meant she should switch into attack mode. If she could remember attack mode now, huddled into her collar, something in her mind calling plaintively into the night, Daddy? as if he would come and save her, as if she could erase forever the name he couldn't possibly have called her. Still walking, she took a deep breath and blew it out. O-kay.

Her steps were almost soundless, but Mike knew where she was. So did Whitey, presumably. He had frozen in mid-stride and was holding Mike close against his body. Listening. Interpreting. Girl on the street alone. Prey, not predator, but the canny rapist will avoid calling attention to himself, even if she is only a girl. They're unpredictable, girls, tend to scream, even though it's unlikely anybody would hear, or think much if they did hear.

And who would hear? Mike asked himself, still clearheaded: needlessly, futilely clearheaded. Certainly not Hill and Walinsky and the two patrols, all of them huddled around an old beige Buick parked two blocks away. His right hand, still in his pocket, still gripped the stock of the Smith & Wesson. What price moving now? he asked himself. Whitey's hand moved up from his crotch, slid across his chest, began moving down his right arm. Copping a feel. Feeling a cop. What's that in your pocket, sonny? As he stood with the exploratory fingers probing through leather, Scilla moved into the light at the foot of the pier.

She had picked out the spot the moment she realized something was wrong. That pier. Dark. Good idea. It hadn't struck them when they had come in, but at that time there was still some sunlight and the aquarium was still lit up. Hard to envision what possibilities for long-term assault will open up in the dark. Whitey had envisioned them. Had visited this place already, when he followed Odabashian to work. Had it all figured out.

She was lucky that her night vision was so good because even though she was looking for the two figures, she almost missed them now, deep in the shadow cast by the curio shop on the edge of the pier, as close together as dancers or lovers. The face looking out at her was Mike's. He was shielding Whitey very effectively, she noted; no shot there, no reason for bright girl cop to blow her cover and go charging down the walkway yelling banzai or Geronimo. The great thing about rape was that it was so intimate. If interrupted, you had your hostage right there where you could keep your hands on him. One move, copper, and the faggot gets it. Although the place was too public for rape, really. He'd be headed back behind the curio shop. If this little huddle of buildings was anything like the restaurant they had just left, there would be a loading area back there. A nice clear space. Open to nothing but water. She kept her face impassive and allowed her gaze to sweep the sidewalk ahead.

Her flinch was real when the car horn honked. She drew up her shoulders, picked up speed. Not interested. Leave me alone. Walk on by. The car moved past, picked up speed.

The pier lay behind her now. Nobody in sight, no cars on the street. She kept walking. Out of range. Out of sight. Out of mind. Another pool of light, step off into shadow, keep on walking. Now she was behind the flank of the next building jutting out from the next pier. She stopped.

And heard behind her the muffled clink of metal striking concrete, a hissed expostulation, the muted scuffling of feet in running shoes, in outrageous spike heels.

She crept back around the corner of the building, keeping in its shadow. They had moved farther down the pier, farther into the shadow thrown by the curio shop. She looked around, then ran down the bright sidewalk and slipped into the shadows of the pier. She could hear the slosh of water against wood, nothing else. The whispery rubbing of planks against pylons. Nothing more. Or were they in fact whispers? She reached into her coat, under her jacket, under her vest. Pulled out her pistol. Edged toward the walkway where she had seen Mike's face looking out at her.

She could see it in the spill light from the streetlamps, there at the end of the walkway. Mike's pistol. She assumed it was Mike's pistol. Her back pressed against the wall of the curio shop, she moved quietly crabwise. Not the fastest way to travel but probably the safest under the circumstance. Considering that she was the only one. The whispers were unmistakable now, whispers and thumps that were probably blows. She didn't wince; she needed all her concentration. If Mike was unconscious, the other one wouldn't be whispering, would he? Whitey wouldn't. She hoped he wouldn't. She really didn't know what Whitey would do. As her father said, you thought you knew them and it turned out you didn't know anything.

"Faggot!" Not loud, but partly vocalized. A good sign, she told herself. He thought he was relatively safe. "You going to *shoot* me, you fucking faggot?" A thump followed by a moan. "Shut *up!*"

She stopped at the corner, back against the building, pistol up. One more moment. O-kay.

"Who's that?"

She froze. Nothing moved. A long silence, too long. She shifted her weight. Under her foot, a board creaked.

Nothing for it now, she told herself. Face-to-face. Fair fight. And stepped around the corner.

There was enough moonlight to make a tableau of it, Mike in front with his right arm pulled behind his back, the nightmare figure behind, twisting Mike's arm with one hand, the other pressing the knife against Mike's throat. The head hovering above Mike's shoulder seemed impossibly large, especially given the weirdly domestic detail of a flowered scarf. It struck her as a particularly intimate stance. She said very clearly, "Whitey, don't be crazy. That's a cop."

Under the scarf he stared back at her, apparently uncomprehending. She hadn't even raised the pistol. It was too risky.

She felt as if she would spend the rest of her life meeting those pale, blank eyes. Staring at her as though she were speaking another language. As though he didn't know her. Power games, staring contests. Costume party. Drag races.

She would never be sure if he slipped, if somehow he changed his mind or changed it halfway, or if Mike himself made a move. There was a blur of motion traversed by the slow slide of the knife, and Mike shouted "My eye!" and spun away, both hands to his face. As he fell, Whitey bolted toward the other side of the curio shop, skirt billowing, high heels kicked away. There was a splash as one of them broke the surface of the bay. She leapt past Mike before he had even hit the boards and rounded the corner with the pistol gripped in both hands. As she had thought, it was a narrow walkway like the one at Malvolio. "Whitey!" she called. "Stop or I'll shoot!"

He was running but he turned his head, the scarf coming undone over a wig that was slipping over one ear. "You cunt!" he shouted, the voice unexpectedly high and hoarse for such a big man. "You libber! You got the disease, you know that? You cunts all got the disease. Like Annie. She fucks fruits, you know that?"

She slowed, for only a moment, but it was enough. He had

leapt around the corner of the building, was on his way down the sidewalk. "It's not a *discussion,* Scilla," she muttered, picking up speed again. She'd match Whitey as a sprinter any day. You don't have to sort out the strands, she told herself; you don't have to say to him that's Annie, she's sorry, but you're a fruit, too, Whitey, face up to it, and this libber business, that's very misinformed. She never had been able to tell them anything. Whitey or her father, either one. Indulgent laughter. Write her off. That's what they'd done of course. Written her off. And now? Was she showing them? At what cost?

She stopped, bent her knees, gripped the pistol, took aim. He was going to cross the street. If he crossed the street there was a strong likelihood she would lose him in the shadows. Her backup was still two blocks away. "Stop or I'll shoot!" she screamed again, the last word erased on the night air by the sudden explosion of her warning shot. He was fast for someone his size. Not to mention his sartorial handicaps. Full-skirted, stocking-footed, the wig gone somewhere in the race off the pier, he turned now and gave her a long stare. She was looking along the barrel of her pistol at his face. She knew the face. He spoke very quietly. "Just a chip off the old block, aren't you? Do you have any idea how much your daddy hates what's happened to you?"

When they're escaping, you're supposed to aim for the legs unless there are extenuating circumstances. Unless aiming for the legs might injure innocent bystanders. It flashed across her mind that there was still traffic on the Shore Drive. A little traffic. A car now and then. Innocent bydrivers. He was standing perfectly still. Then as she sighted along the barrel he turned slowly away. The bullet caught him between the shoulder blades and flung him facedown into the street just as the first squad car came careening up the Shore Drive, siren wailing. She stood very still for one heartbeat. She thought, a chip off the old block. She thought, me, Scilla, a pig. Then she turned and ran back up the walkway.

"Mike!" He was splayed out on the pier, his face so dark

with blood that for a moment she thought she was looking at the back of his head. He didn't move. She dropped to her knees and pulled the silk scarf off her head. As she wiped, she examined the cut. The eye might be gone. It was impossible to say. He was losing a lot of blood, and she wasn't sure how you stopped this kind of bleeding. Lousy training, she told herself, wondering if she should try to hold the wound shut with her fingers. She really didn't know. Had the other eye been open before?

She realized he was looking at her. "Mike!" she cried, bending over him. His lips were moving. She leaned closer.

"My hero," he whispered. The eye closed again.

"Damn it, Mike!" she cried. "Don't you do role reversals on me, it isn't funny! You hear me, Mike?" But it was clear that he didn't hear her. She herself could hear several pairs of feet pounding up the walkway toward her, help on the way, but she lifted his head into her lap anyway and began to scream, shrilly and pointlessly, just like a girl.

Twenty

Scilla made it back to her own apartment at 4:20 that morning. After an ambulance ride in which she shared with an irritable attendant the lurching space between Mike and Whitey Hunter, both of them unconscious, both of them attached by hygienic white webbing straps to hygienic white stretchers, both of them bleeding through bandages that the irritable attendant had to keep changing. She had spent several hours pacing up and down between the familiar chrome and plastic couches and chairs of the intensive care waiting room like an expectant father. Her own father had preceded them to Overlook in a patrol car, had been checked over by a male emergency room nurse who was not Bruce Levine, and had been driven home by his wife. Neither had Carmody requested to speak with Detective Third Grade Priscilla Carmody, who was at least in certain respects responsible for their presence at Overlook. Detective Carmody, on the ninth floor, did not request to speak to her parents. That would all have to be dealt with later.

At some point—Scilla was not sure just when—she was joined by Anna Blessing, and the two of them marched in ponderous silence back and forth across the pebbly gray-and-white linoleum until a nurse, female, came out and told them that Whitey would have to undergo a series of operations, the bullet having made a mess out of one lung and produced a number of bone splinters that were currently hiding out in parts of Whitey's torso like proverbial needles in a proverbial haystack. Mike, on the other hand, was out of danger. The knife had barely grazed his left eye. Anna blew out her breath with an obscene whistling sound and hustled Scilla down the elevator to the first-floor lobby where a uniformed patrol officer, male, was too absorbed in a copy of *Cosmopolitan* to notice their arrival until Anna had coughed in his ear.

The uniformed patrol officer and his partner, both clearly nonplussed to find they had been directed away from the scene of the most important arrest in the last year in order to spend the rest of their shift acting as taxi service for their lieutenant of detectives, drove down Temple Way and Eastern Star Drive and negotiated the snarl of freeway and bridge entrances into Fairbridge without once turning on the revolving lights or sounding the siren. Anna slumped in the backseat in massive silence until they were barely two blocks from Scilla's apartment. Then she remarked conversationally, "Some fuckup, huh?"

Scilla shrugged. Judging from the state of their backs, the two patrol cops had gone completely rigid. "I don't know," she said. "I thought I might kill him."

Anna accepted this explanation without commenting on its ambiguity. "I'd rather he weren't shot trying to escape," she said. "Self-defense would have been better. But that's hard to claim, under the circumstances. Still, I don't think there'll be any call for an investigation."

Scilla shrugged again. Shrugging was about all she felt like doing. The possibility of an investigation did not trouble her. Presumably it might trouble her if it came about. "Mike, now," she went on. "You see, I thought *he'd* been killed. I still don't understand why he wasn't. Whitey had the knife at his throat. I don't see how he came to cut his face."

"Killing a cop's pretty major," observed Anna.

"Cutting a cop's pretty major," said Scilla. "I can't imagine he's banking on public sympathy."

"No," said Anna slowly. "I can't imagine that." They had pulled up in front of Scilla's building. "He'll have a hell of a scar," she added.

"Mike will."

"Yeah."

"Yeah," agreed Scilla. She looked down at her vest and pants with some surprise. "I've got blood on me," she reported.

"It's probably dry by now," Anna reassured her.

"Mike's blood," said Scilla. She considered the dark patches seriously. "It's hell to get out of gabardine."

"Here," said Anna suddenly and thrust something into Scilla's lap. Peering at it in the spill from the streetlight overhead, Scilla saw that it was a white plastic bag of the sort used increasingly in unecological supermarkets. "Ron Odabashian's jacket," Anna explained. "Walinsky drove him home, by the way. He wasn't very happy about the way things turned out. Odabashian wasn't. Walinsky's unhappy, too, but that's because he's part of the fuckup. In that he's responsible, in all likelihood, for pulling your dad in. Maybe even for telling Pat that we suspected Whitey of being the rapist. So Charlie's probably unhappy, but he isn't doing his complaining to me. That would be another investigation, you see. Which, frankly speaking, I'd be just as glad to avoid. Cutting as it would into the general atmosphere of triumph, not to mention competence." Scilla did not comment. "Odabashian, now," Anna continued, "he's got a right to complain, considering the way people just walked off with an item of his clothing. "You can get it back to him, can't you?"

"Sure. We should get it cleaned." It seemed to be the appropriate thing to say. Scilla felt as if she were operating her body from a very great distance. She moved her hand from the door handle to her lap and was pleased to note that her fingers had grasped the bag.

"Oh sure," said Anna generously. "You can bring me the receipt."

"Thank you," said Scilla. She pushed the door handle. The door swung open. "Thank you for the ride," she said to the two patrol officers.

"No problem," said one of them.

"We'll wait till you get in the door," said the other one.

It struck Scilla that their consideration was somewhat after the fact, but she nodded pleasantly and stepped out. It took her some time to locate her front-door key, but she let herself in and waved to let them know she was all right. She was all right, she reflected. She needed some sleep, of course. And a bath. The lobby seemed deserted, but she knew better than to let her guard down. Just because you'd caught one of them, it didn't mean you were safe. You were never safe.

After she had entered her apartment and reset the police lock, she stood still for a moment looking around. The living room was still neat, still undisturbed. It interested her that the light on her answering machine was blinking. She stared at it for a moment, then crossed into her bedroom and took off her jacket, shoes, vest, trousers, shirt, and socks, in that order. Her underwear was still clean, she told herself. Of course, underwear was never clean after you'd worn it all day, but what she meant was it was relatively clean. It didn't have blood on it. She went back into the living room and pressed the Play button on her answering machine.

There was only one message, from Missy. "How come you let him get cut?" it began. Scilla pressed the Pause button and considered the question of Missy's sources. They worked in mysterious ways, she decided. That was all she was going to know about them unless she was willing to risk the trust she had built up with Missy. She pushed the Play button again. "He had such a cute face," Missy continued. She sounded personally affronted. "I'm beginning to think you guys can't put out a decoy without fucking up," she continued. There was a long pause on the tape and Scilla considered the similarity between Missy's and Anna's choice of terminology. "On the other hand, there's something about a man with a scar," said

Missy. There was a click on the tape, followed by a beep from the answering machine.

Scilla reached for the telephone book and looked up the number for Chez Plush. Missy picked up on the first ring.

"Look." Scilla felt as if she were speaking under water. Her lips seemed to be moving very slowly. "I know you're busy, but just talk to me for a minute," she said.

She heard Missy draw in her breath. "I can talk," she said. "You went to the hospital?"

"I just got back. He's okay."

"I know that," said Missy impatiently. "When do they let him have visitors?"

"Why do you want to know?"

Missy's voice was sharp. "I can call the hospital, you know. Remember that I'm asking you first. Because if you try to put me off again, I'll be there as soon as they let me. I can help him, Scilla. I'm going to help him, too, unless you decide you don't want me to. It's about time you decided, one way or another."

Scilla sat down carefully on her rug and crossed her legs. Good legs, she thought, with detachment. She seemed to be wearing a bra and bikini panties. "Why do you think it's about time?"

Missy's breath rattled the receiver. Exasperation, Scilla interpreted. She herself was not tracking, she gathered. "He's *ripe*," said Missy. "That marriage of his is dead. Stone dead. If you weren't so damned *naive*, you'd have figured that out just from the stuff you've told me."

Scilla considered the information. It ought to interest her, she felt. "Marriage is a sacrament," she murmured.

"What are you going to do, revert?"

"Listen," Scilla said with sudden urgency. "I don't know what I'm going to do. Do you understand? I shot Whitey. There was no cause. He said my father hated me, so I shot him. He said that and turned his back. I was *aiming* at him, do you understand?" There was no response. She added pathetically,

"I've got blood on me." She hadn't put that well, she recognized, but it seemed impossible to put it better.

There was a long pause. So long that Scilla thought she could hear a variation in the static on the line, a regular rise and fall, like waves lapping the shore far away. After a while it occurred to her that she was hearing her own blood surging in her ears in time to her own heartbeat.

"Call me tomorrow," Missy said finally. "Don't say that to anybody else until you talk to me again, okay? In the meantime you have to get some sleep. Then call me. Not too early." She paused and Scilla could hear her breathing out. Cleansing breath. O-kay. "I won't go see him tomorrow," she said.

"All right," said Scilla.

"Don't call in the morning. I won't be up in the morning."

"I'll call you in the afternoon," said Scilla.

"Not too early," said Missy. She hung up.

Scilla put the receiver back on the hook and examined her right thigh. She did have blood on her. It had seeped through the fabric of her navy-blue pants, leaving a sort of flush, not unattractive. Mike's blood, she told herself, but it was hard to comprehend what that meant. Blood is blood.

The telephone rang again. She let it ring one more time before she picked it up.

"I suppose you think it's over."

She didn't, she realized. "You helped finger the guy, Bruce," she said into the receiver. "You passed on the word about Ann Hunter. We needed that."

"Now we get to deal with the confidentiality statutes."

For starters, she thought. He might refuse to be tested. Oh, he might very well. Given even an imbecilic lawyer, he'd refuse. And then what did you want to say? That some people don't have a right to confidentiality under some circumstances? Which people? Which circumstances?

"Where do you stand on that, Bruce?" She honestly wanted to know.

"Where do you *think* I stand, Scilla? I'm on my side on this one. If I turn out to be HIV positive, proving transmission is going to be hard enough. I don't want to have to *hypothesize* he's positive, too."

She could see the lines being drawn. "You people may split pretty badly on this one."

"What is this, 'you people'?" His voice was very level, very flat. "You really think you can control this one? You think you can restrict this one to a closed set of deviates?"

"We," she corrected herself. "We're going to split. I want to get him, too, Bruce." He didn't say anything. "Look, I've been tested," she told him. "Twice. So far."

"Good for you. You'd better keep on getting tested, too, Scilla. It takes quite a while for the virus to show up. But then you know that."

"They're talking repeated intimacy now," she said.

"You've been reading the *Advocate*," he observed, but she thought he sounded fractionally warmer. "Listen, Scilla. This repeated intimacy business. That's only odds. It isn't as if, oh, you had to have a *critical mass* of spermatozoa. You understand?"

"There are odds, though."

"Right. Don't think I'm not working them out all the time."

"Bruce," she said. "It's not over. But it's a start. We got him. We got the killer."

The minute she said the words she realized she had put her foot in it. But he was in a gentler mood now. "No, you didn't," he said, and she felt he was pulling his punch. "The killer is still at large," he said.

When the squad car pulled up in front of Anna Blessing's apartment building at twenty minutes before five, the sky above the Masonic Temple, visible from the street as well as from Anna's picture window, was a strange opalescent gray. Monsoons due shortly, Anna observed, waving the car away while duly noting the presence of an ancient Volkswagen

Beetle at the opposite curb defying the alternate-side-of-the-street parking regulations that applied to the whole of Victorian Hill. She stood with her hands in the pockets of her flapping uniform jacket until the patrol was out of sight. Then she beckoned to the Volkswagen, although there was no sign that anyone was inside it.

The passenger door creaked open and Rita Freeling slid out, feet first. She looked rumpled but unsurprised.

"Sleeping?" Anna greeted her.

Rita stretched. "Is it true he's a priest?"

Anna snorted. "You think you can *goad* me, that's what you think."

"He's at O'Dea, right? So is he a priest?"

"He's a coach," said Anna with disdain.

"Priests aren't coaches?"

"Listen," said Anna. "You're after a scoop again."

"I told you. We don't get scoops. We're a weekly. We don't come out for six days. We have to go for depth."

"So get deep," Anna said. "You got something *heavy* to ask me, go ahead."

"How am I going to know what's heavy if I don't know what's going on?"

Anna turned toward her apartment building. "Read the papers."

Rita crossed the street with miraculously renewed energy. "It's important to get at the issues underlying the flashy stuff, the big hunt for the rapist," she told Anna's back. "A lot of people have a stake in what's going on here, Lieutenant. More than you'll ever suspect."

Anna spun around and faced her with magnificent disdain. "Yeah, I know. You're everywhere."

Rita stopped and watched Anna's jacket billow and then flap closed again, like a tent in a high wind. In many ways, she reflected, Anna was an absurd figure, somebody you might want to ridicule very slyly, very subtly, in a long exposé article. In-depth reporting. Something that might pick up an award somewhere down the line. You'd be crazy to try it, too. She was much too smart and she knew how to get back, this fat old cop woman.

Aloud she said, "You figured out who told Bruce and Nancy to feed you doughnuts." Anna only smirked at her. "Have it your way," she said. "You ever consider becoming an investigative reporter?"

Anna snorted. "Investigative *reporter?* What's that? The reporter comes after the investigation. I follow the rapist. You follow me. You're the one who depends on me, and don't you forget it. I'm the thing itself." She yawned magnificently; like a lioness, Rita thought. "I'm the Big Lady," Anna pronounced with satisfaction. "Now I'm getting some sleep."

She turned and stumped up to her door. When she got there, she turned around and waved.

Rita watched until the door closed. Then she took her notebook out of her pocket and began jotting down the conversation. Any information, no matter how fragmentary, might come in handy at some point. And it was useful, if potentially actionable, to have on record that the lieutenant of detectives had referred to herself as the Big Lady. Or perhaps the Pig Lady. As always, it was impossible to tell.